LAST TRAIN TO DANVILLE

A Harriet Roth and Don Gannon Novel

3RD COAST BOOKS
HOUSTON, TEXAS
2020

R. M. MORGAN

3rd Coast Books
19790 Hwy. 105 W. Ste. 1318
Montgomery, TX 77356

www.3rdCoastBooks.com

ISBN's

Perfect Binding — 978-1-946743-25-1

eBook (ePub/mobi) — 978-1-946743-26-8

Project Coordinator — Ian W. Gorman, Associate Publisher

Editor — Ian W. Gorman

Cover Design — Fiona Jayde

Printed in The United States of America

READER TESTIMONIALS

"R. M. Morgan has done it again! After writing the riveting detective mystery Crown Hunt, *he tantalizes us with* Last Train to Danville. *Again, he incites readers to sleuth for the truth!"*

—Leonard Szymczak,
bestselling author of
The Roadmap Home: Your GPS to Inner Peace
and Award-winning author of Kookaburra's Last Laugh.

"For me, two things stand out about Mr. Morgan's Last Train to Danville. *The first is the nuanced, quirky characters populating this "who dun it." The second is the authentic local color that only comes from personal knowledge. Mystery lives in the mountains of North Carolina, too. An enjoyable read!"*

—Dirk B. Sayers,
author of *Tier Zero, Vol 1 of the Knolan Cycle.*

"This would make a great movie! I am amazed at how many characters there are, and they are fleshed out. As in the last book, I like all the history. I am very fond of the main characters. So much so, I don't want to see anything bad happen to them."

—Barbara Hennessey,
beta reader of *Last Train to Danville.*

"R. M. Morgan has a knack for placing intriguing characters in unlikely situations. His hard-to-put-down writing style keeps his readers riveted to the story in Last Train to Danville. *"*

—Craig Wells.

CONTENTS

OTHER BOOKS BY R. M. MORGAN

Crown Hunt

ACKNOWLEDGEMENTS

This tale of events in the Civil War and the camp at Ravensbruck is a work of fiction. In researching the events underlying this story, I read numerous books. For readers wishing to peruse historical fact, I suggest the following books as a starting point:

Hanna, A. J. *Flight Into Oblivion*. Baton Rouge: Louisiana State University Press, 1999.

Saidel, Rochelle G. *The Jewish Women of Ravensbrück Concentration Camp*. University of Wisconsin Press; New edition, 2006.

Winik, Jay. April 1865: *The Month That Saved America*. HarperCollins Publishers, New York, 2001.

Coski, John M. *Capital Navy: The Men, Ships and Operations of the James River Squadron*. Savas Beatie LLC, New York, 2005.

Sohn, Mark F. *Mountain Country Cooking*. New York: St. Martin's Press, 1996.

My writing coach, Leonard Szymczak, guided my absorption of the writing craft and fueled my enjoyment of fiction writing.

Special thanks go to the Morgan kinfolk (Travis, Tyler, Debbie, and Ida) who encouraged me and conceptualized with me on the story. I benefited from the encouragement and reviews of Mel Zimmerman, Craig Wells, Dirk Sayers, Mary Keown-Watkins, Jacki Hanson, David Andrews, and Sheila Larson. Mary Harris carried out an outstanding manuscript critique and edit.

Ron Mumford and Ian Gorman at 3rd Coast Books cheered me on and buttressed me in so many ways. Fiona Jayde did an excellent job on the cover design.

LAST
TRAIN
TO
DANVILLE

"For there is nothing covered, that shall not be revealed; neither hid, that shall not be known."

– Luke 12:2

1

FRENCH BROAD RIVER NEAR ASHEVILLE, NORTH CAROLINA — SUNDAY

Twisting and turning through the woodland, Digger jogged up and down the trail of dirt and flat rocks. He felt pleased with his life, his spirits lifting as he listened to an old Hank Williams' song, "Baby, We're Really in Love," through his earphones. The October foliage—yellow Black-Eyed Susans, thick and skinny trees with leaves changing color, small green shrubbery—lay around and before him. His life was heaven on earth.

Nature's beauty distracted him from the growing ache in his legs and chest. Slowing his pace, Digger leaned forward and forced his legs to thrust, pushing him to the top of the rising trail. Triumph. He bent over, his heart thumping. To catch his breath, Digger stopped running, removed his earphones, and rested his head against a sturdy tree. Panting, he gazed down at his yellow vest, worn to alert the hunters now that hunting season had started. He sucked in clean air through mouth and nose and listened to the slight ripple of the French Broad River a hundred meters or so to his left.

His eyes noticed a slight movement on the ground. A turtle, upside down, its feet waving in the air, trying to upright itself. He bent his knees, turned the green-tinged shell right side up, and gently set the creature beside the path. "Thar my friend. You're good to go."

In his late-twenties and healthy, Digger's breathing slackened, easing his chest's agony. He should push off and drive along the trail, but his body, savoring the respite, resisted. *I'll rest a moment longer,* he thought.

Straightening, he looked toward the river, catching the rays of the sun in his eyes. A metallic sound—*Click!*—pricked the silence.

He twisted toward the noise, gazing up the slope beside the trail, at the green shrubs and the fall-colored leaves.

Pow!—a projectile punched the tree next to him. Flying wood fragments flayed his skin—pain and terror.

Used to deer hunters in the autumn, he didn't hesitate, throwing himself off the path. Falling among bushes and a small tree, he realized someone had shot the tree beside him. Without conscious thought, he shoved his torso and forehead through the brush onto the ground, its earth populated with late-season ants.

Pow!—a second shot.

Digger couldn't believe the hunter hadn't seen his bright yellow garment, visible in the morning light. His pulse accelerated; his ears strained to gather any sound. Digger, motionless, thought the shots, the noise, had come from the trees above him, up the slope. He raised his head. The far trees were a fusion of colors: green, yellow, orange, and red. *Where am I?* he thought.

He lowered his head—*Pow!*—followed by the splintering of a tree branch. Confusion. Shock. *Get the hell out of here,* he thought. *Down to the river. It'll cover the sound.* Digger glanced to his left and low-crawled to a fold in the ground, leading off in the direction of the French Broad River, the main river through Asheville. Fog blanketed the lower part of the incline. He pierced the first haze of the mist.

Another discharge behind him—*Pow!*

Quiet.

Covered in fog, Digger rose to a crouch and moved as quietly as he could toward the flowing river. Rising, he tried to continue quietly down the hill, increasing speed, folding the mist around him. He started running, ignoring the ache in his chest. Worn rocks, interspersed with dirt, lay along this side of the river.

No one fired at his back. He spotted his home. He wanted his rifle. He rushed through the front door, past his dog barking and scampering in circles. He sat on the floor, watching both his front door and the door from his rear porch, holding his Remington Model 700 BDL SS with a box of .30-06 cartridges beside him. He hugged his dog, a Border Terrier. The terrier leapt in his arms and licked his face. His clothes hung heavy, soaked with sweat.

Digger made two phone calls: the first to the Buncombe County Sheriff's Office in Asheville and a second to his fiancée, Lilith Johnson.

"Baby, it's me," he said to Lilith.

"Honey, what's wrong?"

"A hunter kept shooting at me. I had to run."

"Call the police."

"The Sheriff's deputies are coming."

"I'm coming over."

"No. I've got my rifle."

Two Sheriff's deputies responded quickly. More deputies came and followed Digger to the trail beside the river. Observing through the trees, he watched the deputies—in black shirts with long sleeves and black pants—combing the upper slope for the sniper's location. Occasionally, they would push aside the bushes and pick up some object, which they placed in a clear evidence packet.

An older officer separated from the deputies and walked to Digger. The man's build had started to expand, his height reached a little above average, and he appeared powerful with a wide stance and his hands on his hips instead of at his sides. His hair, including mustache and goatee, had turned white, his eyebrows remained brown with streaks of white, and his eyes studied Digger. "I'm Chief Deputy Sheriff Goodman."

"Thanks for coming."

Goodman pointed at the ground. "You stood here when the attack began?"

The memory of that moment made Digger shiver. "Right there."

The Chief Deputy glanced at the Spanish coin on a chain around Digger's neck. Then Goodman studied the tree beside them and pulled out a pocketknife to dig at a hole in the trunk. "The first bullet hit the tree here?"

Still clad in his sweatshirt and jogging trousers, Digger replied, "Uh-huh."

"Do you know the perpetrator?"

"Didn't see the shooter."

Goodman pulled his goatee. "Who has a motive? Someone who hates you?"

He lifted his shoulders in a half shrug. "I don't know."

The officer wrote in a notepad. "You got a hunch? A person we ought to interrogate?"

Digger hesitated and fidgeted with his coin and chain. "My former partner, Johnny Hayes."

"Threatened you, did he?"

"Not threatened. Hayes took something from me."

Goodman scribbled on his notepad. "Who witnessed this attack?"

"No one."

"You jog most mornings?"

"I do. Most mornings."

"Many people know this?"

Digger gave a half shrug. "Family. Friends."

Goodman cocked his head at him. "What's your profession?"

"I search for fortunes."

Goodman gave him a hesitant stare. "You're an archeologist?"

Digger shook his head. "I search for valuables, antiques."

"For yourself?"

"For myself."

"That's your job?"

Digger pulled on the chain around his neck. "That's right. Things buried in the ground."

The officer continued writing. "We found the spot where the shooter waited for you. My deputies found ejected shells; pistol cartridge casings."

"What's that mean?"

The Chief Deputy locked eyes with Digger. "Not a hunter. Hunters use rifles, not pistols. Also means you're in real danger."

He patted the rifle strung over his shoulder. "I'm safe now. Have my gun."

Goodman cocked his head. "Until we find the guy, you'd better cut out the jogging."

The Chief Deputy hesitated to scratch his goatee. "Funny thing. Let me show ya something." Goodman pointed to a bloody form in the brush off the path. "What's that?"

Digger recognized the remains of the green-tinted armor of the turtle: shattered and covered with blood. "It was alive this morning. I picked it up."

"When you escaped to the river, the shooter chased you, tramping through the brush and firing at you."

"Lost me and shot that poor turtle outta spite."

"One heartless piece of trash," Goodman said and closed his notepad. "Here's my card."

Goodman turned and walked back to his deputies. The solitary figure rubbed the coin on his chain and hiked back toward his house, scanning the trees and undergrowth for a sniper.

# # #

Two days later on Tuesday, making his breakfast, Digger listened to the birds and the rhythmic roiling of the French Broad River just down the riverbank from his house. In his kitchen, he placed a plate, silverware, and a sugar bowl on an old table covered with a stained tablecloth. Starting a pot of coffee, Digger felt a refreshing breeze through the door, slightly ajar, out to the rear porch.

He sat down and began eating eggs and bacon. His thoughts jumped to the puzzle on his mind: Who shot at him? Anything to do with one of his treasure hunts? Was his sniper a poor sharpshooter or a good shot deliberately missing as a warning? The coffee finished percolating. Digger grabbed his coffee mug and walked to the cabinet for cinnamon powder and sprinkled a lot of it into his drink, as he did each dawn. He sat to continue eating, a dirty baseball cap with a hardware-store logo perched on his head.

Goodman had phoned and asked Digger to stop by the Sheriff's Office. He wanted to interrogate Digger further. Digger, stirring the coffee mixture, planned to share his suspicion about events a week back. Digger had gone through the attic in his old family house. He had a hunch the shooting tied back to what he had found. He turned his focus to picking out a location to dig tonight. While he consumed his breakfast, he—gaunt-looking, from missing sleep recently—read a timeworn journal and map. He wore clothing appropriate for excavating: blue overalls, a long-sleeve maroon shirt, and a white tee shirt peeking through his shirt collar.

In the front room, his dog barked, maybe sensing someone near the house. The barking continued, joined by a sound of furniture scraping along the floor. Digger put down his fork and went to investigate. His dog shoved his snout under a couch. Digger raised one end of the sofa. A chipmunk scurried across the floor to the TV. Securing his terrier to the furniture, he grabbed a blanket, chased the chipmunk around the living room, and tossed a blanket over it. He released the chipmunk outside, praised his dog for defending the house, and returned to his breakfast table.

He reheated his coffee in the microwave and pored over the map. As he considered where to probe the ground that night, his mind wandered, speculating how a chipmunk got into the house. He had never seen such a rodent in his home. His thoughts switched to Lilith, his fiancée, his Babe. Thoughtful, soft-spoken, and practical, she was his delight. He loved her infectious calm, occasionally interspersed with a short temper flash. She had told him about her pregnancy; he would be a father. He felt the encircling pang of responsibility and joy of awaiting fatherhood. He couldn't stop himself from weeping, tearing with happiness.

His coffee tasted a little bitter; he added more cinnamon powder. Returning to his maps, he chose a location near the railroad tracks for tonight. Getting up and carrying dirty dishes to the sink, he noticed a strange taste in his mouth.

His tongue felt peculiar—growing numb, insensitive to touch.

His abdomen tingled as if insects crawled on his body. He stood and checked under his shirt—no bugs.

A cold and clammy feeling started at his arms and progressed to his torso. Digger turned his head and retched on the floor.

He clutched his stomach; he struggled to breathe; his vision blurred.

Digger grabbed at the table—too late—he collapsed to the floor, pulling the tablecloth, journal, map, and sugar bowl onto the floor. No feeling in his face. Lying on the floor, he wondered, *Am I dying?*

As spasms wracked his body, he thought of the shooting in the woods, connecting the dots—*attempts to murder me.*

He tried to crawl to the phone in his living room, but he didn't have the strength.

As he lay prone, sugar—from the upended sugar bowl—covered the floor before his face. With effort, Digger smoothed down the sugar mound and drew a face with eye sockets and two crossed bars behind the head. He slumped motionless with a hand at the edge of the sugar.

# # #

In the early afternoon, Lilith found Digger's body sprawled upon the floor. The afternoon sun showed through the kitchen window illuminating a trail of vomit going from his mouth to a final pool. She was aware of a slight odor of body waste filling the air. Overcome by a dizzy spell, her hip bumped a cabinet and she sat down on the floor.

Lilith crawled over and slipped her arms around him and tried to hug him back to life. He, Digger, had left her, leaving behind his stone-cold face and unfeeling body. She held her fiancé, wiped his face clean with her sleeve, and wailed. Lilith poured tears onto the lenses of her glasses until they flowed over the edges of her black, plastic rims. The child within her, foretold by early-morning nausea and vomiting, would never meet its father.

An hour passed. Lilith—with gummy eyelids, a runny nose, and blurred vision—lay her Digger down. She lurched into the front room and phoned the Sheriff's Office. During the next fifteen minutes, her hands squeezed into fists, other muscles tightened in readiness, and she settled on an intense sense of purpose. She determined nothing would stop her from finding Digger's killer. She wouldn't hold Digger ever again. Someone had poisoned him and they would pay for this. "Damn you!" With that shout, Lilith's heart filled with poison.

2

RIVERSIDE CEMETERY, ASHEVILLE — FRIDAY

A police vehicle led a procession of cars with headlights turned on in the dim daylight. The police car headed the cheerless line into Riverside Cemetery, winding over narrow, asphalt-paved roads, passing rhododendron bushes and oak trees, going by granite tombstones and the occasional vault. On a level stretch, the line twisted to the shoulder and stopped. In the middle of a field of headstones and mausoleums, an open grave waited, roofed by a canopy stretched on aluminum poles.

Along with other somber pallbearers, Bruce and I—in dark overcoats and without hats—bore Digger's casket to his graveside. In years past, the three of us had grown up at the same Asheville high school, spending many hours on the football field behind the school, learning to play together as a team, and forming lifelong bonds. Bruce and I excelled in those long-ago football games, while Digger, smaller and slower, only entered the contest when the score was lopsided. Time had flown by; those days were ten years ago.

Once the graveside service concluded, I stood quietly with Bruce off to the side, remembering Digger. We always got to school before classes started and sat on the gray brick benches along the wall in the rotunda, laughing and watching the girls go by. I would lend Digger a hand with his math homework, pulled him through trigonometry. In the fall, we'd dress for football practice in the gym with its progressively gross smell. On the weekends, we'd drive through the burger drive-ins along Tunnel Road, seeking girls. We had been pals. Now he's gone. Jeezus, I'm going to miss him.

Bruce, my sidekick, said, "Heard Digger died at his home."

I glanced away because I didn't want him to see me take a swipe at my teary eyes. It wouldn't be manly. "That's my understanding too. Don't know what he died of."

That's when the woman, who would turn out to be Lilith, left the main body of mourners, strode in a line straight as an arrow's flight directly to Bruce and me, and kicked off the case.

I recalled well this moment and my first perception of her: white woman, short, plump, wearing large-framed glasses, and dressed in a baggy peacoat. My initial moniker for her, wrong it would turn out, was Milly Milk Toast. I would come to rue my failure to spot a fierce, unbending spirit behind a false front of blandness.

The woman stopped before me and wiped her eyes with a tissue. She spoke softly. "Are you Don Gannon?"

Who was she? I didn't recognize her. Did Digger have a sister? He had never mentioned a sister. "Yeah. I am."

"The detective?"

I still didn't recognize her. "The one and only."

"I'm Lilith Johnson. I was Digger's fiancée."

I peered at brown eyes behind her thick-rimmed glasses and her helter-skelter blonde hair and reflected: she might turn out to have the soul of a beautiful swan, but she dressed as a scruffy duckling.

"My condolences." I pulled a hand out of my overcoat pocket and gestured toward my partner, a black man of average height with an amiable smile, standing beside me. "This is Bruce Seeker."

"I'm sorry for your loss," Bruce said. "I grew up with Digger, all through high school. He was my friend."

Tears dripped down her face. "I loved Digger. I am pregnant with his child."

I felt awkward. "I'm sad about your hurt." My throat tightened in a painful spasm as I brought Digger to mind.

She nodded and then paused, like someone preparing to spring off a diving board. "Before Digger died, he grew frightened, skittish."

Digger hadn't told me he got engaged. What did she want? Should I calm this grief-stricken woman? Glancing over Lilith's shoulder, I spotted the Chief Deputy standing among the mourners and staring at our small group.

She again wiped her eyes. "Digger told me—if something ever happened to him—to go to you. You're a private investigator."

"Why?"

"You would avenge him."

Bruce ran his hand through his corkscrew curls and glanced at me, raising his eyebrows.

Lilith appeared upset. I wondered if she thought straight. "Didn't know someone murdered Digger."

She turned from me and pointed toward one of the groups at the funeral. "That tall man with white hair is Deputy Chief Sheriff Goodman. He suspects someone poisoned my fiancé."

I spotted Goodman, his back to us. The Chief Deputy talked to a man and woman, who might be in their late seventies. The older man, in a dark jacket, appeared bereaved. The white hair of the elderly woman showed under a black hat. She seemed disinterested, not grief-stricken.

"I know Harry Goodman," I said. "A skillful investigator."

She blew her nose into a tissue. Beside me, Bruce said nothing, standing like a black statue.

"What is it you want me to do?" I asked. "Harry's a pro, and we have a history. He won't appreciate me looking over his shoulder."

She raised her chin. "Get the proof and jail Digger's killer. I can help. I know who did it."

Did she expect me to work pro bono? Roth, my boss, wouldn't approve. Or did Lilith have money to pay me? "I'm grateful for my old friend's confidence in me, but we should let the Sheriff's Office manage the inquiry."

She pulled another tissue out of the pocket of her dark blue peacoat. "You must help. What can I do to convince you?"

I glanced at Bruce, inviting his input. "She has to talk with Roth. The Boss told us no moonlighting."

I took a moment to consider, glancing over the many trees in the cemetery and the rolling hills. Roth always fretted about coming up with her payroll and took money any way she could. Avarice is a narcotic to her, clouding her mind, her beliefs, in her quest for wealth. To investigate Digger's death would bring her money, but she had to command me to do it. Lilith had to talk to Harriett Roth. "Come to Roth Security tomorrow. It's at 2050 Deerhaven Lane and talk with my boss."

She wrote down the address. "When?"

I used my mobile phone to call Roth and, after talking to her, asked Lilith, "Ten o'clock?"

"I'll be there." She turned and walked back toward the remnants of the funeral crowd.

Bruce pulled at my coat sleeve. "Here comes your good buddy, Goodman."

The Chief Deputy walked up to Bruce and me and shook our hands. Goodman came from another time, trained in the Army, the infantry, during the Vietnam War, spoke directly without guile, and looked straight into the eyes of his listener. His formerly full head of hair, receding on the crown, had grown white. These days, he sometimes hesitated in his speech, hunting for a word. Old age had slowed a once forceful man. I caught the overpowering scent of Goodman's aftershave, Aqua Velva. "It's a sad day, gentlemen."

I felt a drop of rain on my face. I glanced at the overcast sky. It didn't seem dark enough for a full-blown storm. "That it is. Heard you suspect poisoning."

"A local lab discovered the crime. They found aconite—comes from the plant monkshood—in Digger's coffee." Goodman rubbed his goatee and continued. "The state laboratory in Raleigh is confirming that finding." Lilith might feel emotional about her former fiancé, but she got the poison part right.

I guessed about the elderly couple who had been talking to Goodman. A sad man. A superior woman. "Those the parents?" I hadn't seen them in a while.

"The old man is Michael Harper," Goodman said. "Do you remember he adopted Digger after his brother, Digger's father, and Digger's mother died in a car crash."

I nodded my head.

"What's the age of Digger's adoptive father?" Bruce asked.

Goodman gave a half shrug. "His adoptive father is eighty. He walked across Europe in the infantry in World War Two. The stout woman is his wife, Bertha Harper."

"What are they like?" I asked.

Before replying, Goodman waited a long moment. "He's a little wacky, like an absent-minded professor. He's also the dazed, pained father. She's annoyed by the inconvenience of Digger's death."

"She's cold?" I asked.

"Cold? Not sure she knows what it means to care for another human."

The Chief Deputy tightly pressed his lips together and switched subjects. "So, what did Lilith say to you?"

"Wants me to investigate the death. I assume you would rather I didn't muck around in your case?"

"Have at it. We've known each other long enough. You will share all your information with me, right?"

Goodman removed his hand from his coat pocket and rubbed his goatee. "Don't tell my Sheriff I said that. He thinks you're cheeky. If he sees me talking with you, he's sure to chain me to a desk answering the fricking tip line."

"Given the lab confirms poison," I said, "do you have a lead on solving the case?"

"Digger argued with another treasure hunter, Johnny Hayes. Lilith says he was after Digger's gold."

"What do you think?" I asked.

Goodman shook his head. "Don't feel right. Johnny Hayes is mean enough to kill. But he's also big-hearted enough to shoot his victim in the back, not poison him."

As Bruce and I talked to the Chief Deputy, I viewed the last of the grievers drifting away, trudging back to their cars. It took me a moment to hear the squabbling noise shatter the mourners' quiet. A ruckus as out of place as mud-wrestling in a church. Across the cemetery, about the length of a tennis court away from me, Lilith waved her arms and yelled at a bear of a man.

The man bellowed, "You witch!"

Goodman had left us, racing toward the two.

Lilith pointed and screamed, "Murderer!"

Bruce and I glanced at each other and then ran after Goodman.

The top of Lilith's head rose to the man's red-faced chin. He seemed to be shaking in rage. Lilith pushed the man, to no effect.

Two additional men ran up into the fray, shouting and circling Lilith and the big man, dancing aimlessly like kids in their first soccer game. The stocky man pulled back his arm as if to punch Lilith.

I sprinted past the Chief Deputy and grasped at Lilith, missing a grip on her dark-blue peacoat but yanking a clump of her blonde hair.

She squawked and fell backward, away from the angry man. I grabbed the big man's arm and held him away from her. He had the tiny eyes of the madman, set in a puffy face, blazing the hate of a nasty rodent. I saw pudgy, about 240 pounds, but strong. He stared at me but hesitated.

Goodman burst into the uproar, shoved the other two men away from Lilith, and pushed the big man back toward the line of parked cars. "This is a funeral, you ass. Leave." Bruce and I stood by the Chief Deputy.

Lilith stood behind the Chief Deputy, rubbing her sore head and shouting, "He murdered Digger. Arrest him."

The big man hissed, "Get that crazy woman away from me."

The three men hurried away, zigzagging around tombstones. After the scuffle, Lilith left too.

"Who were those guys?" I asked Goodman.

"The big one's Johnny Hayes. The other two are his flunkies. Their job is to trail behind him."

"Their clothes are shabby, like the gravediggers," Bruce said.

"Can't charge them with Digger's death just because they're worthless." Goodman hesitated and then continued. "But my hunch says Hayes might not be the culprit for this one."

Bruce and I walked back to our parked vehicle. Tomorrow, Roth and I needed to question Lilith. Harry was unsure about the killer, but she was confident she knew. Why?

3

ROTH'S MANSION, ASHEVILLE — SATURDAY

A few minutes before ten, as I finished brushing my teeth, the doorbell rang. Our visitor had arrived on time. I bounded down the stairs and opened the mansion's front door. Lilith, wearing a white safety helmet and a yellow rain jacket, stood before me. She had parked a navy-blue Vespa scooter on the driveway in the nippy weather. She stepped inside, dripping rainwater, and gave me a closed-mouth smile. Bundled in layers, Lilith removed her helmet and then took off her wet rain jacket and leather coat. Whilst I hung the garments on a clothes tree, she wiped the water off her black plastic-framed glasses.

She said, "Hope this'll work," and strode with me to Roth's office. Seated at her desk on the far side of the room, my boss raised her head, covered by a long black veil, and put down her book. She observed Lilith for a moment and then motioned the young woman to sit in front of the desk. Lilith plopped down and glanced around. "Bruce isn't here?"

I sat to the right side of Roth, my boss. "He's working on another case just now." I took out my notepad and pen.

Roth spoke not a word, cloaked in black with white hair, her dark eyes examining our visitor inch by inch. No one talked. Then Lilith took off her glasses and cleared her throat. "Your black tunic's remarkable. It's silk?"

Roth gave Lilith a tight-lipped grin. "Silk. I'm afraid my sartorial tendencies are to the baroque and the dark."

Lilith arranged her glasses back on her nose. "Ms. Roth … you dress in black. Are you like a Puritan?"

My boss beamed; then emitted a full-bore *whoop!* I had rarely seen her laugh so hard. There had been one previous occasion: after Roth solved the Mountain Feud case and we downed countless glasses of wine to celebrate, she had laughed at jokes, retold old stories. When she stopped laughing at Lilith's question, I thought I saw, through the net of her veil, a tear remained on her cheeks. "My clothing choice is a long story. Maybe we can discuss it further another day. For now, how can I help you?"

"I want to find who poisoned my fiancé. I won't give up."

Roth nodded. "You mourn Digger Harper's death. You're frustrated the Sheriff's Office hasn't charged anyone?"

Lilith brushed her flaccid blonde hair with a hand and lowered her eyes. "I was going … to spend my life with him."

Roth's face showed grim. "Love. It's magnificent. As two grow old together, he looks at you in a way saying he still sees you as he first saw you."

What the hell had I just heard? Roth never spoke like a romantic. When I think I understand her, I see I merely beat about on her surface. Thought-provoking, that's what she is.

Lilith pointed at me. "My fiancé told me, if anyone hurt him, go to Don," Lilith sobbed. "Johnny Hayes stole from Digger." She wiped her eyes. "He murdered Digger."

I realized Digger had been right. I needed to; I wanted to track down his killer.

Lilith, with her leisurely rhythm, had finished. Roth watched for half a minute and then spoke. "You judge Mr. Hayes guilty. Why? What motivated him to slay Digger?"

Lilith stopped, composing herself. "Hayes is a scrounger. He stole coins—and other things—from Digger during their treasure hunts."

Roth began quietly tapping on her desk. "You told the Chief Deputy about Hayes?"

"Yes, ma'am," Lilith said, "I did."

"And?"

Lilith raised her head and clenched her fists. "Goodman wastes time. He hasn't arrested Hayes for the poisoning."

I had begun to understand Lilith: patience wasn't her strong suit. She didn't appear to give up easily, but to bulldog her way past difficulties. Her remark about the Puritans intrigued me. Most people thought Roth dressed as if going to a funeral. Why had Lilith thought Puritan, a reference from ancient history?

Roth continued drumming. "You don't wish to wait on Goodman. You want us to solve the case?"

"I do. It'll work."

Roth laid her finger across her lips as if in thought. "Tell me more about this Mr. Hayes."

"Like what?"

"What was his motivation to murder Digger?"

Lilith fixed her eyes on Roth's face. "Someone shot at Digger last Sunday. The motive—to steal Digger's great-great-grandfather's gold, hidden in the Civil War."

My head jerked. Was Lilith making another vague accusation? I sensed a snag. My boss had a faraway, blank expression, perhaps showing she no longer focused on Lilith's problem. Roth might be choosing either *pay attention* or *flight*, a variation of the better-known *fight* or *flight*. My boss's tapping had increased, and I suspected she had decided not to take on Lilith's case. Luckily, Lilith abruptly switched to a subject Roth loved: *money*. "I know I'm asking Don to find a killer. I can pay you because we sold the Bechtler gold coins. Ten coins got us ten thousand dollars."

Roth blinked at Lilith. In that second, I recognized the shine of avarice in my boss's eyes. I had heard the name, Bechtler, before. Trying to recall where, I sat up straight and searched through my memory of Colonial America. Christopher Bechtler was a German jeweler, watchmaker and gunmaker who came to America in the early eighteen hundreds. He settled in—*oh where was it?*—Rutherfordton, some forty miles southeast of Asheville. Until the California gold rush started, that area of North Carolina led the nation's gold mining. In those bygone days, miners had no government mint in the Southern states. Bechtler cast the miners' gold into his coins.

Roth stopped tapping. "Were Bechtler Coins counterfeit?"

"The coinages didn't copy the government coins," I said, "because they had the name Bechtler inscribed on their surface."

Roth turned back to Lilith. "Where did you find these coins?"

"Digger found Bechtler had a young apprentice. This trainee learned to mint gold coins. His coins disappeared during the Civil War." Roth had stopped tapping and leaned forward in her chair. Lilith had bagged my boss.

"Digger hunted down ten gold pieces," Lilith said, "at the apprentice's crumbling house in Rutherfordton. Found the coins buried under a rotting porch. We sold them to coin dealers."

I scribbled away on my notepad. My old friend, Digger, had been resourceful. He was always fun to be around. It had started to hit me how much I missed him. Roth leaned back in her chair and asked me, "Does the Chief Deputy have a suspect for the poisoning?"

I gave a half shrug. "Goodman told me he's investigating, which means he hasn't gotten far."

Roth turned back to Lilith. "Tell me clearly why Mr. Harper's death occurred?"

"Digger told Johnny Hayes about the buried treasure. Hayes wanted to steal the gold. That's why."

"You mentioned treasure. Are there more Bechtler coins?"

Lilith took off her glasses and absentmindedly pushed one of the temple tips into her mouth. "No more Bechtler coins. I mean Confederate coins."

Roth began tapping again. "Get to the point."

"My fiancé had a great-great-grandfather who was a Confederate midshipman in the Civil War. In 1865, he buried Confederate coins near Morganton, North Carolina. Digger found this ancestor's diary in the attic of his old family home."

"This family home is where?"

"Old Fort, North Carolina. Those attic records say where the great-great-grandfather hid the gold."

My boss considered what Lilith had just said. "Surely the midshipman dug up the coins after the war?"

Lilith shook her head. "He died at the Battle of Swannanoa Gap, shortly after Lee surrendered to Grant. Doubt he had time to return for them."

Roth glanced out a window and tapped away. "Your fiancé found records of a hidden hoard. He told Hayes, and both began searching. Do I have the progression correct?"

"Yes, ma'am."

My boss frowned and little by little shook her head. "That's a flimsy motive. If no one has unearthed the cache, why kill? Just keep searching for the coins."

"I have a bad feeling about this," I said. "I grew up in the South. Most of those tales about Confederate gold were hearsay."

Lilith frowned at me and sat up straight. "Treasure hunting is what Digger did. He knew what he was doing. That hillbilly killed him."

"Do you know this Hayes explored for the treasure?" Roth asked Lilith. "Did he dig in the ground?"

"Digger saw Hayes excavating around Morganton. My fiancé—as he was dying—told us who did it. Digger drew a skull and crossbones in the spilled sugar."

Roth pursed her lips. "Hmm, why does a skull and crossbones mean a Civil War treasure?"

"It means buried in the ground, like a pirate treasure."

"I can think of other meanings," Roth said. "The symbol means poison. Maybe Digger wanted to make plain he had ingested a deadly mixture."

Lilith hesitated and then continued. "He threw up. Why would he use his dying energy to write the obvious?"

"In ancient times, the skull and crossbones marked a church's cemetery," I said. "Fraternities and sports teams adopted the symbol as their icon."

Roth shook her head. "Who had poison? Do we know if Goodman found any at Digger's house?"

Lilith appeared to take time to think before she answered. "Chief Deputy Goodman told me he didn't find any."

Listening to Lilith, I accepted Johnny Hayes was a mean hillbilly, but she had only a hunch Hayes killed her fiancé.

Lilith's face began to take on a red tinge, as she appeared to grow frustrated with Roth questioning her. "I'll write a check now. You find who murdered my love. It'll work."

Roth smiled. "Write out a check for five thousand dollars—to start."

Lilith retrieved her leather coat, pulled a checkbook out of her pocket, and wrote the retainer. Roth took the check in her right hand and tapped one edge against her desk. "The important thing is to nail the killer, but what if we find the Civil War gold in the process?"

Lilith jerked her head up to face Roth. "I don't care. Prove Hayes killed Digger and don't quit."

Roth put the check in a desk drawer. "This gold might not exist but if it does, I suggest we split it: half to you and half to Roth Securities."

Lilith removed her glasses and wiped them again. "Okay."

Roth gazed at Lilith for a moment. "You know where the gold is?"

She hesitated. "More or less. Nathaniel Harper told me."

"In his journal? You read his words?"

"In his April 1865 diary."

"And you have this diary?" Roth asked.

"I do."

Lilith's epiphany surprised me. She had chattered on and on about Hayes; I had missed the vital info in the journal. Now Roth would concentrate on gold coins like a hawk after a rabbit.

"Let's meet tomorrow," Roth said. "Bring your fiancé's documents, his great-great-grandfather's journals."

Lilith put on her outer garments, picked up her helmet, and left. I watched her ride off on her Vespa and then I went back to the office. "You did well to bring Lilith to me," Roth said. "Gratifying."

She stared at the ceiling as if in deep thought. "Let's go through Digger's documents with Lilith tomorrow."

"Yes, ma'am."

Roth glanced at the bookcase at the front of the room, where a small camera for a CCTV system lay hidden. "Mickey, come here."

Her third operative, Mickey Ploughman, a muscular man with brown eyes, short black hair, and sparse goatee and mustache, entered the office. "Ms. Roth."

"You saw everything?"

He nodded.

Roth pursed her lips. "Did Lilith gain by Digger's death? Trail her and find out where she goes and if Digger's death brought her wealth, like a life insurance policy."

"Yes, Ms. Roth."

"And get Bruce to run a computer background check on her and Digger."

Mickey jotted in a notepad, nodded, and left the office.

I twisted my college ring around my finger. "What are my instructions?"

Roth turned to me. "Same as always: sleuth for the truth."

"Why didn't Lilith tell me in the first place she had a description of burying the gold?"

Roth held her hand up with its palm facing me. "Doesn't matter. Tomorrow, begin your hunt for the Confederate coins. Tomorrow, find out how and where the gold got buried." She picked up her book, dismissing me.

I thought, *Roth wants to find coins. Lilith wants to find a killer.*

4

ROTH'S MANSION, ASHEVILLE — SUNDAY

The next morning, under a light-blue sky and cold air, Lilith puttered to the mansion on her scooter. She untied a box from the rear section of the seat and handed the carton to me. "My files."

I took Lilith and the box to Roth's office. Roth, in a maroon tunic with a white transparent headscarf, faced Lilith. "Why couldn't your fiancé taste the poison?"

"Cinnamon-flavored coffee masked the poison's flavor, a bitter taste. The coroner and the state laboratory in Raleigh both found aconite in Digger's body."

Roth pursed her lips in a puzzled expression before she asked me, "What do you know about aconite?"

"Claudius, the Roman Emperor, might have been poisoned by aconite. His wife—"

Roth snapped. "Are we trying to solve the murder of a long-dead Roman emperor or track down Digger's killer? Ask Taylor to join us. She has practical knowledge of our mountain flora."

I fetched Taylor Ploughman, our cook, a petite, attractive woman with blue eyes and red hair. Roth waved her to a chair and introduced her to Lilith. "Taylor was born in the high mountains, to the northeast of Asheville. Taylor, tell me about aconite."

"Aconite a-comin' from da plant monkshood. It sprouts in da wild. A blue flower, a-growin' among rocks."

"And do pharmacies sell aconite?"

"Naw, idn't nothing but a poison. You'ns get it free in the woods."

Roth leaned forward in her chair, her eyes narrowing. "A blue flower, you say? Does it grow everywhere, like dandelions?"

Taylor shook her head. "It are blue or purple-blue. Don't grow everywhere. A-wantin' sun an' moist, well-drained soil."

My boss drummed her fingers on her desk. "Taylor, for everyone involved in the Digger case—Johnny Hayes, the Harper family at Old Fort, and Digger—search their neighborhood. Verify whether they have monkshood growing nearby. Don will give you the addresses."

"Yes, ma'am. If you'ns a-finishin' with me, I need to fix a passel of food fer lunch."

Roth learned back in her chair. "Taylor, go fix a passel."

At Taylor's departure, my boss reached for her coffee cup and sipped. "Most murders reflect the killer. I'm guessing your Johnny Hayes would be more likely to lie in wait for his victim and beat his head to a paste with an axe handle than poison him. Too bloodless for a thug." Roth looked at Lilith and cocked an inquiring eyebrow.

Lilith nodded. "He would."

Roth continued tapping her fingers. "Humor me. Tell me again why you believe Hayes killed Digger."

Lilith removed her plastic-framed glasses and sucked on a temple tip. "My fiancé tracked down lost fortunes. He unearthed antiquities, old coins, and Native American artifacts. He found one of his relatives hid Confederate gold in Western North Carolina."

Roth held up a palm to stop Lilith. "Confederate gold reached Western North Carolina?"

"It did," Lilith said in a calm voice.

Roth dropped her hand. "You think Hayes killed Digger to prevent him from finding this wealth?"

Lilith nodded. "I do."

"And why do you think he'd kill him *before* he found it? Wouldn't it make more sense to wait until he had it and then off him?"

Lilith frowned. "Hayes did the killing."

Roth compressed her lips. "How did the gold arrive?"

Lilith lowered her head and appeared to study her feet. "As the war ended, the Confederacy sent the remaining treasury from Richmond to Danville, Virginia. Some of the coinage went on a train to Morganton, North Carolina."

I tried to recall how the war finished. I remembered reading the Confederacy had fled farther south in its final days. I remembered Danville was in Virginia a few miles from the North Carolina border. Morganton sat southwest of Danville, not south. "Why that particular city?" I asked.

"It's in the diary of Digger's great-great-grandfather, Nathaniel Harper," Lilith answered. "He rode the railroad to Morganton, where the tracks stopped in eighteen sixty-five. When he couldn't get wagons to transport it farther west, Nathaniel hid the treasure there."

I didn't see a link between Digger's death and a legendary Confederate treasure. "Yesterday, you said Digger found his ancestor's records. Old accounts left in the attic of the Harper family home."

"My fiancé found journals. And a map."

Roth stopped drumming on her desk. "Do you have these documents?"

"Yes, ma'am. I have some of 'em. Here in this box."

Roth stood up, rolled the long sleeves of her maroon tunic higher up her arms, and cleared a space on her desk. Lilith laid out the journals on the cleared surface. The room grew quiet. For some reason, Roth had stopped, as if to think. She might have been figuring how Digger's gold hunt affected our case. "The page where Digger's ancestor hides the cache. Show me."

Lilith dug through the box and extracted five journals. She opened one of them. "Midshipman Nathaniel Harper started his final diary in January 1865. It ended the following April."

"I want Don to examine the documents for genuineness. Were they made circa Civil War?"

Lilith handed the manuscripts to me. "Be gentle. The pages are brittle."

I turned the books over in my hands and told Roth what I found. "I smell must. The covers are of hard cardboard in a muted black color." I opened a diary. "This paper has a clear grain direction. The moving belts of machines began to cast paper about the start of the 19th century. The pages are white with a sepia tint." All five diaries were similar in paper and handwriting. "These journals appear to be originals, old."

"Civil War old?"

"Yeah." I returned the diaries to Lilith. "So, Digger spent his time going through old documents?"

She smiled with a pleasant grin. "My fiancé spent his time gazing headfirst into yesterday."

She picked up the last volume entitled, *Diary 1865,* thumbed past a few pages, and found an entry where Nathaniel Harper wrote:

> April 7, 1865 - Our train stopped in Salisbury, North Carolina. Happy to get out of our cramped railcar and stretch our legs. Captain Parker ordered us not to stray. We had to be ready to continue to Charlotte. His mission was to store the reserves in the government mint tomorrow.
>
> Spoke with Captain Parker. Explained we ought to plan for the years of war ahead. Fight the Yankees by hiding in

the woods and coming out only to attack them. I wanted to take hard currency, armament, and ammunition westward to support partisan resistance. He approved my plan and set aside a railcar for my journey.

Union forces under Stoneman attacked some nearby towns, but the rail line still operated to the west from Salisbury. My rail car was detached from the main train and added to another one going toward western North Carolina. My railcar contained gold, guns, and ammunition for partisans to use in the mountains for the defense of the Cause.

The main treasure train set out for Charlotte to the south. My short train departed to the west.

Lilith placed her thumb on the diary page as a bookmark and raised her head. "You see, his railcar carried gold."

"Who's Parker?" I asked.

Lilith stopped to straighten the bangs of her blond hair, perhaps trying to recall who Parker was. "A naval officer in charge of midshipman education. Where Nathaniel buries the gold is a page or two further." She picked up the diary, flipped through two pages, and continued reading:

April 9, 1865 - Train arrived at Morganton. The rails ended here. Sought a wagon with oxen to carry our cargo. No suitable cart found—after four years of war, the Confederate Army had begun to run out of men and transport to requisition. My small group buried our baggage beside the tracks—for our return later. I marked its location on a map on the next page.

My Old Fort home stood about thirty miles west of Morganton.

Lilith turned the diary to face Roth and placed it on her desk.

I moved to study the map over my boss's shoulder. "The *X* beside the train tracks marks where Nathaniel buried the gold. There are no obvious topographic features. The only way to locate the cache would be to dig up all the land next to the tracks."

Lilith stuck her finger on the *X*. "The diary proves he buried the gold."

I shook my head. "Weak at best. It says he hid cargo. To assume your midshipman buried gold is—a stretch."

"The gold is there. It has to be," Lilith said.

"Has a single gold coin been found by anyone near the old Morganton train tracks?" I asked.

Lilith crossed her arms over her chest in a gesture of defiance. "No."

"If rationality were the reason for things occurring," Roth said, "the world wouldn't have babies. Don't dismiss Lilith so quickly."

"But why murder anyone?" I asked. "No one knows if the treasure even exists."

Lilith tenaciously defended her view. "Hayes believed a treasure exists. He killed Digger to stop him from getting it."

I brushed my cowlick, trying to grasp the reason for Lilith's animus toward Hayes. "Did Hayes threaten Digger?"

Lilith bobbed her head multiple times as if she were twitching as she thought. "Weeks ago, Digger and Hayes drank beers downtown at Carmel's Restaurant and Bar at The Grove Arcade. Digger told Hayes about the gold, showed him the map."

"Why did Digger do that?"

"He were drunk as a skunk. Had a copy from Nathaniel's diary. Hayes snatched the map out of Digger's hands."

"You were there? You witnessed what happened?"

"Saw everything. Digger jumped up, pawing at Hayes' arm, trying to grab the map back. Hayes was bigger than Digger."

"Digger had brought a copy," I asked. "He didn't bring the original map from the diary?"

"A copy. Hayes grabbed Digger's throat and choked him," Lilith said.

I stared at her with my mouth gaping. "What happened?"

"I slapped at Hayes, and people pulled his arms away. He ran off with the map. Digger recovered."

"This is why you blame Hayes?"

"He doesn't think. He flies into rages."

I considered what Lilith had told us, and then changed the subject. "Confederate gold's an old wives' tale. No one would kill for an unproven map. This treasure hunt is a pipedream."

Lilith slammed the timeworn diary down on Roth's desk. She seemed determined to convince me she was right. "Wasn't early archaeology a treasure hunt?"

"Maybe, but did archaeologists kill each other?" I asked.

Lilith would let me know when she thought me wrong. To my admiration, she avoided hateful looks, didn't stare daggers at me. She carried an expression of closed-mouth determination. She had limited formal education, but she didn't back down when she thought she was right.

Roth pursed her lips, waited for quiet. "Don is a very competent investigator. Like all competent investigators, he comes with a healthy measure of open-minded skepticism." Roth's left eyebrow tilted upward. "He senses he should follow other paths in addition to the Confederate treasure and I'm inclined to agree."

Not letting me reply, she turned to Lilith. "You believe the killer was following Digger's map—to get the Confederate cache. Right?"

"My fiancé knew, Ms. Roth," Lilith answered. "He had brains. He drew the skull and crossbones in the sugar."

Roth raised a hand to appease Lilith. "Don will tackle this from two angles. He'll follow his hunches half the time. To investigate Hayes, you and he will pursue the treasure trail for the other half." Roth had a sneaky side. Without telling me, she had slipped into the guise of a treasure hunter. In the minuscule chance the gold existed, she wanted me to find it with Lilith's support. Riches attracted Roth as ice cream drew kindergarten kids.

Taylor had entered the room. "Don. Mr. Michael Harper are a-callin' you'ns. Wants to jaw about his dead son."

Roth transferred the call to the phone on her desk and punched Speakerphone. "Mr. Harper, you're on speakerphone. My condolences for your son's death."

Mr. Harper spoke in a loud and clear voice. "Oh, my poor son, our family pride, he's moved on to the Great Beyond. My heart weeps a thousand tears and then cries again. We must go forth each day into the stings and shots of daily toiling to deliver for our cherished family. To take this debilitating blow drives our hopes and aspirations into the muck of sorrow."

Roth and I turned with bewildered expressions toward Lilith. "That's Michael Harper, my fiancé's adoptive father. He talks that way."

What had Chief Deputy Goodman told me? I tried to remember. Digger's father had the rambling speech of an absent-minded college egghead. Yeah, that was what Goodman had meant. I leaned toward the speakerphone. "Mr. Harper, this is Don Gannon. You wanted to tell me something?"

"Yes, yes, my valued lad. I am pleased to meet you. Digger always spoke in praising—no, in glowing—esteem toward you. Kindhearted of you to take my call; I have important information relative to my son's death. You and I, we together, will work jointly to chase and ride down, to trample, the craven creature who visited this terror on us. What the hell! We'll be two of the horsemen of the Apocalypse falling on the gutless. Come to see me." The call went dead.

Roth pressed buttons on the house phone, turning off the dial tone. "Don, get over to Old Fort tomorrow and question Digger's old man. What does he know about the Nathaniel Harper diaries? Does he believe his ancestor buried a fortune at Morganton?"

I felt I had joined a colony of crazies. The old man had to be mad or mighty strange. Roth had started to lose her mind over imaginary gold. At times, all a map does is tell you you've gone astray. "Yes, ma'am."

"Then on Tuesday, meet Lilith and go through her box of files."

I nodded with a frown. After I had finished interviewing Digger's father, I had to find Lilith and scan ancient chronicles. Old Fort lay about twenty-five miles east of us. It would take me half an hour to get there in the morning.

"Have Bruce search public records and create background files on Digger Harper and Johnny Hayes," my boss continued.

Roth ended the meeting. Lilith arranged for me to meet her in two days' time at Digger's house to review the Nathaniel diaries in more detail, then departed on her Vespa. I planned to leave for Old Fort the next day to question Digger's family. I would be traveling within a labyrinth to solve a murder; I wanted to get going as soon as possible.

5

OLD FORT, NORTH CAROLINA — MONDAY

The next morning, I drove twenty-two miles, gradually leaving the Appalachian Mountains behind and dropping down to the town of Old Fort, a descent of some seven hundred feet. The Harper house had begun as a two-story, wood structure. Later, as the family grew, they had thrust one-story additions out to the sides at various angles, giving it a whimsical but homey look. The original main building, with white clapboard siding and high single-pane windows, was old, going back as far as Civil War time. The attic could have concealed nineteenth-century documents.

Digger's dad and uncle, Michael, opened the door. He appeared close to eighty years old, with salt-and-pepper hair, a hairline just starting to recede, and rimless glasses. He wore a tweed coat, a vest, and a pair of grey slacks, like a college professor. He reincarnated the courtly man.

"Mr. Harper?"

"Yes, yes. It's me in the flesh. I was sitting in my sunroom, reading about the Battle of Shiloh, the first of the slaughterhouses to fall on our nation. I am an ardent student of history. Do you read history, Mr. Gannon?"

After my earlier experience with the elder Harper, I wondered how beneficial it would be to talk with this man? He was eccentric, a rambler. "You called me. Invited me to drive to your house. I saw you at Digger's funeral."

He replied in an engulfing, grandiose voice. "By God! What a gorgeous day it was for the funeral service three days ago. Just marvelous, marvelous. A sweet farewell to my adoptive son. All God's children live—"

I interrupted him, "Lilith Johnson hired me to find Digger's murderer."

"Lovely, lovely person. Lilith was to Digger as Shakespeare's Juliet, a beautiful woman to be wooed. She must be—"

"Remind me," I broke in again. "Was Digger adopted?"

"Yes, yes, my destiny was to guide him through life. After that horrible day when his father died in an automobile crash,"—he stopped speaking and stared at the ceiling for a moment—"I adopted my nephew. It aggravated my wife, Bertha. She didn't adopt my son with me, didn't want him around the house. Her decision caused my heart to ache—"

I couldn't be sure when he planned to stop talking. Roth had taught me to slow down an excessive talker by interjecting a question. I drew in my breath and pushed forward into Michael's gale of chatter. "Was Digger's great-great-grandfather a midshipman in the Civil War?"

He blinked, pausing for a few seconds. "Yes, his name was Nathaniel Harper, my great-grandfather, my noble ancestor. Nathaniel lived in the original part of this very house, with his wife, young son, and parents. He set out to be a midshipman in the United States Navy but joined the Confederate Navy when North Carolina joined the rebellion. Alas, an unfortunate day. Come and meet Nathaniel."

Puzzled, I followed him out of the front parlor toward a den at the rear. The house had a chaotic layout. The furnishings seemed to be at war with each other, with early American and German furnishings shoved together in disharmony. I found prints of historical battle scenes, cuckoo clocks, old colonial kerosene lanterns, a shotgun on a wall, German beer steins on a mantel, a spinning wheel, pictures of old Munich and Heidelberg—on and on.

Michael stopped before an oil portrait of a serene-looking man, clean-shaven with medium-length, brown hair, standing with his right arm propped on a table behind him. It was a formal picture of a man wearing a gray, double-breasted frock coat with two rows of buttons down its front, a dark cap roughly four inches in height, and a saber. Over a hundred years after the painting of his portrait, this ancestor had led Digger to search for hidden treasure.

He had his shoulders back, and his chest pushed out. "Meet Nathaniel Harper, my great-grandfather and Digger's great-great-grandfather. In April 1865, when Richmond fell, he was in the James River Squadron. What a glorious adventure that must have been. If only his portrait could talk."

Michael's eyes were bright, reflecting his joy in recounting the family's Civil War tales. Thinking he might inadvertently say something useful, I let him ramble. When he paused for breath, I asked, "Why did you call me?"

He stuck his right index finger in the air as if he had the answer. "Lord save me. I want to add my payment to Lilith's; to hire you to pursue my son's assassin. I'll increase—dollar for dollar—what she pays you. Send me the bill. Don't tell my wife, Bertha. She forbade me to spend money seeking justice for my son. 'Let the Sheriff's deputies handle it,' she said."

Michael went silent and lowered his head. His shoulders slumped. "Oh, a horrible day my son died."

Continuing his monolog on the Harper family history, Michael led me through a warren of rooms. I paused at a wall to view a battle-scene drawing, a portrayal of a squadron of wooden and iron ships sailing up a winding river. Peering closer, I saw smoke—maybe cannon fire—from high bluffs on both sides of the river.

My brain numbed, overcome by sorting out all his utterances. I held up my palm to stop him from dumping more words on me. "What's this?"

"That is the Battle of Drewry's Bluff, back in May 1862. Union warships sailed up the James River, on their way to Richmond. My ancestor, Midshipman Harper, commanded a Confederate cannon on the bluff."

Michael rambled onward in an overwrought dissertation on the early sea battles in Virginia and the bravery of Nathaniel Harper. A photograph of what appeared to be a European town stood next to the battle sketch. "What's this?" I asked.

Michael blinked, first at me and then at the photograph. "The town of Furstenberg, Germany. Bertha was born there. Just after World War II, I had been stationed nearby, with my army unit."

He led me to a patio off the rear of the house. I sat and glanced down at a creek along the back of the house.

"My son had fantastic accomplishments during his short life," Michael opined about Digger. "He made me, his adoptive father, proud. He studied history like his father—"

"Who killed your son?" I asked.

Before speaking, Michael fiddled with a watch-chain fob connected with a gold-cased watch in his vest pocket. "No idea who the cold-hearted monster is; may he rot in Hell. It's pitiful. Good-natured Lilith thinks a cache of gold is involved. The thing is, since Digger found that old map in the attic and made copies, someone like Johnny Hayes would search for the gold, not poison my son. Furthermore—"

"You suspect anyone?"

"Don't know. Chief Deputy Goodman doesn't know either. Lilith asked me to join her in hiring you."

Michael went back to fiddling with his watch-chain fob. He seemed sad. "I am an amateur historian, no college degree. Delight in reading about the past. I passed my love of history to my nephew. We, father and son, spoke unceasingly of history and our forbear, Midshipman Nathaniel Harper. Often in the evening, out on this very patio—"

"Could I see the attic?"

Michael took me up to a loft lying under an A-framed roof. The family had stacked boxes, trunks, and rubbish to overflowing on a planked floor. I sniffed a stale smell but didn't notice a moldy scent.

"Digger spent a week hunting through the family castoffs, tossed aside through decades. In the middle of this debris, he found a steamer trunk of old papers belonging to Midshipman Harper, a dusty trunk, locked with no key to open it. My son broke open the lock. He found Nathaniel's journals and diaries, including a hand-drawn map. Digger was an explorer, going where no one had gone since Nathaniel Harper died. His mind constantly sought answers to why things happened and how. His curiosity had always been indefatigable and he—"

"Did you read the diaries?"

"We read the journals together. Thrilled at the stunning adventures of Nathaniel Harper. Digger explored all over the attic."

Michael glanced over the attic and fingered the chain attached to the fob in his trousers. "But Bertha complained my son had created a mess going through the old boxes. She ordered him out of the house. They had an immense quarrel, shouting and screaming. Digger left our home. He took the journals and diaries with him and renewed studying at his home on the French Broad River. I attempted to appease Bertha, but she wouldn't relent. She had—"

"Your son ever have any trouble with the law?"

Michael led the way out of the attic. "Not my hardworking son. He testified in a trial about the desecration of a Native-American mound. My son appeared for the prosecution. Digger had high respect for the Cherokee culture. Often, he hiked through the Cherokee Reservation, in awe—"

"I hope you'll talk with me again, about your son's murder?"

We headed toward the front of the house. Michael talked too much, but he had bonded with me, and he might still have information that would be useful. From my experience with him at Roth's office, I had been dreading this meeting. I left pleasantly surprised. "Got to leave," I said.

Michael walked me to the entrance. He took a handkerchief out of his coat pocket to wipe his glasses and blot at his eyes. "Mr. Gannon, find my son's killer. I loathe him."

His wife pushed in through the front door. About the same age as her husband, she was taller and more massive. I smiled and greeted her. "I'm Don Gannon. Been talking with your husband."

Bertha stared at me; her jowls hung down in an unending frown. She brushed past me and turned to Michael. "What's he doing here?"

I noticed Michael stepped back, deflating under her gaze. "Investigating your adopted son's death. I work—"

"Wasn't my adoptive son. I didn't ask you. I asked my husband." She bent toward Michael. "Well?"

Michael took a moment to answer. "Mr. Gannon is a detective probing my son's death. Lilith is paying him."

She deepened her frown, aimed at her husband. "Don't you give him any money. The sooner you forget Digger, the better." She turned and left the room.

My eyes followed Bertha without a turn of my head. I sensed a prickling of the hair on my neck. I shook Michael's hand. "I'll be in touch."

Before driving away from the Harper's home, I sat in the Mustang and wrote up my impressions in a case notepad. How could he stand her? I saw her sole reason for existence as a forewarning of the hazards of marriage. Starting the car, I set out for Roth's mansion. Tomorrow, I would meet Lilith at Digger's house to go deeper into Nathaniel's journals and the map. Did those documents figure into Digger's death? How?

6

DIGGER'S HOUSE, FRENCH BROAD RIVER —
TUESDAY

"A remnant of the Confederacy Treasury exists or does not,"
Roth had said. "Find out which! Do not disappoint me."
I sighed. My shoulders slumped. For the lure of a
treasure that might not exist, I would have to quiz Lilith and listen
to her incessant claims Johnny Hayes killed her fiancé. Where the
temperaments of humans are entangled, life is a game of chance.

But as I did not know who killed Digger. I might as well talk
to Lilith.

I arrived at Digger's home on the river. The house stood a
doughty old lady, two stories with weathered wood siding and a
metal roof. The French Broad River roared past 500 feet behind
the structure. Stepping out of my Mustang, I strolled over a gravel
parking area to a rustic building with an open porch in front and a
screened-in porch in back. I knocked and Lilith came to unbolt the
door, her white-knuckled hand squeezing its edge. Her hands moved
in jerks, and she couldn't stay still, a strong woman concentrating on
her crusade to avenge Digger. Her blond hair was natural, the same
light shade as her eyebrows. She dressed modestly in blue jeans, a

black blouse, and those black-rimmed glasses, like a blithe soul, not a clothes dame.

Lilith had spread the old Nathaniel Harper journals on a coffee table in the living room. She had done her homework, setting up for our discussion. I took out my pen and notepad, and said, "How did Digger hunt for treasure?"

"Digger would identify a cache. Buried money left by bandits, pirates, or someone in the madness of war. He researched a past event and nosed around the actual site."

"How would he research?"

"He would find witnesses and go to the library."

I glanced up from my notepad and tilted my head to one side. "Digger extensively studied a site?"

"Digger did careful research—he'd try to understand what the people had been thinking and doing. He became a historian, burrowing in libraries, searching on the Internet, and poking about in attics and basements."

Leaning forward, I slid my chair closer to Lilith. "Tell me specifically how he searched for the Bechtler coins."

"Digger talked with surviving families in Rutherfordton, North Carolina. He located the old home of the apprentice. Over several nights, he went with his colleague, Johnny Hayes to the site and explored until he found the coins."

I raised my eyes from my notepad and frowned at Lilith. "The same Hayes you suspect of murder? He and Digger were partners?"

Before answering, Lilith took her plastic-rimmed glasses off and chewed on one of the temple tips. "Hayes did little to find the coins but demanded half. He took half, and my fiancé never trusted that snake again."

My posture slumped. "But Hayes didn't kill Digger for the coins. Why would he kill your fiancé over an unconfirmed map?"

"I'm wasting my breath, aren't I? You don't believe me."

I didn't answer. I hesitated to disrupt our meeting by quarreling with Lilith. Had she condemned Hayes because of an old grudge? She was an obsessive woman. I changed the subject. "Do we know Nathaniel's map is the real McCoy?"

Lilith pointed at the diaries on the coffee table. "Digger stumbled upon these long-lost journals in a locked trunk in the family's attic. The Harper family had handed down an oral history. In their folklore, the midshipman had guarded Confederate gold taken from Richmond."

She leaned over the journals on the coffee table. "Let's read more about the lost treasure?" Several journals, for the years 1862 through 1865, lay before her. The last being the one she had read from when she met Roth.

A surge of adrenaline alerted me. Roth would want a report on what Lilith was about to say. "Guide me through the significant parts of his journals," I said. "Where does Nathaniel cross paths with the Confederate Treasury?"

"Grant attacked Petersburg in June 1864—opposed by Lee," Lilith said. "The struggle grew into the siege of both Petersburg and Richmond. In late March 1865, Grant broke through Lee's overstretched lines, pushing the Confederates to withdraw from Richmond."

Lilith pushed her glasses up on her nose. "I'll read what the journal says about the capital evacuation." She started:

> April 2, 1865 - Sad day for James River Squadron.
> Navy Secretary Mallory informed us General Lee had
> started withdrawing from Richmond. Got my orders.
> Destroyed our small wooden gunboats and ironclad
> ships to prevent capture by the Union Navy. Fired our
> vessels, sending them down to the river bottom near
> Chaffin's Bluff.

With other midshipmen, gathered provisions and arms. We expected to join General Lee's army in the field. Arrived at the Richmond train depot. Late afternoon.

I glanced at what Lilith had been reading. Nathaniel's handwriting on this page appeared hurried. "Did your fiancé check these journal entries against historical facts?"

She smirked, didn't like me interrupting her. "Hell, yes. Digger confirmed the Confederate Navy scuttled their James River Squadron on the second of April."

She continued reading the journal:

Mustered at Richmond depot as ordered. We were now in the infantry—sixty men. Captain Parker wanted us midshipmen to lead the enlisted seamen taken off the scuttled gunboats and ironclads. I felt disoriented and excited by this new mission. Heavy smoke in the air. Richmond burning. What a shame. The beautiful city had held out for so long.

Captain Parker received orders from Secretary Mallory. Guard one of the trains with our midshipmen. Parker was still the superintendent of the Confederate States Naval Academy—our commander. We marched to a siding where negro workers loaded boxes and barrows onto a train. Crowd had formed around the engine and boxcars. I assigned our contingent into watch rotations and specified guard details. Our arrival kept people from rioting. The cargo was cumbersome, dozens of boxes and crates of hard currency, some bullion, and jewelry donated to the Confederacy. I took charge of one boxcar. A government clerk revealed we guarded last monies of the Confederacy.

A train departed with President Davis, his cabinet, and other government officials. About midnight, boxcars loaded. We guarded the cargo as our train left the station. Ours was the last to quit the depot for Danville.

"I wonder, was this really the last train to leave the station?" Lilith's eyes flared at me. "Why don't you believe me?"

I winced. "I'm just establishing the diary is accurate." I had begun to understand her: she wouldn't back down.

She removed her glasses and glared at me. "Library studies confirmed the last trains left Richmond—for Danville, Virginia—close to midnight. The Treasury and midshipmen were on one of those trains."

"Your fiancé's library research backed up Nathaniel's journal entries?"

Her voice remained tranquil, but her mouth turned down in another smirk. "Do you have wax in your ears?"

I stifled a witty retort and yielded. Wanted to keep Lilith reading. But the journal seemed a dead-end as a tool to find Digger's killer. "What happened next?"

She turned a page and continued reading:

April 6, 1865 - Arrived in Danville. People greeted us warmly. Ate cornbread and hardtack. There was a coffee-like drink made from acorns. Captain Parker inspected the train and ordered we watch each car.

General Lee's army withdrew west across Virginia—fleeing the Union army. Some said our military would

no longer fight in military formation. Had to break
up into countless guerilla bands, like General Mosby's
Raiders. I talked with Captain Parker about the
soundness of this tactic used by our hit and run raiders.

Our orders said to transport the treasure to the
government mint in Charlotte. We got provisions from
the storehouses in Danville. Train set out for Charlotte.

I frowned at Lilith, a quizzical expression. "I recall Mosby led partisan raiders in Virginia. What does Harper mean by countless guerilla bands?"

"Digger told me Lee had the choice of surrendering at Appomattox or dissolving the army into many small guerrilla units. Lee elected to surrender and begin the peace."

"Hmm, was guerilla warfare a serious consideration?"

"My fiancé read that—after Richmond had fallen—President Davis wanted to switch from defending territory to attacking with small units, which would then blend back into the countryside."

"You know history," I said. "Did Digger tell you or did you study it?"

"Digger taught me a bunch. I didn't get a whole lot of formal schooling."

Just because Lilith was as immovable as a stone wall didn't mean she was thick as a stone. She wasn't dumb. But she was street smart, not book smart.

She returned to the journal, "The next entries on April 7th and April 9th are the ones I read out at your boss's office. Do I need to repeat them?"

"No that's fine," I said.

Lilith had a gleam in her eyes like she felt proud of her fiancé, the skilled treasure hunter. I sensed she had more interest in Digger getting credit for finding the map than in claiming gold for herself. This woman felt strong loyalty toward her friends.

I splayed my hands wide on the coffee table. "Please tell me what happened after Midshipman Harper made his map."

"You don't have much patience, do you?" She turned to the page following the map and read:

April 12, 1865 - Reached my family home.

April 17, 1865 - Have now spent five days with my kin. I am going to join our Army at Swannanoa Gap to defend against Stoneman's raiders. Leaving this journal at home for safekeeping until I return.

I realized the diary contained no further entries. "What happened to our midshipman?"

"The journal had been left at the Old Fort home. Nathaniel died at the Swannanoa Gap Battle, the last engagement of the Civil War. No one at the battle knew the war had ended."

I continued to wonder how this got Digger killed. "Your fiancé began digging around Morganton?"

"Using a hundred and thirty-five-year-old map, Digger started looking. He dug near the old railroad tracks. He made a mistake: got drunk and showed Hayes a copy of the map."

I glanced up from writing in my notepad. "Digger didn't find the treasure?"

"Digger's dead. Hard to hunt treasure dead."

I bit my tongue, an approach that had served me well during my time in the Military Police. "But Digger and Hayes both had hunted this hidden treasure?"

She nodded. "They dug at night. Separately."

As she closed Midshipman Harper's diary, I realized there was another notebook on the coffee table. Lilith saw me glancing at it. "Digger's workbook. About what he found in the Old Fort attic."

"What kind of finds?"

She opened the bound notebook to an arbitrary page. "He researched Bertha Harper, the wife of his adopting father. Born in Fürstenberg, Germany. In 1945, after the war ended, she served drinks and simple meals in a German village."

I brushed down my cowlick and interrupted Lilith. "I met her. She's austere and introverted."

She narrowed her eyes and grimaced. "Bertha can act standoffish. She disliked Digger."

Lilith turned back to Digger's working journal and summarized. "Digger's father, Michael, was a Jewish soldier at a U.S. army base nearby. He met and married Bertha. After the army discharged Michael, she moved to the U.S. with her husband."

Lilith closed and stacked the journals. "I work at a mail store. Got to go to work. Take these documents and make any copies you need."

She waited as if she wanted to ask me a question. "Why doesn't Ms. Roth leave the mansion to do the investigation herself?"

I got this question a lot. "Roth is brainy, but she's also impatient and anxious."

Lilith wrinkled her nose. "What do you mean?"

"Roth has agoraphobia, a type of anxiety condition where she is afraid to leave her mansion she knows to be safe."

Lilith's eyes opened wide. "She sends you out and you report back to her, tell her what you see and hear."

I grinned at Lilith. She was quick-witted. "I am like a roving detective. I do the legwork for a detective genius."

Lilith wrinkled her nose again. "And she provides room and board for you?"

"She's fidgety. She wants us at the mansion so she can get hold of us immediately to work on a case."

So far, Lilith hadn't convinced me Hayes killed Digger for a Civil War map. She had told me a sad tale about a man she loved. She did have her facts straight. Could Lilith be right? Could Johnny Hayes have decided the treasure existed and killed Digger to keep it all? Maybe. Maybe not.

I still didn't know who poisoned Digger, so my next step would be to pick the brain of my boss. What did Roth know about the poison aconite, used to kill Digger? Where did the killer get it?

7

ASHEVILLE — TUESDAY

Early afternoon, I pulled into the garage at the back of Roth's mansion and walked in through the basement. Taylor, our chef, her red hair fixed in a French braid, stood in the main hallway. "Howdy, Don."

She'd been watching for me. I didn't like this. "What's up?"

She smirked like I imagined a crocodile does close to pouncing on a zebra at a waterhole. "Miz Roth a-wantin' to see you'ns."

"What's up?" I repeated.

She had turned her back on me, heading toward the kitchen. "You'ns will find out."

"Damn it. Tell me what I'm walking into." She had long been my pal, but I stuck out my tongue at her back. Forsaken, I poked my head into Roth's office. "Want to see me?"

Roth glanced up, put down her book, and began her impatient, left-handed tap on the desk, never a good sign. Under her pageboy-cut white hair dropping straight down to her shoulders, her eyes glared. "It has been said, 'There are two theories to arguing with a woman. Neither one works.'" She stopped tapping. "Our client is furious with you."

I glared back at her. "I never argued with Lilith. Explaining facts is not arguing."

Roth slammed her palm on her desk, the long sleeve of her dark-green, glossy tunic pulling back from her hand. "Dense as a granite slab."

Pressing my lips into a thin line and pushing my palms against the edge of her desk, I waited for her to expel her frenzy.

She rolled her eyes at the ceiling. "Listen carefully. Here's what I want."

I leaned rearward and crossed my arms. "I await your pronouncement."

Mad as a bride abandoned at the altar, she bored into my eyes with hers. "Make nice with Lilith. Her story bubbles gold. If it exists, find it."

My jaw dropped; she persisted in chasing a phantom. "I'm busy searching for a killer."

She stood and placed both her palms on the edge of her desk. "Keep Lilith happy," she shouted.

I leaned forward and bellowed back, "It's a mirage."

"You think nobody cares about money? Try missing a couple of your paychecks."

We faced each other, scowling.

She sat and picked up her book. "You may go."

I walked into the hallway and entered my office next door. My chair stood behind my desk and in front of windows facing out over the rear lawn. With my feet up on a bottom ledge, I reclined and stared out the windows. My boss had an insecure fear of poverty. Her anxiety had driven her to talk nonsense with me. *Cool down. She's eccentric.*

My throbbing pulse slowed. I heard the doorbell ring. Let Taylor answer it. I continued to calm down by following two ravens, walking with their odd gait outside on the grass. My eyelids began to droop.

"Oh, Don." Behind me was Taylor. I rotated my head to face her, as she stood, smirking in my doorway.

Now what?

"Roth are a-lookin' for ya."

"Thanks for prepping me for my earlier meeting with Roth."

There was her smirk again. "You'ns got a surprise coming."

"What surprise? Damn it, Taylor, you're not funny."

As she turned toward the kitchen, she waved her left hand over her shoulder. "You'll see."

I muttered at her back and headed to see my boss. What had I done now?

I stopped inside the office door. A visitor, her back toward me, her brown hair barely extending above the top of her chair, sat facing my boss at her desk.

"Here he is now," Roth said, waving me in.

The woman turned in her chair. Her face showed a mischievous elegance reminding me of those legendary actresses in old Hollywood movies from the forties and fifties. I knew her. Her visage—should she fire up her smile—could jolt my heart.

"Hello, Donnell," she said.

Carla Diaz was an irrepressible bundle of energy and enthusiasm in a small, Hispanic package. I froze. I might be dense about the female of my species, but I grasped they bristled with more weapons than the male in the battle of the sexes. The most dangerous would be the queen of the chessboard—a stunning woman with beautiful legs and brains, like the one in front of me.

Carla waited. Adrenalin flushed through my body, brought on by my deep-seated male emotion: fancy or flight. I last saw her, when was it, three months ago? Back when we parted.

She stood up, in a dark-blue, close-fitted dress with a high neckline. Her eyes scanned me inquisitively. She walked over and hugged me, more a sisterly hold than a cling.

When she pulled back, I finally spoke, "C-c-carla, you look wonderful. Didn't expect to see you."

She laughed, a throaty, menacing snort. "Good to see you too."

She spoke not another word and fluttered her eyes. At that moment, my brain stopped dead; nothing came out as I opened my mouth. How had Taylor known I was in trouble before I knew?

Roth spoke up, covering my verbal embarrassment. "Carla is our new office manager. To help me with everyday tasks."

"Wonderful," Taylor startled me from behind. "Where does she start?"

Roth pursed her lips. "She'll help Don work with Lilith."

Taylor chuckled and leered at me. "Lucky you."

Roth told Taylor, "Show Carla the mansion. Get her settled in her room and take her around to meet Bruce and Mickey."

Leaving with Taylor, Carla whispered to me, "You never called or wrote. I guess love doesn't conquer all?"

Chattering amiably, they left me with Roth in the office. Roth waited. I moved to Carla's vacated chair. "How did Carla get here?"

"She phoned for you," Roth said. "We talked. I hired her."

"But you don't know her."

"She's smart, curious, and aggressive. All qualities I want for my office manager. As I said, she called by chance and I engaged her."

"But we were seeing each other, pitching woo. She was my Hunny."

"Too loud." Roth pointed to the front of the room. "Close the door."

I shut the door and returned to the chair before her desk. She leaned forward. "Hiring Carla isn't about you. It's about what she wants."

I fiddled with the college ring on my left hand. "What do you mean?"

"Someone put it in her head investigative work is exciting." Roth gave me a deadpan stare and shook her head. "I wonder who that was?"

I remembered talking to Carla about my job. "Don't blame me. She'll find investigation isn't fun; it's writing never-ending reports and standing in the cold and rain to do surveillance."

"Fine, you didn't have anything to do with it," Roth snapped at me, "but she's here now. She's clever, inquisitive, and wants to learn more about being a private eye."

I got up and whirled toward the door. "Fine. Hire her." I stopped with my hand on the doorknob. "What am I supposed to do?"

"Start her reviewing your cases: files, invoices, and microcassette case recordings."

I left the office and swung by the kitchen-dining room where Taylor brewed fresh coffee. I took a cup out to the flagstone patio where I paced back and forth, thinking about what to do next. I'm a gumshoe, a good one, but people drain my time, peppering me with snags like a summer shower. I'm not a people person. Lilith, a fanatical woman, is going to drive me into a nervous breakdown. Carla is alluring and scary. Did Roth hire Carla to get even with me for past defiance? An early-afternoon sun hung in a clear sky to warm me, relaxing me in one of the wrought-iron chairs spread around the patio. Bruce, his black, corkscrewed hair fluffed out, took a seat beside me. "You done got your fingers in the wringer."

"You heard?"

Bruce laughed. "Everyone heard. I was all the way around the mansion in the computer room."

I waved my left hand dismissively. "She's greedy. Wants me to follow the gold. Its glitter blinds her."

He nibbled the cinnamon roll he had brought from the kitchen. "Guy, tell me your investigation is going better than it sounds."

"Need other suspects. Lost treasure keeps popping up because I have no other prospect."

Bruce nodded. "Remember when we ran with Digger? He always got into trouble. Lilith probably doesn't know half the things he did."

I rubbed my cowlick. "Would you use your computer to check for federal and state criminal charges against Digger?"

Bruce shook his head. "I'm busy. Afraid you'll have to do it yourself."

"Hmm. Your search. I'll pay for beers next time we're at the Naughty Hops."

Bruce finished his pastry and wiped his lips. "Okay. Besides, Roth told me to charge some of my time to your case. What about da Hayes guy?"

"Check him out too."

A light breeze drifted over the patio. He turned to me. "What did Goodman say about the crime scene?"

"Did we give him a case of scotch whiskey?"

"Guy, I'm checking the criminal records for Digger and Hayes. Can't do all the work. You need to meet with the Chief Deputy."

Bruce got up and left.

Before questioning Hayes, I needed to speak off the record with Goodman about the murder. If he had solved the case, he would have passed the info to the District Attorney's Office, and the DA wouldn't share anything with me. But, at the funeral, Goodman denied having identified the culprit.

I felt no rush to leave the courtyard, with its light breeze and warming sun. My thoughts turned to Lilith: take her with me to meet Goodman? No, that wouldn't do. He would clam up, not wanting to talk to Digger's fiancé, a suspect.

I went back inside the mansion. Carla sat in an office at the rear. Perched at a big desk, she had unpacked some of my old case files. I tried to explain my brilliant sleuthing, but she wanted to analyze the information on her own, chasing me away with waves of her hand.

I phoned the Chief Deputy and found him in his office. He gave me the can't-contaminate-an-ongoing-investigation evasion but agreed to meet me. I drove my Mustang downtown.

#

Now that October had arrived, the tourist crowd had shrunk. Goodman was in the beautiful Buncombe County Courthouse, a seventeen-story building, faced with cream-colored brick and finely dressed masonry. Others had told me the lobby had a Neo-Classical interior. It contained a sweeping marble staircase, a ceiling with sunken panels called a coffered ceiling, and a mosaic tile floor. It was a magnificent endowment from a bygone era.

On one of the upper floors, Harry Goodman sat at his desk, slowly stroking his white goatee. "You working for Lilith?"

His office had a chill. I kept on my double-breasted half trench coat and sat down before him. "I'm on a quest for Roth."

He lowered his eyebrows in a questioning expression.

"Want to take a break? Run over to the Tavern?" I asked.

Harry stood up. "You buying?"

"Does it rain in Asheville?"

Goodman grabbed a canvas bag with his spare clothes and went to the men's room to change out of his black winter uniform. I followed Goodman—in his civilian clothes—out to the square. We walked to the Tavern on the Square, an old, red-brick building, and found a table, avoiding the long bar at the rear of the tavern.

I ordered beers. "Want something to eat?"

"Just a beer ... maybe two."

Goodman gazed out at the street through a long row of windows, his head motionless, and his eyes unchanging. "Ah, Don, time is tearing by—like a steady whoosh of wind in winter. I remember when you were a young kid shooting out streetlights. You were a juvenile crime wave until I figured out it was you. You promised me you wouldn't do it again, and you didn't."

I thought back to my old Daisy BB gun and smiled. Our beers arrived, and I took a sip. I didn't remember Goodman ever speaking so poetic when he was younger. He had grown long in the tooth.

Maybe he had become melancholy and thought about retirement. He picked up reminiscing again. "Later you played football with my son, who was too lazy for the game. Today, he manages a big box store in Charlotte, and you're a hotshot P.I." He took a sip of beer. "Known you so long—you rascal."

We always had to play a pecking-order game. I was forever the wet-behind-the-ears kid, and he was the elder of detective investigation. "I'm not a rascal—give me an example."

Harry did his drawn-out stare before replying. "Back in your senior year in high school, didn't you wrestle a bear at the county fair?"

His memory was still good. "Bear was smaller than me."

"Answer the question."

"Yeah."

"You're a rascal."

"Doesn't make me a rascal."

"You're a rascal."

"Do okay. Right now, I'm stuck on Digger's murder. Tell me about the crime scene."

He wiped beer off his white mustache. "I know your grandmother taught you to respect older people."

"Sorry. Please tell me what you found, sir?"

He took a gulp and set the mug down. "Two days before the poisoning, a person, unknown, shot at Digger in the woods. Scared him but missed him. My deputies found shell casings and a bullet for a pistol, a Sig Sauer P239. We ain't got a suspect."

I took a small swallow of beer. 'A P239? Don't often hear that around these parts."

"Yeah. The Swiss make it, A semi-automatic light-weight handgun."

I recalled Sig Sauer had recently started producing the P239. "Heard about the shooting. You still think Hayes didn't do the poisoning?"

"I told you I doubt it. He's a person-of-interest, but he doesn't feel right. He's a cruel, macho lummox, but is he a poisoner?" Goodman shook his head.

"Lilith says he did it."

"Based on Digger always whining about Hayes stealing his valuables. Stealing isn't killing! Morning of the poisoning, our nasty hillbilly and his two accomplices were together, hungover from a night of drinking at Hayes' grimy shack."

"Any clues at Digger's house?"

Goodman emptied his mug with a long gulp. "You know aconite poison was in Digger's coffee cup, and we found no aconite in the cinnamon container or anywhere else in the house."

"Tell me what I don't know."

"Living room furniture was a shamble, which Lilith said was unusual." He signaled for a second draft. "That morning, I think Digger ran into his front room. Then someone sneaked into his kitchen, put aconite in his coffee, and skedaddled out the back door."

"Fingerprints?"

"Only those of Digger and Lilith."

"Surely, you found something."

"The techs found a partial muddy footprint on the floor of the screened-in rear porch. Appeared fresh but didn't have a distinctive pattern."

I sipped my drink. "Who did it?"

"You do your job, Hotshot. You tell me what you find, and I'll tell you if you're right."

"Hmm, thanks for sharing, I think."

Goodman remained quiet for a moment, watching the pedestrians out on Pack Square. "Let's trade? You phone me with your clues. I warn you about Hayes."

"I plan to see him next. What about him?"

"Watch his dogs. They're dangerous."

I gave him a blank expression, a puzzled glance.

Goodman finished his second beer. "Don't turn your back on the canines."

Was he kidding me? What kind of dogs were we talking about?

8

RURAL BUNCOMBE COUNTY — WEDNESDAY

On a two-lane road somewhere above Hayes' shack, my partner, Mickey, parked his Explorer. The road struck me as wretched. Potholes in the road, drainage ditches clogged with plastic trash bags and abandoned couches screamed, "I don't care anymore." Parking near a mailbox with peeling paint and a door that wouldn't close, we got out and waded through a field of tall grass. An ancient yellow school bus rusted next to a woodshed whose blistered paint exposed gray, dry-rotting slats, already tilting toward the bus. It would collapse next year or maybe the year after.

My face tightened, and my eyes narrowed in response to the dumping. "Except for the debris, this would be a cheery meadow."

Behind me, Mickey made a *tut-tut* sound with his mouth. "Need to catch the dumpers and thrash 'em."

I searched the area ahead for Hayes' shack. "Closed-minded Fascist."

Mickey—a bear of a man at 210 pounds both muscular and hefty—followed behind me, making little noise for a big fella. "Mushy-headed liberal."

After another fifteen minutes of slipping through the woods, we spotted the shack off to the side and down a slope. We halted at the edge of the scrub forest.

Mickey sat down with his back against a small tree. "You're just gonna walk up to his door and knock?"

"Yeah."

"Reckless. This guy, Hayes, won't talk."

Maybe Hayes would speak with me. Maybe not. I had planned for my interview with him: getting Mickey to accompany me, strapping a dog-bite cover on my arm and under my jacket, and placing my M1911 pistol in my belt holster. Even if he refused to meet with me, I would have learned more about him.

Mickey sat on the ground. "We're spying on Hayes?"

"Detectives don't spy, we investigate."

"This is stupid. Wait till he's in a bar, with people around, and walk up to 'im."

Before replying, I scanned the broken-down shack, its silvery-colored chain-link fence enclosing the entire trash-strewn yard. The enclosure appeared a pen for dogs; there were dirt patches and dug-up holes all over the enclosed area. I didn't see them; I guessed Hayes stuck the mutts in the main hut. "Serves me right for bringing you along. You don't like my direct approach to gathering intel."

"Direct is meeting this guy in Starbucks. Stupid is confronting him in the woods when he has a pack of wild dogs."

I sat and crossed my legs. "Hell's bells—you used to have a backbone—before you married Taylor and became an old man."

Mickey reached into his long duffle bag and pulled out a crushed package of pastry. "Speaking of my wife, she wants to know how you talked Carla into coming to Asheville?"

"Didn't talk her into anything. Roth hired her."

Mickey paused eating, brushing his mustache and goatee clear of crumbs. "Taylor says you're Carla's type, tall, buff, and shy around women. Says you need to show a little passion—enchant her."

"Shut up. I should have brought Carla instead of you." Mickey paid me no mind. I glared and flashed the palm of my left hand at him. I heard the caw of crows. Two were in a tree above us. They waited to scavenge any food my partner dropped.

"What about you?" I asked. "Didn't Roth tell you to investigate the fiancée, Lilith?

"Lilith works at a mail store. While she worked, I went through her papers at Digger's house."

I gave him a dazed stare. "You can't just break into our client's house."

Mickey gave me a shy smile. "Roth said to find out if she's cheating."

"She's living in Digger's house?" I asked.

"Her clothes and shoes and papers were there."

"What did you find?"

"No insurance policy for Digger. No stray, unexplained pile of cash."

I raised my eyebrows at Mickey. "Spied on her? Followed her around?"

"She works and goes home. Doesn't fool around with a lover."

"You put everything back in its place at Digger's house?"

Mickey smiled again. "Everything. My investigation must be well done. Especially when I break the law."

"You informed Roth?"

"She knows."

The wire fence circled the house, an enclosure topped by a No Trespassing sign, surrounded to the sides by thickets of vines and shrubs. My partner put the remaining pastries back in his haversack. I stood. "Let's get started."

I left the tree line and headed toward the structure. Dogs barked inside the shack. Stopping outside the fence, I called, "Hayes! Johnny Hayes!"

The dog noise masked my hollers, but anyone inside had to know I stood before their dwelling. Minutes passed. The barking subsided a little. A stout man came through the front door. I recognized him as the man I had grabbed at Digger's funeral, identified as Hayes.

He stepped aside to let three eighty-to-ninety-pound mongrels rush past him to snarl and snap at me, exposing open mouths around pointed canine teeth, their ears flattened against the sides of their heads—nasty brutes.

The fence stretched and bent as the canines pounded it but stood.

The pudgy man's eyes held my attention. The white part of his eyes was prominent and spread around the colored pupil region, giving him a bug-eyed look. A warning reaction, fear, diffused through my frame. My situation could get out of control quickly.

Pudgy stood behind the dogs. "What ya want?" he yelled in a rough, raspy voice.

I moved my right hand inside my jacket. "Are you Johnny Hayes?"

I could barely hear him above the snarls of the dogs. "None of your business. Now git."

"Want to talk with you."

He stared at me with those crazy eyes. "I mean it. Git."

The dogs stayed in their fury. Hayes didn't talk like a hillbilly. Nor did he dress like one; he wore a black, fleece jogging outfit.

"I want to ask about your late business partner."

"I'm counting to ten. Then I'm opening this gate. Turn the dogs loose." He moved toward the fence gate.

The dogs looked much more bloodcurdling in real life than what Goodman had hinted. I pulled my pistol from my holster and turned, so my left side and the dog-bite guard around my left arm were toward the dogs. I worked to keep my hands steady as I racked the slide.

"I'm leaving. Release those dogs—I shoot them."

Hayes and the dogs stopped in a cluster of fur and fleece at the fence gate.

I backed away, keeping my left side turned toward the pack on the other side of the fence.

Hayes kept his hands fixed at his sides while I retreated. His wide-open, scary eyes fastened on me. But then they shifted and gawked behind me. I glanced to my rear.

My partner stood with his Remington 870 shotgun, its muzzle up, its barrel across his body.

We backed up the slope from the hut, keeping our eyes pinned on the dogs. Our retreat continued through the woods to the Explorer and away down the trash-strewn road.

Turning toward my partner in the driver's seat, I said, "Thanks. I'll talk with Hayes when he doesn't have his dogs with him."

Mickey snorted. "Maybe you'll listen to me next time?"

I chuckled. "Chief Deputy Goodman has a point. Hayes doesn't act like a poisoner."

Mickey glanced sideways at me. "More the direct type?"

"Yeah."

"Too bad Hayes chased you off before you could question him."

"Not all bad. Hayes is a real whack-job—crazy enough to kill."

9

ASHEVILLE — WEDNESDAY

When Mickey and I got back to the mansion, Taylor had begun to serve lunch, a casserole of fried chicken livers baked with rice. Mickey left his shotgun in a corner, and we joined Roth and Carla at the table.

Carla glanced at the gun. "Been hunting?"

"Dog," I said.

She knitted her brow but said nothing.

I took a seat next to Carla and helped myself to the casserole. Mickey sat across the table from us. "How was your first day?" I asked Carla, stealing a peek at the swell of her breasts, straining against her Oxford shirt with the top two buttons open.

"Everyone is friendly. The house and grounds are beautiful."

"Well, Don can use your help," Taylor said as she refreshed the glasses with iced tea. "He need a partner with tact."

Carla showed a shocked expression and switched to a smile. "I've found Don tactful."

Mickey snorted. "Especially with the ladies. Heard his nickname, in high school, was—"

"Carla doesn't want to hear old-school tales," I broke in.

"I'd love to hear. I see Don's blushing."

Taylor had circled the table, filling glasses. "He should be."

Roth, who wore a full-length black dress, hooded collar, and long sleeves, scanned the table. "Where's Bruce?"

Taylor stopped circling and answered Roth. "He asked to be excused. Wanted to see a ball game on TV in the media room. I fixed him a tray."

She glanced down at her plate, spooned casserole on it, and switched topics. "Let's discuss the poison."

She gazed at Taylor, who had changed to collecting plates at the table. "You told me one couldn't buy aconite at a pharmacy. It comes from the plant monkshood—have to grow it."

"Yes, ma'am."

"Hard to grow?" Roth asked.

"Grows in da wild. Likes da sun but is shade-tolerant. Folks know never to let hounds eat it—poison da hound."

"Would it be reasonable to guess the killer has monkshood plants?"

"Yes, ma'am."

"Remember I want you to visit the neighbors around Johnny Hayes's shack, the Old Fort home, and Digger's home. Does monkshood grow nearby?"

Taylor nodded. "I'll go there and keep my sight berries peeled for monkshood."

"Go incognito. When you search for monkshood around Johnny Hayes's house, take Mickey and don't go near the dogs."

"What dat word, incog—?"

"Hide who you are."

The doorbell rang. Taylor left the room and returned with Lilith, wearing a black blouse with frills at the sleeves and blue jeans. Roth introduced Lilith to Carla. A color combination had set me to thinking: both Roth and Lilith always dressed in dark colors. Lilith dressed to grieve the passing of her fiancé. Did my boss wear black for the same reason? If so, for whom? She supported the people around her but shrouded her past in secrecy bordering on opaque.

Taylor served coffee to Lilith, who draped her leather jacket over the back of a chair and turned to me. "You questioned Hayes this morning. Do you have proof he killed my Digger?"

I put down my fork. "Didn't talk with Hayes. I left when that nutcase threatened to release a pack of dogs on me."

Mickey hooted. "Man's in the wrong business. Should be breeding guard dogs—big ones."

Lilith glared at me through her black-rimmed glasses. "Do you believe me now? He's horrible."

Remembering Roth's instructions, I attempted to pacify our client. "You're right. I can see he's dangerous."

Lilith leaned forward over the table. "Dangerous? He killed Digger."

My client was determined. "I believe that's possible, but we'll need more evidence to convince the Sheriff's Office."

Carla glanced back and forth between Lilith and me. Roth came to my rescue. "Don met with Chief Deputy Goodman. He's not positive who killed your fiancé."

Lilith remained petulant. "You have to prove Hayes did it."

I spooned more of the chicken livers and rice onto my plate. "I should consider all suspects."

Lilith grew red in the face. "Suspects? He's the only one accused."

The room went silent. Lilith took off her glasses and glared at me. "No one else had a reason to kill."

Roth pursed her lips. "We've uncovered other suspects. This morning, Bruce, my computer specialist, dug up criminal activity in Digger's background."

Lilith settled back in her chair, giving Roth a raised-eyebrow expression. "What do you mean?"

Roth twisted her head to view Carla. "Get Bruce to join us. Tell him to bring his findings."

Carla left and—after several minutes—returned with Bruce. He carried folders and loose papers and seemed nervous.

Roth turned toward her computer whiz kid. "Bruce, you've been researching the public records for Hayes and Digger Harper. Report."

He sat and stacked his folders and papers on an empty chair. "The county and city arrested Johnny Hayes multiple times for fighting. The county took him to court cuz of nonpayment of property taxes. The authorities often detained two other individuals, along with Hayes, also for fighting."

Bruce tended to slip into what I called his vernacular when he got tense. Once relaxed, his voice reflected his college education. "Dovetails with what Goodman told us about Hayes," I said. "Anything on Digger?"

My partner, Bruce, beamed. "I found two court cases. One involved Digger. Both be about taking Indian relics from the Cherokee Reservation."

He paused, maybe to let us absorb what he had told us. "The tribal police arrested an individual on Cherokee land. Paul Atsadi, a member of the tribe, dug into an ancient Indian burial mound. At night."

Bruce had awakened my curiosity. Carla stared at Bruce. Lilith listened.

"Digger saw Atsadi tunneling through the burial site and reported the damage to the tribal authorities. The tribal police arrested this Atsadi for digging up the graves."

Carla interrupted. "Why dig through an Indian mound?"

"He's a tomb robber," Roth replied, shaking her head. "Unusual as that would be for a tribal member in good standing."

"The tribal police searched Atsadi's house and found dug-up Cherokee relics," Bruce said. "Had a drug habit, methamphetamines. Sold relics from the burial grounds—for drugs."

"Where is he now?" I asked.

Bruce searched through his papers. "Digger testified against Atsadi in court. The courts tried him and convicted him. He served three years and got released on parole last month."

"The penalty for drug possession is severe," Roth said. "In which court was he tried? Federal, state, or tribal?"

"The tribal police arrested Atsadi, and the tribal court system tried him."

"Well done, Bruce," Roth said. "Did this Atsadi know Digger tipped the police?"

"Yes, Boss."

Roth nodded to Bruce. "Maybe this tomb robber had more reason to kill Digger than Johnny Hayes did. Carla, make copies of Bruce's records and distribute them to the rest of us."

Lilith grunted. "Why are we talking about this person? He didn't poison my fiancé. Digger never said anything about him."

No one replied to Lilith.

"Good work, Bruce," I said, "you're finally earning your paycheck."

He grinned at me. "Look and learn, my friend."

Roth steepled her fingers while she thought. "What was Digger doing on Cherokee land? How did he happen to see this tomb robber burrowing into a mound? How did the tribal council handle Digger's presence?"

Bruce scanned his papers. "Ain't known. But Digger didn't want anyone to know he was there. According to court records, he wore a ghillie suit, allowing him to see Atsadi but Atsadi couldn't see him."

Carla stirred beside me. "What's that?"

"A concealment outfit, to make the wearer appear like dense shrubbery."

"Why?" Roth asked.

Bruce seemed taken aback. "Why what?"

"Why was Digger in a ghillie suit on Cherokee land?"

Bruce paused. "Maybe hunting for treasure? The tribal police kept mum about why Digger happened to be there."

"Did your fiancé tell you about this episode?" Roth asked Lilith.

Lilith took some time to answer. She twisted strands of her blonde hair and fretfully pulled on them. "I remember nothing."

"Why didn't Digger turn a blind eye?" Carla asked. "Why accuse Atsadi in front of the police?"

"Digger was a student of history," Lilith said. "Maybe he was upset by a tomb robber spoiling a prehistoric structure."

Roth placed her fork and a used napkin on her plate. "Atsadi is a suspect. We need information about him. Where do we begin?"

Lilith stood abruptly, sending her chair toppling to the floor. "Hayes did it! We don't need to consider this tomb robber." After grabbing her leather jacket, she stamped her right foot on the floor— *Stomp!*—and ran from the room, with Taylor stepping out of her path to avoid a collision.

Roth pointed at Carla. "Try to catch her before she gets to her Vespa. See if she'll come back?"

I admired Carla's curves as she rushed to catch Lilith. Thank goodness, I had been born into this world after the invention of stretch pants.

Sipping her after-lunch coffee, my boss paused. "We'll continue to investigate Hayes because our client judges him the killer. But don't neglect Mr. Atsadi, who maybe had a stronger motive. Also, why were the two at the same Cherokee burial mound in the middle of the night?"

She looked around the table. No one answered her question. She sighed and faced Bruce. "Tell me about the second court case involving Cherokee artifacts."

He seemed relaxed and thumbed through his papers. "A year after Atsadi went to jail, three Cherokee Indians were caught digging up Indian artifacts."

"Who masterminded this second crime?" Roth asked. "Were drugs involved?"

Bruce shook his head. "The tribal police suspected a collector funded the thefts. They called him 'Mr. *X*.' Never found who he was."

Roth finished her coffee. "That's vague."

"All I have, Boss. I'll try to find more."

Roth tapped the table with her left hand. "I am disappointed no one identified the collector. The distance between success and failure is measured in persistence."

Carla returned. "Lilith left on a motorbike. Is she a problem?"

I chuckled at Carla. "I'm beginning to understand Lilith. She's seeking to avenge, not to be a problem. She's persistent: trying to accomplish one thing, revenge."

Roth got up from the table, issuing orders as she stood. "You know what to do. Investigate Mr. Atsadi. Find if this Mr. *X* exists."

Roth paused, staring out the windows as if thinking about something. "I wonder. Was that a skull and crossbones Digger drew in the sugar on the floor? Or was the drawing of bones like in an Indian burial chamber?"

Carla turned to me and mouthed, "What skull and crossbones?"

I mouthed back, "Later."

Roth got up to leave the room. "Hell's bells, Digger was dying, painfully spewing his guts on the floor. What was he trying to say with his sketch?" The silence was her only response. She left.

#

I had insomnia, flipping and rolling under the sheets, so when the phone rang, my eyes were open in the dark. I fumbled around my nightstand and answered on the second ring.

A voice—could have been a woman—slurred, "Ooh … ooh …agh."

The call seemed genuine. Not a prank by Bruce. "Hello? Who's there?" *Someone's suffering*, I thought.

Silence, then, "Ooh … ooh," followed by a hush.

I sat up on the edge of the bed. "Who are you?"

No answer. It had sounded a little like our client. "Lilith?"

Someone answered in a muted voice, "Damn them."

She needed help. "Lilith, I'm coming. I'm going to hang up. Call nine-one-one."

I ran down the hall in pajamas and knocked on Bruce's door. "Wake up! Crisis!"

I got the nine-one-one operator and asked for emergency medical services at Digger's house. Our household awoke; Carla answered my knock and said she was dressing. I put on pants and shirt and pulled my pistol out of its lockbox. On my way out, I passed Roth in the hall. She closed the lapel of her long, black robe and said, "Inform me when you can."

Carla and I joined Bruce in his Jeep and left the mansion for Lilith. The area around Digger's house lay in pitch black at a time, as I used to say back in the military police, of oh dark thirty. His house, of weather-beaten boards, planks bleached a mixture of light brown and dark-brown blotches, had a metallic rooftop. I saw a single light high up at the roofline. The Jeep's headlights illuminated the darkness more than the house light.

"There she is," Carla said. "Three o'clock."

Off to the side of a gravel parking area, Lilith lay on the ground partially wrapped up in a torn, plastic bag. Her head poking through a slash on the side of the black bag, Lilith still wore the leather coat she dressed in to ride her Vespa. Carla rushed to her and supported her in a hug. Hate streaked from Lilith's eyes. She grumbled but didn't appear to be bleeding or have broken bones.

Beside me, Bruce held a pistol and a flashlight. "I will be seeing if anyone else is here."

I bent my head toward Lilith. "Carla and I'll find out what happened."

Bruce slipped away. I eased the big black bag off Lilith. I supposed her attackers pulled the bag over her head and torso and knotted its plastic straps to enclose her. She had escaped by tearing a gaping hole in the elastic material. I noticed she held her mobile phone in her hand.

Carla sat on one side of Lilith, and I seated myself on the other. Our client said, "Damn," and tightened her fists. Whatever happened hadn't shaken her confidence; I had never seen her back down from anything.

After a while, Bruce's flashlight shone around the house, and he stopped in front of us. "They are gone." He settled himself cross-legged on the ground.

The emergency medical service ambulance drove into the parking area. A paramedic and technician determined Lilith had been slapped and choked but had no visible lacerations, or, it turned out, fracture or sprain. She said her attackers hadn't raped her, only grabbed her, smacked her, and stuffed her body in a plastic sack. The emergency team applied ice to her facial bruises and helped her into the house.

Lilith reclined on the couch in the front room and stared straight ahead. Digger's old terrier went back on its hind legs, wined, and licked her hands. As she composed herself, I searched Digger's kitchen cabinets and found an open bottle of bourbon. I poured a drink for Lilith and called Roth. I explained our client appeared physically unharmed and we planned to talk with her. We disconnected.

"Must have been Hayes," Lilith said. "I should have expected this."

Carla appeared calm, holding Lilith's shoulders to comfort her. Bruce and I sat and watched. "The shits popped up and attacked me."

Lilith muttered something incomprehensible under her breath and hugged herself. The dog and the rest of us waited. "There were three of them, waiting for me in the dark."

I took out my notepad and started writing.

"I felt"—she began to shake—"helpless. I was mad."

Carla glanced at me and shook her head. Although our victim had experienced minor physical injury, I wondered how she might react to this long-term. I leaned back and studied her.

"I came back home from my mail-store job. Men grabbed me as soon as I got off the Vespa. They wore masks."

I glanced up from my notepad. "Masks? Wore a sack with eye holes?"

She gave a dismissive wave of her hand. "Like a Halloween mask."

I recalled the Vespa lay on its side. "You fought, and the motor scooter got knocked over?"

Lilith bobbed her head. I turned to Bruce. "Would you see what you can find outside?" He left.

She continued her tale of the attack. "One man was big … Big as two men. Three of them."

The terrier whimpered and moved in circles. "What did they say?" I asked.

"The big man told me, 'Shut yer mouth. Or we'll come back.'"

"What did they do?" Carla asked.

"The big man held me. Others put that plastic sack over my head. I had difficulty breathing."

"I rolled over inside the bag, pushing and stretching the sides. I got my back on the ground and kicked the plastic around me. The side ruptured, and I got my head out into the fresh air."

She breathed rapidly. "They had gone. I sat on the ground and called Don."

Bruce returned. "The grass and brush are trampled down. Nothing left behind—no cigarettes or candy wrappers."

"Fingerprints on the plastic bag?" I asked.

"No prints on the plastic, its surface was smooth or scratched up by the brush. The attackers probably wore gloves."

Lilith turned her face toward me. "Thank you for coming, Don. I knew I could count on you."

Lilith appeared exhausted, and her head had begun to slump. "Carla, we better get her to bed," I said. "Could you stay for what's left of the night?"

"I'll remain with her."

"I'll head back to the mansion. In the morning, I'll report the attack to the Chief Deputy." Bruce and I climbed into the Jeep and departed.

10

CHEROKEE, NORTH CAROLINA — THURSDAY

"Are you sleeping?"

Until she spoke, I hadn't seen Roth in the doorway. I jerked my head up, taking in her maroon tunic and a white lace headscarf. "I'm reading a map."

"With your eyes closed?"

I had been slumped over my desk, flipping pages of a travel Atlas, familiarizing myself with Cherokee, North Carolina. Paul Atsadi's house lay there along a rural road. The distance from the mansion to his home looked to be about forty-five miles. I had decided to make a cold call at the house. I saw no point phoning for an appointment: why would he see me? My plan aimed to leave shortly and arrive late morning. I yawned and brushed my cowlick. "Is there some purpose in your tiptoeing into my office?"

"When are you interviewing the tomb robber?"

"Just about ready to leave."

She pursed her lips. "Take Carla."

I twiddled the college ring on my left hand. "I work alone."

"Not anymore. Take Carla."

I frowned. "She's not trained. Don't know what will come out of her mouth."

Roth stepped in and closed my door. "Keep your voice down. Taking her is only a suggestion but try to remember your boss is asking."

Annoyed, I rolled my eyes back and glanced at the ceiling. "Whatever you say ... Boss."

She walked farther across the floor and stood before me, tapping her fingers on my desk. "She'll do okay."

"Guess I'm taking Carla."

She turned and left, smiling, a playful grin. I watched the folds of her full-length tunic disappear around the door frame and then exhaled. I went to get Carla, who sat at her computer going through my old case files.

"We're driving to Cherokee."

She stood, excited. "My first investigation."

I eyed her black turtleneck jersey, beige slacks, a necklace, and dress shoes with short heels. She had dressed up, expecting—before I knew we were going together—to go with me. I'm a detective. I detected a hint of trouble coming my way.

# # #

A little before midday, Carla sat in my car, ready to go. "Thanks for picking me up last night at Digger's house."

I grinned at her. "When Goodman said his deputies would check on Lilith throughout the night, I could understand why she told you to go home." I hadn't heard from the Chief Deputy since last night.

"Should we stop by Digger's," she asked, "and check on her before we leave?"

"Yeah. We should."

A chill was in the air, leading me to keep the windows raised and turn on the defroster. The sky was gray, and a drizzle dropped. At

Digger's home, Goodman had parked his white Crown Victoria to the side of the house. He opened the front door. "Come in. She's okay." We followed him into the kitchen, where Lilith sat. The terrier had greeted us, chomping on a toy bone and trailing us into the kitchen.

Lilith had Digger's rifle close by, resting on a counter. Her black, plastic-framed glasses set askance on her nose, but the thick frames hadn't broken. The two bruises on Lilith's face—below the line of her glasses—had a red-black color. Her expression brightened when she saw me. "That's my hero. He knew it was me on the phone."

"Lilith, you're smiling. Last night didn't shatter you."

She rose from the kitchen table and hugged me. "Hayes is a snake. He don't scare me. You prove he killed Digger."

"I drove to Hayes' shack," Goodman said. "He and his crew claimed they had been there all night."

"Isn't there some way to protect Lilith?" Carla asked.

"I got Digger's gun. Don't need no protection."

Goodman cleared his throat. "Our deputies have started to swing by this house in their nightly patrols. We're watching for Hayes."

Lilith stared up at the Chief Deputy's face. "Arrest him for Digger's murder, and I wouldn't have this problem."

Goodman covered his eyes with a hand. "We've been over this. I have no evidence to charge Hayes with poisoning Digger."

"What about my attack?"

"If he attacks you again and I catch him, I'll throw him in jail."

Lilith shook her head up and down. "See that you do."

I told Lilith, "Glad to see you've recovered," and hugged her shoulders. Next, I strolled past Carla. "Let's pay a visit to Mr. Atsadi."

# # #

Driving my silver Mustang with Carla as my navigator, I pointed it toward I-40. I wore my laidback private-eye ensemble: black jeans, a dark-blue shirt with small white dots, a light-brown sports coat, and sunglasses. I wondered what we would find: Atsadi might have the persona of the lawyer he used to be or an unkempt ex-convict.

I hadn't thought about taking Carla, but she had to start sometime. Then again, I didn't fancy her interviewing without rehearsing first. On the drive, we discussed how our tomb robber might react to finding us at his door. Carla agreed to follow my lead as the curt detective while she would act in a calming role.

She grinned. "Understand. You're bad P.I.; I'm good P.I."

Closer to Cherokee, deserted motels with iconic neon signs appeared along the two-lane highway, supplanted by modern three-story chain hotels. The forsaken neon signs showed images of Indian braves, wigwams, Indian headdresses, and cabins.

"You probably think my move to Asheville is about you?"

My heart rate jumped. I glanced sideways. Carla's expression betrayed no emotion. "I don't know," I said.

She frowned at me from the passenger seat. Should I have said I was happy to see her whatever the reason she had come here? My chest tightened.

"You had three months to contact me," she said. "You didn't."

Sweat rolled down my back. I studied the Oconaluftee River beside the road, a river about three feet deep, a good-size stream meandering along. I thought I was smart enough to avoid Carla's wrath, but I had gone belly up. I had to answer, but what to say?

Carla continued staring at me, absent her usual sweet smile. "You didn't send your contact information—you promised me you would."

I saw little, flashing spots in front of my eyes and swallowed. Since Carla had arrived at the mansion, I had enjoyed her company.

Didn't want to irritate her. "I kept meaning to call you, but the time slipped by."

Carla cocked an eyebrow and sighed. She concentrated on navigating the rest of the way to Atsadi's house.

He lived in a brown, wooden single-story with a covered front porch and an undernourished lawn. I saw a car parked on the grass to the right side. We got out and headed for Atsadi's front door.

Carla tugged at my sports coat. "Can we break in on him? Won't he call the police?"

"He's on parole. Won't want to involve the cops."

The man who answered my knock had medium-length jet-black hair, combed straight back, and the spooked eyes of a rabbit. He wore a black suit and a charcoal polo shirt. At first glance, he appeared more a professional man than a drug addict. His quizzical expression turned into a frown. "You aren't a Bible thumper," he said, "and you aren't my parole officer. Who are you?"

The man facing me might be indigenous to the North Carolina mountains: brown skinned but not too dark, high cheekbones, and straight hair. He had a stocky frame and viewed me with uncertainty. "Mr. Atsadi?" I asked.

He tried to shut the door, but my foot lay against the door frame. "Are you too thick to understand? Go away."

"Could you help me?" I asked.

He stared at me without responding. I ignored his glower and remained in the doorway. "I'm investigating Digger Harper's death."

His expression didn't change. "He testified against me in the tribal court."

"You need to talk to me."

His eyes dilated, and his face grew red. He had become angry and had decided to hit me. I braced myself.

"No." He jammed an open hand against my chest and pushed.

I didn't move and shoved back with both my hands against his shoulders. He stumbled rearward into his house. I held the door open for Carla, who had stood to my side as I had instructed her, and we walked into a wood-paneled room with a gray rug. I scanned the man and his surroundings for a weapon, finding nothing.

He swung his right fist at me. I took his blow on my left forearm and moved forward a step.

He tottered backward, landing in a rocking chair. The chair tilted sideways, dumping him onto the floor. Atsadi must have decided I was too big to push around because he stayed down and remained still. "Damn you. Who are you?"

"Don Gannon, P.I."

"Hi. I'm Carla Diaz. I'm Don's assistant."

"Well, Gannon, why don't you and your pretty lady turn your tails around, and get out of here? Crap. I'm calling the tribal police."

Atsadi gathered his legs under his body and sprang up, trying to ram me with his head. "Get out."

I bent my knees and pushed his shoulders, sprawling him onto the hardwood floor. I righted the chair, lifted him by the lapels of his suit jacket, and dropped him in the rocker.

He rose to get out of his chair. I shoved him back down into the rocking chair. "Stop pushing me."

"I plan to stay here until you talk to me," I said, "or you can tell us what we want to know, and we'll leave. Over in ten minutes."

Carla stepped past me and placed her hands on my shoulder. "Don, leave Mr. Atsadi alone. Give him time to catch his breath." She turned her mega-bright smile on him. He stared at me with beady eyes but stayed seated and waited. Carla and I sat on a frayed, gray couch, facing him.

"Digger died in the morning, in Asheville, Tuesday, eight days ago," I said. "Where were you that morning?"

He hesitated, with his left eye twitching. Then he gazed over my shoulder as if thinking. "I had a closing that day, with a client at the escrow office."

Beside me, Carla grinned and asked, "Early morning?"

He smiled back at her. "Office secretary was there. Two agents were too." He recited the names of the people at his real-estate office that Tuesday morning. I jotted them down in my notepad.

Atsadi sat in the rocking chair, his legs rigidly set on the floor, and smoothed down his ruffled hair. "I'm a realtor. Obey the law. No longer take drugs."

"After your parole?" Carla asked.

He nodded. "After I got out."

He lowered his head and wrung his hands. "When I left the Craggy Correctional Center, I had determined to go straight, to work as a realtor." Atsadi glanced at her. "You get the idea?"

"Did you hate Digger?" I asked.

He did his glancing-over-my-shoulder movement before answering. "I served my time—stinking day after day. I hated me. Depressed and miserable."

I felt he had started the felon scam, pulling at my heartstrings. I'd let Atsadi talk: to see if I would believe him or not.

His left eye twitched again. "Before I used drugs, I got a law degree. At Campbell University. The Bar Association disbarred me after the tribal court convicted me."

Carla raised her eyebrows. "Where's Campbell?"

"It's in Buies Creek, North Carolina," I said.

He rocked and stared out the front window. "In prison, I took online courses. Got my realtor certificate. Couldn't work because I was in prison."

I fiddled with the college ring on my left hand. "About Digger. Did you hate him?"

He shook his head. "I'm explaining. The Bar Association disbarred me. But when I got out of Craggy, a Cherokee realtor company gave me a job, a chance."

"My question has a simple answer—*yes* or *no*."

"No." He raised one side of his mouth and scowled at me, a glare of annoyance. "Digger didn't make me steal or take drugs. I did. I was always between drugged stupors."

"Mr. Atsadi, you're working your way back, aren't you?" Carla asked.

"I'm off drugs. Leading a straight life. Staying out of trouble."

He had a story. It might be true. Carla and I needed to check with his realtor company. "Know anything about aconite?"

After hesitating, Atsadi said. "It's a plant. Has blue bell-shaped flowers. Why?"

"Just wondering. Been to Asheville lately?"

He glanced at his wristwatch. "Two weeks ago. Picked up a couple at the airport. They wanted to buy a house in the mountains."

"A few years back when you went on the reservation to steal—"

He stiffened and stared at me.

"Were you hired to steal artifacts?"

Atsadi appeared defiant. "Don't do that anymore."

"Who paid you?"

He glanced over my shoulder again, maybe thinking. When he resumed talking, he went at a careful, slower pace. "I don't know. An intermediary—always the same man—met me in public places."

Maybe he feared something or someone. Carla jumped in with a question. "We heard there was an unknown man, a Mr. *X*?"

Atsadi shrugged. "I think so."

"You don't know who he is?" I asked.

He glared at me. His eyes held some emotion, maybe frustration, maybe fear, and he shook his head.

"Did Digger make deals with Mr. *X*?" Carla asked.

Atsadi shifted his gaze to his watch. "Don't know. Maybe he did."

He had to go somewhere, maybe his realtor office. I put my notepad in the pocket of my sports coat. "You and Digger never worked together? Never searched for the same artifact?"

Atsadi held his head as if in pain. "I didn't. I've answered your questions. Got to go to work." He rose up and opened his door. "Leave."

Walking out of his home, I thought about him. He showed no symptoms of a return to using meth. He didn't seem underweight or gaunt. When I wasn't shoving him into a chair, he appeared calm and not unusually nervous or anxious.

Atsadi didn't have a dog; it would be easy to come back later and get to his vehicle without him knowing. He impressed me as someone following the law. Should I inform Chief Deputy Goodman of the link between Digger and Atsadi?

When we got to my car, I told Carla, "We should check his alibi at the realtor office: was he there Tuesday morning, eight days ago?"

She got in on her side of the Mustang. "What do you think?"

I glanced about and located Atsadi's car next to a thicket of trees. "We're coming back tonight."

"Why?"

"Put a tracker on his vehicle."

Carla ran her fingers along her neck. "Because you want to know where he is. Is he digging up Indian artifacts?"

"Want to know if he drives to Indian mounds at night."

"Is it legal for you to mount this tracker on his car?"

I didn't answer her.

Our return ride from Cherokee took place in silence. Perhaps she continued miffed with me for not contacting her during the three months we were apart.

When I got back to the mansion, I walked into Roth's office and found her reading a book, *Beowulf* by Seamus Heaney. She lowered it and told me to report. I gave a verbatim account of our meeting with Atsadi.

"How did Carla do?" she asked when I finished.

"She talked at the right time and kept quiet when she needed to be quiet."

Roth nodded. "We don't have a contact in the Cherokee tribal police. To investigate Atsadi's recent activity, Chief Deputy Goodman has better connections than we do. Call Goodman and ask him for a trade. Exchange the Atsadi link for his help in getting assistance from the tribal police."

"Yes, ma'am."

She picked up her book and resumed reading.

Dinner was Taylor's sautéed trout, which she did lightly fry. I pulled the meat from the bone at the midsection. After dinner, Taylor told me Carla had gone out to the pond with a blanket and a book. I walked to the small lake, with its elongated shape, hemmed in by deciduous trees on all sides, where Carla sat on a blanket reading.

"Hey," I said.

She glanced up and patted the blanket next to her. "The sun is setting. Sit and watch." The sun was going down somewhere over the trees, its rays reflecting off the clouds directly above with colors of orange and yellow, those colors offset by the darker shade of the clouds closer to us. After fifteen minutes, we gathered up the blanket and headed back to the mansion.

"Where do we get a tracking device?" Carla asked.

"Mickey and Bruce are assembling it in the basement. Uses the new GPS."

When we reached the patio, she stopped me by pulling my arm. "I want to help in planting the device. How do I dress?"

I gave her a short account. "We don't want to leave any traces or be seen. Wear dark clothing and gloves."

"What else?"

I picked a piece of lint from my sleeve. "Don't leave any fibers; they might connect us to the scene."

"Is that all?"

I shook my head. "Tonight, we'll leave the car at the playground down the street from Atsadi's house. We'll work out an escape path from the house back to the car." I left Carla inside the mansion. "Get a nap."

# # #

Mickey, Carla, and I arrived back in Cherokee at two in the morning. Crickets chirped, and the night had a chill and a blackness, except for a slight glow from an occasional peek of the moon through a hole in the clouds. To improve our night vision, we sat in darkness for fifteen minutes.

Mickey turned toward me. "We ready?"

I adjusted a black ski mask over my face. "You come with me. I'll attach the box to the car. Carla, you stay here and watch our vehicle."

Carla opened her door and got out. "Coming with you. I'm supposed to be learning."

I cursed under my breath, "Hell's bells." She had walked off, heading in the direction of Atsadi's small house.

"Women will drive you to drink," Mickey said. "Oh, wait. You already drink." He followed her.

I shouldered a canvas bag of spare tools to attach the tracker and trailed Carla and Mickey through the trees. As expected, the house was dark. I crawled from the evergreen trees to the rear of his vehicle, on the opposite side from the bungalow. Earlier, I had gone to a used-car lot—to find a similar model—and identified an excellent location to mount the tracker. I pulled wooden stays out of my bag and placed them on one wheel to prevent the car from rolling over me.

I squirmed partway under the car, relaxed, and used my fingers to locate the metal structure to seat the magnet. I attached the plastic box with the magnet holding on to the metal. In response to the push of my finger, the tracker held fast. My flashlight had tape over a portion of the face cap, limiting the amount of emitted light. I did a quick check to view my tracker box.

Something didn't appear right. I studied the area where I mounted the box. The slight flashlight glow illuminated the contour of my device—and a second bump. I scrunched farther under the rear bumper and peeked closer at the bulge. I cursed silently: "Darn, darn." The bump turned out to be a second tracker box like the one I had attached. God had just given me a clear signal bad luck had started.

My crawl took me back to the woods, where Mickey kneeled, watching the house. "Something wrong?" he asked.

I moved closer to Mickey and Carla and whispered, "There's already an electronic device on his car."

Carla's face lay hidden in the darkness, but her voice rang clearly. "You told me you knew what you were doing?"

A momentary urge to strangle her by her beautiful neck plunged through my body. It turned out she is a lot better than I thought. I couldn't grasp who put the gadget on the vehicle, but I wouldn't let this newbie know. "It's just a bit more complicated than I thought."

She snickered.

We headed back to our vehicle. "Who's trailing Atsadi?" Carla asked.

"As I said, it's complicated." I smiled. "But we'd best find out."

11

ROTH'S MANSION, ASHEVILLE — FRIDAY

Taylor rushed into the kitchen-dining room, where I ate breakfast with Mickey and Bruce. "Don, come now. Lilith are in Miss Roth's office an' plum a-havin' fits."

My fork, still holding the scrambled eggs, dropped on my lap. *For Chrissakes!* Another go-around with Lilith, our client. To prepare my nerves to squabble with her, I slowed my breathing, took a last sip of coffee and glanced out the row of windows overlooking the blue-tinted flagstone patio in front of the mansion. Fog spread away from the house, obscuring the lawn. Why couldn't Lilith let us work the case?

In Roth's office, Lilith sat, haranguing Roth across her desk. "I don't go after no red herrings. Johnny Hayes killed Digger." Her skin had a florid tint.

Roth had half-closed her eyes and inclined her head at me as I entered the room. "Yes, Lilith, you've expressed this thought before—"

"I know more now." Lilith shook her head so that her flaxen bangs jumped up and down. "I've been going out at night. Been following Hayes on my Vespa."

Lilith had a deep love for her fallen fiancé, but she needed to develop a fear for her safety. Like when she had accused Hayes—to his face—of killing Digger. Now she had tailed that brute in the dark. I shook my head.

I said, "Hello," to Carla sitting beside Lilith, and took a chair next to Roth's desk. My boss wore black today, headscarf and tunic, and tapped on her desk. As Lilith rambled on, Roth put her hand over the side of her face and mouthed, "Calm her," toward me.

Lilith stood to remove her brown leather jacket. A discouraging sign; she planned to stay for a lengthy badgering about Hayes. After folding the coat over her left arm and sitting, she pointed her right forefinger at me.

"He doesn't believe me. He wants to study Indian grave robberies in Cherokee." She wasn't going to drop her rant.

"The grave robbery is not a red herring," I said. "Yesterday, we talked to a guy, Atsadi. Had the motive to kill Digger. Digger reported Atsadi's larceny to the tribal police."

She plopped her coat on her lap. "Last night I tried to follow Hayes. He went out like he does every night. I couldn't keep up with him on the Vespa."

She infuriated me. But I had to admire her spunk, puttering after a pickup on a scooter.

Her voice grew loud. "That's right. With my fiancé out of the way, Hayes is after Digger's treasure."

Lilith paused. Two lines of tears started down her face. She removed her black, plastic-rimmed glasses and again hollered at me. "He's going to find the gold and slip away. You're too slow to catch him."

Carla had been quiet, sitting back, maybe gauging Lilith. Now, she reached out and squeezed Lilith's shoulder. "I haven't been here long. But the other men say, 'Don can hunt.'"

Lilith put her thick-rimmed glasses back on. "Don't need a stalker. I got instincts."

Carla moved closer to Lilith and patted her shoulder. "Give Don time to solve this case. He'll catch up with the killer. He has to prove to Chief Deputy Goodman, what he knows."

The red tint of Lilith's face began to lessen.

"Where does Hayes head at night?" I asked. "Morganton?"

She hesitated and then answered. "Went in that direction. Hayes and two other men."

"Lilith, please be patient with me," I said hoping to avoid further argument. "You and I will follow the Confederate-gold path—the midshipman's journal—and any other leads we uncover. One day I'll tap Digger's killer on the shoulder, and I'll say, 'Got you.'"

Lilith stood up and put on her leather jacket. "I better go now."

Carla and I tagged along with Lilith to the front door. The morning fog had lifted. I could see the mansion lawn and the trees off at a distance. As our client drove off, I smiled at Carla. "You calmed her."

She ran her hand through her ponytail. "Lilith has to vent her anger. Just listen to her and nod."

"Yeah. Well, she needs to stop following Hayes."

Carla touched my shoulder to get my attention. "After Digger died, I'm guessing she began to shut down. She can only focus on revenge." She turned to the second-floor stairs. "Talk about Digger and the Confederate gold with her. That'll keep her busy and away from Hayes."

I rejoined Bruce and Mickey at the dining table and blew air out my mouth. Bruce glanced over his newspaper and asked if I had calmed Lilith. I frowned and shook my head.

"Don't get distracted," Mickey said. "Keep an eye out for that Hayes fellow."

Bruce read aloud from the paper. "America Online is now the biggest and most successful Internet Company—30 million subscribers worldwide."

I scanned my watch. "Guys, I need to make a call, change clothes, and start my morning jog." I went to my office and called Harry Goodman, the Chief Deputy.

"What do you want?" he said. "I'm busy."

"Hey, busy man. What's happening with Hayes? Have you wrapped up the Harper murder?"

"Heard about your visit to see Hayes' hound dogs. You're none too smart."

"Think I got Hayes' attention?"

Goodman snorted. "He's furious."

"Have you heard of a Mr. X?"

Goodman laughed at me. "Afraid not. Need to get back to work."

"Wait, Harry! Don't hang up!"

"Make it quick."

I explained that Bruce had found the tribal court case concerning Digger and Paul Atsadi and uncovered reports about the Cherokee Tribal Police searching for an unidentified individual, Mr. X, suspected of hiring grave robbers.

"I know about Atsadi and Digger," Goodman said, "but hadn't heard Digger robbed Indian tombs. Didn't know about a grave-robbing ring."

"You agree I just slipped you useful info?" I asked.

"I'll follow up with the tribal police on the Cherokee crime. What do you want now?"

"Does the Sheriff's Office suspect Atsadi?"

"We checked him out. When someone attacked Digger, he had an alibi. Realtors at his real estate firm said he was forty-five miles away in Cherokee."

So the Sheriff's Office had verified Atsadi's alibi. Maybe he had changed. "Do you have a contact at the Cherokee Tribal Police? A name I can call?"

"Hold on a second." The line went quiet, and then he came back. "My colleague is Joseph Kanuna. I'll see if he'll talk with you. Now go away."

"But I told you about Paul Atsadi, and the mystery man financing grave robberies. I'm like your … confidential informant."

"No, you're the raccoon going through my trash cans at night."

I groveled, another of my concealed talents. "Aw, Harry, tell me what you found at the crime scenes."

"Oh, sweet Jeezus. Wait a minute." When Goodman returned to his phone, I heard paper rustling. "The CSI team found no trace evidence. No aconite in Digger's house other than inside him and his coffee cup."

"How did Digger swallow poison?"

Goodman delayed his answer, possibly deciding how much to let me in on. "I think someone interrupted Digger's breakfast and slipped aconite into the cinnamon-flavored coffee."

"Come on, Harry. What did you find?"

"We found latent impressions for the murdered man and his fiancée. Didn't I already tell you that? Oh and lots of folks knew he flavored his coffee with cinnamon."

I had my notepad out and jotted down Goodman's info. "Someone—it could be the poisoner—shot at Digger?" I asked. "Two days before the murderer killed Digger?"

"That's right."

"What did you find at the shooting scene?"

Goodman emitted a low *Umm*. "The rifling impressions on the spent bullet match no other bullet markings in our database or the national database. I already told you the pistol was a P239."

"How'd the lab figure a P239?"

"Based on the rifling twist, the lands, and the grooves of the spent bullet, the laboratory believes that was the weapon."

"And no match with a bullet in the NIBIN database?"

"Still searching but the possible images NIBIN sent don't match the bullet fired at Digger. But the shooter isn't a pro," Goodman said.

"Why?" I asked.

"Because our guy doesn't regularly shoot people."

"How do you know?"

Goodman hesitated. "The shooter stood too far away to expect to hit Digger with a pistol. Should've used a rifle. Not a hitman."

Digger's killer had been smart enough to evade the Sheriff's search but had used a pistol instead of a rifle, a talented amateur. "Hard to believe the shooter left no trace."

Goodman emitted an additional *Umm.* "We have the shell casings. Laboratory couldn't pull fingerprints off the casings."

"No trace evidence? Not even a wrapper?"

Goodman took a long time answering. "When we catch the shooter, you can sue him for not leaving evidence at the scene of a crime."

"Sorry, just asking," I said. "Let me know when you discover something else about Paul Atsadi."

"I will inform the Sheriff you are helping our office. In his eyes, you will likely rise from the degrading level of dumpster trash to diesel exhaust." Goodman made a snorting noise. "Try biting your tongue around the Sheriff. And here's a radical thought — feed his ego. That way maybe he won't ride my ass when he catches me talking to you."

"I'll pass on bootlicking. Thanks for the crime-scene information. I owe you."

I think he slammed the phone down.

I got back to the breakfast table. "Let's go for a run?"

Bruce had picked up another section of the paper. "Almost finished. Wait. I want to go with you."

Mickey, older than Bruce and me but muscular, glanced up from his section. "Me too. Give me a minute."

Getting Bruce and Mickey to move was like corralling rabbits. "Can't wait."

I changed into my sweats and left the mansion. Outdoor, the deciduous trees around the estate were changing color. While I jogged, I saw variations of orange, rust, and some vestiges of green leaves around me. The day was perfect for a run: chilly but not cold. I went across the lawn and into the trees, circling the pond off to the side of the mansion. Because I jogged regularly, my body felt loose and fit.

I followed a worn path through the woods to the edge of Roth's property and around the circumference of her estate, a trail allowing me to check for trespassers and to exercise. I felt the firm resistance of the soil to my lower limbs, viewing the slight accumulation of leaves on the path and scanning ahead for wildlife such as a deer. I fell into a rhythm of sucking air into my lungs and exhaling.

My eyes scanned the path and the bushes and trees, but my mind relaxed and worked on the case. What would be my next step? I had told Lilith I would go over more of the Harper journal with her. Had to keep her happy. I wanted to check on what Hayes did in Morganton, but that could wait. Would go to Cherokee with Carla and talk with the realtors at Atsadi's real-estate—

I didn't see the line across the path. Just before my foot caught on it, I saw a cord like a fishing line.

I face-planted, my right foot tugging on the colorless filament as my body lurched, relaxing in my fall just as my football coaches had taught me years ago. I rolled over and had almost righted myself when the first man struck me.

Spinning into the second man, a slight individual in a Spock mask, I elbowed him in the nose—*Crunch!*—knocking him down.

Someone grabbed my arms, perhaps the first man, allowing a third man to smash me in the face with his fist.

I rotated violently in the grip of the arms holding me and kicked the third man in the side of his knee. I felt his knee give way as he went down.

I rammed the head of the first man into a tree trunk and spun away, landing on my knees. Man number two was up, kicking me in the face.

My vision hazed: trees and two men whirred around in a circle.

Rising, I collared one of my attackers and pulled him to the ground. One of the other men pummeled me, darkness clouding in on my vision.

I heard feet pounding nearby, and my assailants seemed to melt away. I make out a meaty sound—*Thwack!*—followed by the sound of running feet.

"Is he hurt bad?" Bruce asked.

My vision blurred. I could barely make out Mickey standing over me. "Don, how many fingers am I holding up?"

What fingers?

12

MISSION HOSPITAL, ASHEVILLE — SATURDAY

I rose from the bed, seeking the path to the lit room, trying to get there in time. My dorm room confined me, high single-pane windows gazing out on an October day. Made it out of my room, walking down an empty hall, passing closed doors. Outdoors, into the open air, going along the brick path, empty of people. The lecture hall, a red brick building. Please be the right one. Inside, down the hall, into the first room. Empty chairs, no one here. Hurry to the next room, also empty chairs. Keep entering rooms and finding no one. Another door to go through. I see the light; I see motion.

Following a night of fitful sleep, I woke with my legs elevated and a drip tube stuck into my arm. A petite nurse in blue scrubs studied her clipboard. She smiled at me. "Good morning, Mr. Gannon." She considered the monitors attached to the digital monitoring system behind my bed and recorded information. When I wobbled my head to follow her, my eyesight rippled into a blurred vision. "How do you feel?"

My lips stuck together; I ran my wet tongue over them. "Dizzy."

The nurse proceeded to give me a quick rundown on my condition; nothing broken. It looked like I would be in for a few days for scans and observation.

My nurse glanced toward the door. Roth, my boss, stood in the doorway. "Found you. Had the devil of a time." She stepped forward with Mickey following. The nurse moved to block her.

My quirky boss had dressed in her unique way—a long-sleeved, black dress down to her black shoes, dark headscarf tucked under her chin and sunglasses—to travel to the hospital. She rarely left the mansion. Instead, she would send me, as her eyes, to walk wherever she needed me and to report back. As I realized she had left the comfort of her estate to travel outside to see about me, a strong feeling of appreciation coursed through my body.

The nurse stood her ground before Roth, who at five-foot-eight glared down at her obstacle. "You have to leave."

"Why?"

"Not visiting hours."

"Nonsense. The patient's awake."

Roth moved left. The nurse shifted right. "Please leave."

Roth turned to Mickey and dipped her head at the door. Mickey held the nurse's arm and gently pulled her out into the hallway. Then, he stood with his back against the closed door, ignoring the nurse's protests, voiced at a moderate level but intense.

Roth pulled the room's single chair to my bed. "Who did it?"

I raised my head and saw the windows behind her. I had a private room. Roth might chase wealth, but she took care of her people. "They wore Spock masks."

She waited. "You told me Mr. Hayes was big with a crescent-roll physique."

"One guy was big like Hayes."

"You're not sure."

The sun rose outside the windows. I shifted my body to raise my head. "He covered his face."

My head started to ache, but Roth pressed on. "Why would Hayes attack you? Did you see something at his shack?"

"Hayes lost face when I stood up to his dogs. Dog lovers can be protective."

She frowned. "Hmm, you're sassy. You can't feel too badly."

Nurses tapped on the door. "Open this door." Mickey kept his back against it, preventing entry.

Roth pursed her lips as if pondering. "So how do you feel?"

"My body's sore."

"Any fractures?"

"No, but the nurse told me my arms are black and blue."

More pounding on the door. "We're calling security."

"Show me your arm."

I raised a sleeve of my hospital gown.

"Ah! Your arm has turned blue. How is your head?"

"Doc ordered a CT scan and a stay in the hospital for a day or two."

"Bruising appears painful. You feel well enough to continue the investigation?"

"I don't care about a headache. I'll be back tomorrow."

She glanced at my head bandages and viewed the liquid dripping into my arm. "That's the spirit. Get your sleuthing done between beatings."

"I'm okay."

A hush settled out in the hallway.

She gave a dismissive wave of her hand. "Something good could come of this. Unforeseen attacks keep an investigator watchful and quick of foot."

"Did you report the attack?"

Roth nodded. "Chief Deputy Goodman investigated. He wants to question you." She took a break and fidgeted with her headscarf. "We still don't know who gained by killing Digger."

I shifted to relieve my numb rump. "I don't. We investigate the Civil War treasure map because Lilith thinks it's important."

She leered at me, showing what I call her money grin. "We investigate because dumb luck may have sent a treasure to you."

"Ridiculous to believe a lost treasure is still in the ground."

Roth stood. "Doesn't mean it isn't."

Hammering began again on the door. "Hospital security. Open the door."

"I'll leave you to mend."

In a billow of black garments, she left, with Mickey running interference.

Later in the morning, Bruce followed a nurse into my room and snickered at me. "Your left eye resembles a mushy, chocolate-chip cookie."

"Nurse, this dreadful person is badgering me and hindering my recovery."

She smiled at Bruce and left the room after examining the drip tubes.

"Mickey and I rode in like the cavalry in a Wild West movie."

I pressed my hands to my face. "When I'm in trouble, I'll listen for the bugle."

"Smote the bad guys. Done saved your bacon."

"You're a godsend. The cream of our team."

Bruce kept yakking. "Mickey and I were runnin' after you. Came on three men in masks, one down and two grappling with you."

He jabbed the air as if boxing. "They didn't see us. I hit one in the face."

"How did they keep their masks on?"

Bruce took the chair beside the bed. "Masks fit over the full-head. Felt like latex."

He continued gesturing wildly and nearly toppled his chair. "We had knocked them down. You were down."

"I must have blacked out."

"Mickey and I checked you out. Two attackers pulled the third guy up off the ground. Hustled him away."

"They escaped?"

"We busy a-gettin' you back to the mansion."

Carla entered, holding two fists against her face. "Poor thing! Bandages, tubes, and bruises! You need loving."

She wore a form-fitting yellow dress, showing off her figure. I wore one of those cotton hospital gowns open in the back. I pulled the bed sheet higher around me to cover my bare ass.

Bruce stood up to give Carla the chair. He bumped against the bed, pulling on the tube to my hand. *Ouch.*

He jumped back. "Sorry."

I rubbed the top of my hand, feeling a bandage. "How did I get here?"

Carla found a section of my arm without discolorations and held it, sending a shudder up my spine. "After the attack, Mickey and Bruce carried you back to the mansion."

Bruce stuck out his chest. "Used a two-handed seat carry."

"EMS arrived," Carla said. "You appeared lightheaded. They took you to the hospital."

Carla had been kind to me, and I wanted to talk with her, but I felt drowsy. My eyelids grew heavy. I must have dozed because I opened my eyes to find my friends gone.

# # #

By early afternoon, my body dropped off to sleep again. I dreamed of my teenage years, growing up, imagining the old bathroom in the morning. I could smell the Aqua Velva aftershave I used back then. The peppermint scent staggered my sense of smell. When my eyes opened, Chief Deputy Harry Goodman sat in the chair beside my bed. His aftershave dominated the room. He wore khaki pants and a blue flannel shirt; with age his stomach strained against the fabric of his shirt. Goodman fit my vision of a kindhearted uncle.

"What happened, Don?"

I told Goodman what happened. I pointed at a water jug on the table beside the bed; he handed me a glass of water, then leaned forward in his chair. "I went over the ground where they jumped you. Located your blood on the ground and leaves."

"Why not their blood?"

"I'm betting we'll find their blood residue inside the gloves and masks they wore."

"I tripped on a line."

"We found a filament fishing line tied across the path."

"Did you locate the ground where they waited for me?"

"Yep."

"Any trace elements?"

"Nada. Not even a gum wrapper or cigarette."

"Harry, I'm thinking Johnny Hayes and his two friends."

Goodman smiled. "I visited him with one of my deputies."

"Anyone beat up?"

"They were a sorry-looking group. Said they'd been at their shack all night and day—drinking & wrestling."

"What kind of sorry-looking?"

Goodman grinned again. "Hayes sported a swollen face and a bandage around his head. One of his followers had a badly sprained knee—was on crutches."

"Arrested them?"

"Nope. Figured they attacked you, but I didn't have a witness who could identify them."

"Spock masks?"

"None I could find."

"Why'd Hayes do it?"

"Guess you challenged him by threatening to shoot his hounds."

"Think they'll try again?"

"Told them I'd throw them in jail if they did."

We were quiet for a minute or so. I sat up straight, leaning against my pillows. "We know Digger's testimony sent a tomb robber to jail?"

Goodman did his goatee-stroking reflex. "That guy, Paul Atsadi, got out of the slammer last month."

He viewed me calmly, his eyes brown under dark eyebrows, the rest of his facial hair a muted white. "I talked with a colleague in the tribal police. Both times someone attacked Digger, Atsadi was far away in Cherokee."

"Carla and I talked with Atsadi. I figure we ought to check out Digger's activities in Cherokee."

"We?"

"Could use your help."

Goodman nodded. "I'll let you know after I ask the tribal police what they have on Digger."

"Can I go with you?"

He studied me. "When did your doctor say you could get out?"

I tried to brush my cowlick but found another bandage in my way. "Hmm. I reckon I'm staying another day."

Goodman stood. "Have a rapid recovery."

"Don't forget me."

"I'll ask the tribal police to let you come along." He left, leaving the tang of aftershave.

I am a determined being. It's not the size of the unknown in an investigation that counts; it's the size of the sleuth who must solve the unknown. I decided my next step. Lilith had given me Nathaniel's diary and the map to make copies for Roth as she wanted to keep the originals. Roth had mentioned she wanted a history professor to examine those journals.

13

MISSION HOSPITAL, ASHEVILLE — SUNDAY

My limbs had been bruised but not broken. No headache, no fog of bewilderment, no ringing in my ears. The doc released me during his morning rounds. I dressed in the clothes Carla had dropped off and phoned the mansion. Bruce answered and told me someone would come to get me. I waited in my hospital room chair and gazed out the window at a clear sky.

A nurse spoke from the hallway, "Someone to see you."

Lilith stood in the doorway. "You beat up Hayes. You're the best."

I viewed Lilith's tight-lipped smile and big eyes, studying me through plastic-rim glasses. "We hit it off together."

She strolled into the room, holding a scooter helmet in her arms. "Ready to leave?"

"Someone's coming to get me."

She spun back toward the door. "I'll take you. I have something to confess."

Roth had told me to stop arguing and listen to our client, and my ride hadn't arrived. It wouldn't hurt to see what Lilith had to say. I grabbed a plastic bag containing my hospital papers and followed her down in the elevator. Her Vespa stood in a parking space. I had forgotten the smallness of her scooter. Lilith handed me a helmet with a transparent visor. I felt the padding inside the shell to judge how well it might protect my head in an impact. The cushioning was thick. Although the sun shone down and warmed the air, a chill crept into my body: she expected me to jump on the stunted scooter. Visions of an adult straddling a child's tricycle sprung into my head. She buttoned up her leather jacket and put on her helmet. "Let me get seated first."

She mounted the machine, tilted it so she could pull up the kickstand, and revved the engine. Once the motor ran steadily, she turned to me, "Get behind me and balance your weight, so the Vespa doesn't tilt."

"Lilith, I'm big. The scooter isn't. I better wait for my ride."

With her right foot on the ground, she turned her helmet to face me. "Silly. I'll have you at Roth's mansion in no time. Only seven miles away."

"I'm still bruised from my brawl."

She pulled on a strand of blonde hair sticking out from under her helmet. "Riding a Vespa in the city is easy-peasy."

"A car would be better."

I scanned the parking lot for Bruce or Carla; I didn't see them. The sun had stayed out, and no rain clouds speckled the sky. Maybe I could ride a short distance on the little bike?

She grabbed my left hand and pulled me to the scooter's left side. "Put your hand on my left shoulder and swing your body over the rear of the seat. Wrap your arms around my jacket."

Well, Roth instructed me not to argue. I slid the helmet on my head. With trepidation, I squeezed onto the tiny seat and held Lilith around her leather jacket. My perch dug into my rump, like sitting on the fence rail or small-diameter bar. With her right leg on the ground, she balanced the bike and me. She looked over her shoulder, and said,

"When I slow and stop, keep your feet on the foot-pegs. Lean with me—no more and no less than I do."

"Where?"

She twisted the throttle—*Rumble! Rumble!*—and we scooted off, Goldilocks with Papa Bear hanging on behind her. We went down Biltmore Avenue, picking up speed. The noise of the wind prevented me from talking to her. Lilith balanced, and I concentrated on mimicking her body movement. We blew past rows of leafless trees along the street.

My heart rate raced.

Clinching my teeth, I turned my head to view the opposing lane of traffic. Going in the opposite direction, Carla drove past in my silver 1999 Mustang. She gawked out the side window; her brown eyes amused. Shortly afterward, Carla had turned around and passed the Vespa on her way back to the mansion.

I relaxed again when Lilith arrived at the mansion, with my rump cramping where the small-diameter seat poked it. No more headache, but my tail had died. I dismounted and waddled for the front door. "You wanted to talk?"

She followed me. "I want to explain to Ms. Roth and you together."

Bruce waited in the hallway. He turned and draped something over his head. He turned around wearing a Spock mask.

I chuckled. "Whatever look you are seeking, this is a huge improvement. You should consider adopting it."

He placed a hand over his heart. "I'm hurt. Are you crabby from falling out of your hospital bed this morning?"

"At least I didn't fall off the ugly tree, hitting every branch on the way down."

We continued swapping warm greetings until we got to Roth's office, where Bruce took off his mask. Three people clustered around Roth at her desk: Carla and a stately-looking black woman seated in chairs; and Taylor Ploughman, the cook, who stood to serve coffee and tea. The dignified woman had a stiff posture, ramrod straight, and a penetrating gaze, assessing Lilith and me. I noticed a brown briefcase with straps, the type scholars favored, propped against her chair.

"There you are," Roth said to me. "Carla went to get you. She said you already had a ride." I took a chair with Carla on my right. She began to shake and made a noise—*puff!* Holding her mouth and struggling to stop her shaking, she whispered, "You were hilarious on that scooter."

Roth introduced the stately black woman. "This is Dr. Angela Lightfoot, a history professor at the University of North Carolina at Asheville."

After a moment, Roth finished her intros. "The two men entering the room are my investigators, Don Gannon and Bruce Seeker. The woman with them, Lilith Johnson, seeks the identity of a killer."

Bruce gave Dr. Lightfoot a lewd, toothy grin. "Be happy to meet with you, so you know me better."

With a gray Afro hairstyle and wearing a full-length white dress, she smiled. "I'll pass." What did my old friend intend? My guess would be twenty years separated Bruce's age from the older woman. His future actions would bear watching. A wise man once told me older women recognize what matters and what doesn't in life. Bruce could use coaching in life's goals.

I picked up a cup of coffee. Lilith and I pulled chairs into the group as Roth continued. "Taylor found our history professor. Taylor, how did you meet her?"

"Told Miss Roth I knowed a professor named Lightfoot," Taylor said. "She were a-doin' study of early Scotch-Irish people a-settlin' in Appalachia. She were a jasper but learned right fast about mountain people."

"What's a *jasper*?" Carla said.

Taylor grinned. "A person not from these mountains. You'ns a jasper."

Lilith rose up in her chair and cut to the chase. "My fiancé, Digger Harper, died of poison. A map, showing the site of Civil War gold, triggered his death. Do you know early U.S. history?"

Angela nodded. "I research the early American South, North Carolina, and the colonial United States."

My snap judgment reckoned Taylor had chosen well. "Just the individual we need."

Angela stared at me. "You're the detective. Is that why you have a bandaged head, and you limp?"

"A small disagreement over right away."

Roth gave out a grunt. "A glorious fight! Everyone joined in."

Taylor stood up. "I be a-gettin' back to the kitchen." She left the room.

Angela touched the fingertips of her left hand to those of her right, forming a tent. "On the phone, you said you're interested in the events of April 1865?"

Roth nodded.

"The final month of that war was remarkable," Angela said, "shaping the future of our country. Of course, the assassination of President Lincoln by that simpleton Booth was a hideous act."

She rubbed her temples. "I don't operate a metal detector. How can I help your inquiry?" I noticed Bruce grinning over at her.

Roth cleared her throat. "You can examine a journal; to assess its authenticity. We'll pay you."

Angela sipped her drink. "Could I see this journal?"

"Carla," Roth said. "The copies."

Carla handed duplicate copies of the journal to Angela. She viewed the papers and dropped them in her lap. "You have the originals?"

"I have them," Lilith said.

Angela glanced out the windows along one wall before turning to Roth with an ironic smile. "Interesting. You do know that Confederate gold legends from the latter days of the war have proven to be almost always a sham?"

I shifted in my chair, trying to revive my sore rump, which had fallen asleep on that tiny seat. "I share your skepticism."

Roth shot me a stern glance, maybe saying she expected me to find her gold.

Angela lowered her head as if thinking. She glanced up at Roth. "Would you go over the details of what happened and what you need from me?"

Roth reviewed Digger finding the journals and his poisoning.

Roth drummed her desk. "I need a professional historian to confirm the journal is genuine. A fake, a sham, must not dupe me."

Angela listened to Roth, and said, "Study the manuscripts for authenticity? Connect journal events to primary-source events?"

"Exactly."

Angela looked intently at Roth. "Anything specific?"

"Did Midshipman Nathaniel Harper cross paths with the Confederate gold?" Roth said.

Angela raised her eyebrows. "History I can handle. When the action of a single human is mixed in, precise predictions are precarious."

"Can you do what I ask?"

Angela finished her drink. "I can."

Angela reached for the briefcase beside her chair. "If there is nothing else, I'm on my way. I've reading to do."

After she left, Lilith spoke, "Ms. Roth?"

Roth glanced at Lilith and waited.

Lilith, sitting beside me, put her hand on my shoulder. "I wasn't completely frank with Don and you. I omitted something."

All eyes centered on Lilith. "Remember the intermediary?"

Roth leaned forward over her desk. "The man who passed out Mr. *X's* directions to steal Indian relics?"

I exchanged glances with Carla and recalled Atsadi told us a go-between told him what to dig for in the burial mounds.

Lilith stared at the floor with a pensive expression. "Digger dug up relics for an intermediary. I tailed this guy for Digger."

Roth leaned back in her chair. "Digger robbed tombs?"

Lilith went red-faced. "He did. But I loved him."

I rubbed my cowlick. "How did you help Digger with the middleman?"

"Digger wanted to know who hired him. He reasoned the intermediary took the loot straight to Mr. *X* after Digger handed it over."

My respect for Lilith grew. She made things happen. It wasn't her want to sit around and do nothing. "You waited for the middleman?"

"I went to where Digger met him and hid. Then followed the middleman. He drove to his home in a trailer park."

"Was this your plan?"

"I suggested it."

My estimate of Lilith went up a few pegs. Even if she hadn't had the opportunity for lengthy formal schooling, she had street smarts. Back when I first met her, I had sold her short. "You saw him?"

"He and Digger talked together."

"Describe him."

"Older man, early 60s I reckon," Lilith said. "Wore a baseball cap over white hair. Not very tall—slight. I didn't trust him like I wouldn't trust a snake."

I had my notepad out and took down her account. "Who was this guy you followed?"

Lilith took off her black-rimmed glasses. "Wrote down his license plate. Digger used the plate number to identify him."

I leaned forward. "And?"

She took a moment to adjust her plastic-rimmed glasses back on her face. "His name is Andy Murphy."

Carla broke in with a high-pitched voice. "Who's Mr. *X*?"

Lilith shook her head. "We never found out."

I had a lot of work to do. *Should I share Andy Murphy's name with Chief Deputy Goodman or keep this new lead for Carla and myself? Is this Murphy a suspect in the murder of Digger or just in stealing Indian relics? People lie to me and keep me in the dark. It's my curse.* I'd been wondering when a missing piece in the puzzle was going to drop. *But an older man in his seventies. As a go-between?* There had to be more to this. *Right,* I told myself. *But what?*

14

RURAL BUNCOMBE COUNTY — MONDAY

I woke early and stretched, my stiff muscles still aching from the fight three days before. A drawn-out hot shower eased the pain, and I crept downstairs for breakfast. Taylor handed me a plate of scrambled eggs and grits as my phone buzzed.

"Pick you up in twenty minutes," Goodman said without opening.

"Huh?"

"Be ready." He hung up.

I stood in front of the mansion and sipped coffee from a foam cup. On the wide lawn spread before me, a tarmac lane began at a distant point and stretched straight toward me. A tiny Crown Victoria appeared at the far end of the lane and grew bigger. Goodman pulled up, and I handed him a second cup of Taylor's coffee. The two of us drove off in his vehicle. The miasma of Aqua Velva permeated the cruiser.

I coughed. "Did you recheck Paul Atsadi's alibi? For the morning Digger died?"

He gulped his coffee and put his cup in a holder. "I did."

"Tell me."

"Once more, we found he worked that morning in his Cherokee real-estate office."

Atsadi was forty-five miles away when Digger died. "Strong alibi."

Goodman glanced across the car at me. "Maybe. Maybe not. Their office is chaotic."

"You think he did it?"

He shrugged. "Atsadi says he's reformed and legit now."

I smirked. "What else would he say?"

Goodman picked up his coffee. "Don't expect people to always tell the truth. I stay away from the disappointment that way."

"Where're we driving?"

"You'll see."

We rode in silence until he continued. "About the time of his death, what was Digger doing in Cherokee?"

"Does this mean you're not getting anywhere with the case?" I said.

"Whatever. It's my case, and I'm stuck with it."

"What's wrong?"

"Things don't add up."

Where was Goodman taking me? Could be Johnny Hayes's shack. "Like what?"

Harry took another gulp of coffee. "Whoever shot at Digger in the woods left 9-mm shell casings."

"You mentioned that already. Shooter had a P239."

"The thing is—" He paused a moment and continued. "It's a nice gun, but not in any way rare. It's not that expensive."

I listened carefully. "So?"

"They haven't been around that long."

I realized what bothered him. A professional killer tosses their gun after shooting someone. "You reckon the killer got rid of the gun, right? So we'll probably not have a chance of matching the bullets."

Glancing out the side window, I saw we had left behind the malls, gas stations, and chain stores. He turned off toward a rural area, in the direction of Hayes' hut.

"Another thing."

"Yeah?"

Goodman glanced at me. "Remember we talked about what to use to shoot someone from a distance?"

"A rifle."

He turned his focus back on the narrow two-lane road. "That's right."

I finished my coffee. "Who sells ammunition for a Sig Sauer P239?"

Goodman chuckled. "Gun stores. All of them, even Walmart. See Herr Luger designed the 9mm round for his namesake pistol 'bout a hundred years ago. That bullet outlived his handgun, as it's a cartridge widely used in semiautomatic pistols and submachine guns the world over."

"Including our Sig Sauer?"

Goodman nodded.

We pulled off on the side of the narrow two-lane road near Hayes' home. Three Sheriff's Department vehicles were parked there.

"Thought you searched Hayes' shack?"

"After your fight in the woods, we questioned Hayes and hunted for a Spock mask. Today, we search for a connection to a murder."

"Warrant?"

"Got a warrant to search Hayes' home. Based on Digger's death, and a separate drug investigation."

Goodman and I went through the field down to Hayes' house. The Chief Deputy talked to his deputies, who had been going through the home. They wore their summer uniforms: short-sleeved black shirts with a badge over their left shirt pocket and black trousers. I heard Hayes' dogs baying from a kennel behind the shack. Three men, civilians, sat on a wooden bench beside the structure. As we closed on the house, one of the three, an obese, stocky man, got up and stomped toward us. He wore the same loose-fitting, charcoal running suit and high-top sneakers; It was Hayes.

Goodman waited. "You're about to greet Johnny Hayes again, but this time without a Spock face."

After marching up to Goodman, Hayes thrust his head close to the Chief Deputy. "What the hell are you bothering us for?"

Goodman planted his right palm in the middle of Hayes' torso and shoved him back. "Weapons. Poison used to murder Digger Harper."

Hayes jumped forward, again planting his face close to Harry's. "Damn it. Didn't kill Digger. Don't listen to that crazy woman."

Goodman released his belt-mounted truncheon, holding it down along his right leg. "Out of my face. I'll tell you once."

Hayes snorted but backed away. "Had nothing to do with Digger's death."

The Chief Deputy signaled one of his deputies, nearly as massive as Hayes, to help. The two of them marched Hayes back to the bench. "Keep your butt on this seat," Goodman said. "Interfere with our search… and I'll slap your ass in jail."

Once Hayes sat back down with his two pals, Goodman queried the deputy, "Luther, did you find the gun?"

"No P239."

"See any old coins?"

"Nope."

"Notice anything of interest?"

"One of Hayes's buddies limps."

"Maybe he was the attacker I kicked in the knee?" I retorted.

Goodman grinned at me. "You might want to send him a get-well card."

"I'd rather find Digger's killer."

A deputy, carrying a can covered with crud and peeling paper, rushed up to Hayes and thrust the container at him.

Hayes rose and slapped the can out of the deputy's hand. "Get that out of my face."

The deputy shoved him backward. "Stay out of this," Goodman said to me. Then he ran to the tussle, again pulling his truncheon off his belt. "Stand down, Hayes."

Hayes struck the deputy in the junction of his head and neck, knocking him to the ground. The two men on the bench got up and began striking the other deputies.

The Chief Deputy got to Hayes and swung his baton, whacking Hayes on his shoulder. A grimace of pain swept the man's face as he folded his arms around his head.

Goodman struck Hayes on his lower limbs, dropping him to the ground. The big deputy rushed up and fell on him. Together, Goodman and his deputy cuffed Hayes.

The other deputies subdued Hayes' two buddies. With the Sheriff's men in control, I hung back from the fray, happy not to expose my achy body to additional pain.

Hayes shouted from the ground. "I'll sue you. Police brutality."

"Charge him," the deputy said. "He had the poison."

Goodman examined the sides of the can. He shook his head. "Different poison. *Bromethalin* in this container. It was *Aconite* that killed Digger." The deputies placed Hayes and his two men in their cruisers and took them to jail for assault. When Goodman returned to his vehicle, he said, "That was a waste of time. Hayes' lawyer will get the charges dismissed."

On the way back to Roth's mansion, the Chief Deputy talked about his retirement. He wanted to fade away and go fishing. Dealing with so much of the seamy life had left him looking forward to fishing for mountain trout, a desire to step down. He was a comfort to me, a mentor. I would hate to see him leave the Sheriff's Office. After he had dropped me at the mansion and driven away, I found Carla in my office. "Angela wants to see us," she said.

# # #

Carla and I walked into Angela's office on the university's campus. She sat beside a student at a cluttered table. After wrapping up with her student, Angela got us seated at the table and checked the time on her wristwatch. Classy, I noted, with a red band and Roman numerals on its face. She wore a beige sports coat of coarse weave and a black dress, an upscale snappy-dressing professor. "I spent two evenings reading Harper's journal. I want to discuss my initial thoughts with you two."

"Why us?" I said.

"See how what you're seeking ties into what I'm reading."

I pulled out my notepad. "What do you think?"

"It's a primary source from 1865. The writing is consistent with a Midshipman from that time."

I pointed at Nathaniel's journal. "Isn't the wording sophisticated for a sailor in 1865?"

She switched to her quiet, academic voice. "Before email and telephones, we wrote letters and kept diaries. Midshipmen had varied talents—a sailing man, an engineer, and an educated man."

Carla had a question. "So Digger's great-great-grandfather could have written these journals?"

Angela nodded. "As I told you, the wording is appropriate for a Midshipman. I think you have a previously undiscovered diary, describing events in the Civil War."

That was something. Angela didn't immediately find Digger's documents fabricated.

She continued. "Besides this diary, you have other journals written in the years before 1865. I need to check all of them for authenticity."

I stopped writing in my notepad. "Why?"

Angela's lips turned slightly down as if she was dealing with a slow student. "Due diligence."

I dropped my pen on the table. "Hmm, if authentic, does that mean a cache of gold is in the ground?"

Angela frowned. "Perhaps Nathaniel Harper buried something in April 1865."

"The map implies he put containers in the ground where the train tracks ended," I said.

Angela wagged her forefinger at me. "The diary didn't say what Nathaniel buried."

Carla spoke up. "If not gold, what else?"

Angela shook her head. "Maybe guns and powder to carry out guerilla tactics in the mountains."

"So, the story is real," Carla said. "What he left is still in Morganton?"

Angela shook her head again. "We don't know if the soldiers came back and dug it up."

I shoved Hayes into our discussion. "One of our murder suspects may be searching near the old tracks around Morganton."

Angela pondered for a few seconds. "You might want to watch him."

"We'll put a shadow on him," I said. "Check what he's doing."

"You do your probing. I'll read the journals."

I had a thought. "Do we have historical records documenting how much of the Confederate treasure went missing?"

Angela took a moment before she answered. "I'll go to the university library and pull up documentation on lost Confederate gold."

I envisioned that day in 1865, when the last trains left Richmond, as one of total chaos. "Do you expect to find complete records?"

"I'm guessing not."

Carla spoke in her precise, crisp voice. "How do we find if someone already unearthed the hoard?"

Angela placed a finger to her lips to consider the question. "Morganton has a newspaper. Researching the early issues might tell us."

"Can you scan through those old issues?" I asked.

Angela held a hand against her afro while she thought. "This project is growing. I doubt Ms. Roth would want to spend more on research." Angela pulled back from the table. "Your history puzzle is fascinating. Give me a single payment now, but I'll keep searching."

"No additional cost to Roth for the extra work? What'll you get out of it?"

"I'll write an academic paper based on the diary."

"It'll help advance your career at the university."

Angela gave me a knowing grin. "That's right."

I wrote her proposal down in my notepad. "Roth and I'll be in touch."

# # #

That night, I ate with a large group—Roth, Bruce, Mickey, and Carla—at the long table in the kitchen-dining room. Taylor had prepared fried ramps—a wild onion that pops out of the ground when spring comes to the mountains—and roast pork served with stuffed apples. Taylor had frozen the ramps a few months earlier and thawed them out for our meal.

I told them about Goodman's serving a warrant on Hayes.

Roth turned to Carla. "Are you settling in well?"

Carla put down her fork. She dressed classy and casually: wearing a magenta top with a scoop neckline and three-quarter-sleeves, ending below her hip in a ruffled lower hem, combined with blue jeans. "I am. Taylor's food is delicious. Yesterday, Mickey and Taylor showed me around Asheville." A sensation of mild irritation interrupted my breathing with a spasm when I heard Carla went out without me.

Roth continued talking to Carla. "I always enjoy Taylor's meals."

Taylor, who had just carried a bottle of wine to the table, explained her penchant for pork in the fall. "When September and October a-comin' to the mountains, dat when the farmers killed some of the pigs."

As Taylor served the wine, Roth turned back to Carla. "What did you see?"

"We drove about downtown and stopped for beers at the Tavern on the Square. I met lots of people."

Mickey spoke up. "Including a guy who offered Carla a job—can you believe that?"

Roth pursed her lips. "Hmm, who was this?"

"Larry Buchanan," Mickey said. "He builds houses around the city."

Mickey and Taylor's behavior gave me heartburn. They should have taken me along to watch over Carla. No, no, foolish thought. I'm petty. But she should avoid Buchanan. I knew him. That man never gave something away without expecting payback.

Roth sipped her wine, a Biltmore Estate Chardonnay. "How was your visit to see the history professor?"

I swallowed some ramps and faced Roth. "Angela's digging into the journal."

"I don't hold much hope she'll find anything in the journal," my boss said. "On the other hand, I've found when I'm not ready, a surprise can take place."

"Angela suggests keeping track of Hayes," I said.

Roth handed out instructions. "Bruce, tail Johnny Hayes. Where does he go and when?"

"Okay, Boss."

Roth slid a slice of pork covered with wild ramps into her mouth and smiled. Next, she turned and slapped me with an unexpected task. "Don, visit the Cherokee Tribal Police. Digger's death might have a connection with the Indian burial mounds."

15

Roth's Mansion & Cherokee — Tuesday

My cell phone buzzed on my desk. "Gannon here."

"You owe me." It was Chief Deputy Goodman.

"What?"

"You'll meet that tribal police officer."

"The one at the Cherokee Tribal Police?"

"Yep."

I pulled out my notepad. "How well does this guy know Atsadi?"

"He investigated Atsadi three or four years ago."

I twisted in my chair and grabbed a pen. "What's the officer's name again?"

"Didn't hear you," Goodman said.

"What?"

"Didn't hear you say, 'I owe you.'"

I scribbled on my notepad, "I owe you shit," and said, "I'll underwrite our next beer outing. What's his name?"

"*Underwrite*? You have to pay." Goodman was in a rare mood.

"I'll pay. Name?"

"Joseph Kanuna. You remember now?"

Goodman gave me the address of the tribal police station and said the officer expected us in the town of Cherokee this afternoon at two.

"You'll be there?" I said.

"I'll drive separately."

Excited about making a police contact on the reservation, I dropped my feet and spun my chair around. Roth would want me to take Carla. "I'll bring my associate, Carla Diaz."

"Be on time." Goodman hung up.

I checked the time; Roth had a get-together planned this morning.

Angela arrived first for the scheduled meeting in Roth's office. Coming through the front door, she rolled a medium-sized, black briefcase behind her. Lilith appeared next, hanging her safety helmet and leather coat on the coatrack in the hall. Angela dressed smartly in a long-sleeve white cotton blouse with a tie around the collar and long gray cotton pants. In contrast, Lilith appeared frumpy in a baggy, white sweatshirt and shapeless blue jeans. Bruce had run down the hall when Angela came in the front door and followed her. She walked directly to the office, but gave Bruce a slight grin.

Roth waited at a table, our poker table, in her office. She proposed we sit down and go over the Nathaniel Harper diaries in detail. Carla had made additional copies of all the journals. Roth placed them on the table. Angela opened her briefcase and pulled out her scribbled notes. Taylor brought in coffee and hot water for tea. Carla and I grabbed two chairs at the table. Outside, the October dawn was chilly and damp, putting me in a mood to drink coffee and scrutinize the old diaries further.

Roth started the discussion. "Angela, you've read the war-year journals?"

Angela gestured toward the documents in her briefcase. "There's some interesting history here."

Roth raised her eyebrows. "How so?"

Angela poured hot water into her teacup and dropped a bag in it. "In 1861, Nathaniel Harper was seventeen years old and going to be a midshipman at the U.S. Naval Academy."

"Before the war?" Carla said.

Angela nodded and sipped tea. "The war came, and he switched to a midshipman at the Confederate Naval Academy."

Carla leaned forward. "Where was he before 1861?"

The question appeared to stump Angela for an instant. She glanced through her written notes. "His family lived near Old Fort in the mountains of North Carolina."

Lilith opened Harper's first diary. "Nathaniel Harper wrote he was on a tug at the Norfolk Naval Yard. He watched the birth of the Confederate Navy."

"Later, he'd be at its death," Angela said.

Roth asked, "What happened to him at Norfolk?"

Angela placed the teabag on her saucer. She pulled out the 1862 journal. "He saw the wood ship, USS *Merrimack*, converted into an iron-plated ship, CSA *Virginia*."

Angela checked to see she had everyone's attention. "In early March 1862, *Virginia* demolished a Union fleet of wood ships off Newport News. The next day, two ironclad vessels, *Monitor* and *Virginia*, battled to a tie."

It was interesting. "How did our midshipman get to Richmond?" I said.

Angela explained. "The smog of war. The Union army drove toward Richmond and forced the Confederates to burn *Virginia* and retreat up the James River."

I tried to remember my geography. Where does the James River go?

Angela continued. "The Union Navy followed the Confederates up the James River to Richmond."

Carla, listening intently, asked, "This happened?"

Angela grinned. "As my thesis advisor would say, 'It was a magnificent retreat.'"

I envisioned the Confederate ships scampering up the James River like foxes with a pack of hounds biting at their rear ends. "When?"

"May 1862. Nathaniel got swept up in a rush fleeing the Union Navy."

Carla flipped pages in her journal copy to catch up with Roth and Angela. "What stopped the Union ships?"

"It appeared the Union Navy would punch their way to Richmond," Angela said. "Seven miles south of the Confederate capital, a small fort sat beside the James River. Drewry's Bluff rose ninety feet above a sharp bend in the river."

Glancing at her pages of the journal, Lilith carried on explaining what happened. "Once the Confederate ships sailed past the bluff, the defenders sank old wooden ships and trees in the channel. Nathaniel Harper worked to build up defenses at Drewry's Bluff."

Roth cleared her throat. "And?"

Angela stuck her finger in her journal to mark her place. "The Union navy drove on the last hurdle. Between the obstacles sunk in the river and the guns high above the water, the Confederates stopped the Union warships."

"Digger's great-great-grandfather was there," Lilith said. "Firing down at the Union ships?"

Angela picked up the story. "As a midshipman, he commanded a gun. The diary specifies the cannon as a relocated seacoast gun."

I realized the Confederates had been scavenging any cannon and hardware they could find. A poor man's navy, clutching at the sides of the abyss to stop their fall into the void.

Angela continued. "The remaining Confederate vessels, upriver from Drewry's Bluff, formed the James River Squadron. Harper stayed with the James River Squadron until April 1865."

Roth glanced at Angela. "Have you checked Harper's account against the historical records?"

"I've checked many events in the diary against library records. So far, they match."

I fidgeted with my class ring. "What did he do between May 1862 and April 1865 when he supposedly planted this gold?"

Angela placed her finger on her lips, seemed to think, and continued. "Studied at the Confederate Naval Academy and, as I just said, he was a midshipman in the James River Squadron."

I questioned Angela. "I've heard of the Confederate White House in Richmond. Didn't know the Confederate Navy had a naval academy there."

Angela smiled. "They didn't teach Harper in a Richmond building. The Confederate Navy taught their midshipmen on a floating school and dormitory, called the *Patrick Henry*."

"His campus floated on the James River?"

"It did."

Both Angela and I had other engagements. We discontinued the meeting and arranged to resume later. Carla and I left the office.

#

After the meeting, Carla and I scurried down to the garage and jumped in my Mustang. We carried fried catfish sandwiches, fixed by Taylor, in a paper bag. Beside me, Carla munched her sandwich. After a while, she said, "We're going to see Goodman?"

"We are."

"What do we tell Goodman about Andy Murphy?"

When I didn't answer, she continued. "We know he acted as the intermediary between the grave robbers and the collector."

I chewed on Taylor's sandwich. "We'll check out Murphy before we tell."

I enjoyed driving through the mountains to Cherokee. The far hills along the way showed a brown-purple tint, contrasting with the dark green and yellow of the closer trees and the brown of the bare shrubs along the side of the road. Carla didn't speak for a while. She appeared to be reflecting on a profound puzzle. "Ms. Roth doesn't believe the path to the killer is in the journals, does she?" Carla was curious, like the Nancy Drew character she admired.

I tried to describe Roth. "Going down every rabbit hole is pointless, but she does it anyway. Hard work solves the case."

Carla pushed her sunglasses down on her nose, maybe after glancing over them to see if I teased her. "That's all there is? Do lots of mindless iterations?"

I tossed the empty paper bag into the back seat. "Don't know how Roth does it. She unexpectedly has the solution. She pulls a rabbit out of the hole."

The curtain of trees beside the two-lanes began to pull back from the road. Motels and one-story stores occasionally appeared. Carla neatly folded her sandwich bag. "You respect her ... you like her?"

"I can't hoodwink Roth. She's cranky at times. Sometimes, she's a pain in the neck."

She swallowed the last of her sandwich. "I take that as a *yes*."

I drove in silence for a while. "You enjoy Asheville?"

She grinned at me; her dazzling smile froze my spine. "Haven't found a yummy Italian restaurant."

I grinned back. "Let's go out? We'll do the Italian Kitchen restaurant downtown?"

"Can we go the next time Taylor has the night off?" Carla asked.

She had been upset with me when she first arrived in Asheville. Angry because I hadn't called when we were apart. I had just gotten a second chance.

Going into Cherokee, the two, black-topped lanes passed power lines on wooden poles and deciduous trees dropping their leaves— orange and brown leaves swirled in the rear-view mirror. A separate, single-story building housed the Cherokee Tribal Police Department. Goodman's Crown Victoria stood parked before the station.

Tribal Police Officer Joseph Kanuna collected Carla and me at the front counter and took us back to his desk. He had a clean-shaven, oval-shaped face, short black hair, and the confident bearing of a veteran police officer.

I sat between Goodman and Carla at Kanuna's desk and faced the tribal officer. He had tan skin, maybe from the sun, and chapped lips. An outdoor type. "You worked on the Paul Atsadi investigation?" I said.

Kanuna frowned. "Let's understand our relationship. I'm a fifteen-year veteran of the tribal police—served as a patrol officer, juvenile officer, and tribal-complex security. You're a lowly P.I."

I glanced at his desk at the pictures of his family: a wedding with a young wife, and three young children. A family man with ties to the community. "Officer Kanuna, you're working at finding who's stealing Cherokee relics. Chief Deputy Goodman is working on a murder case in Asheville. My interest is helping him find who poisoned Digger Harper."

Kanuna stared at me. At least he didn't throw me out of his station. Getting him to trust me would be a long-term undertaking.

I lowered my head and did my sad look. "The thing is, Digger's fiancée is distraught, and his father is beside himself with anguish."

Kanuna brushed his hand over his short hair. "I'll see if we can work together. If you interfere with my investigation, you'll have to hit the road."

I gave Kanuna my earnest look, firm chin, the super-hero marching into machine gun fire. "I'll make it work." I glanced sideways to see Carla and Goodman nodding their heads in support.

Kanuna took a small tube of lip balm out of his pocket and brushed it across his weather-beaten lips. "What do you want to know?"

I settled in my chair. "Tell us about Digger Harper."

Kanuna hesitated. He didn't seem comfortable talking to me. "We wavered between charging Harper or using him as an eyewitness."

"Wavered?" Carla asked.

"We suspected Harper stole a number of Cherokee relics."

Roth had figured out the link between Atsadi and Digger. "So both Atsadi and Harper stole Cherokee relics?"

Kanuna answered in his unruffled, low voice. "We know Atsadi did. Harper probably did."

"Together?" I asked.

"Separately." Came the response.

"I'm confused. Is there a big market for Cherokee artifacts?"

"A few wealthy collectors—pay well."

Goodman picked up where the tribal officer had left off. "You didn't charge Harper, why?"

"Lacked evidence."

Kanuna believed Digger took relics but didn't charge him. Since then, maybe something happened to change his mind.

"With Atsadi in jail, did the thefts stop?" Goodman said.

"A month later, someone raided the same mound Atsadi had been plundering."

"What happened?" Carla said.

"Robbed of more of its buried objects."

Goodman glanced up from writing in his notepad. "You arrested anyone?"

"Suspected Harper. Had no proof."

I rubbed my chin and thought about the second attack on the burial mound. "You think Digger waited a month?"

Kanuna tightened his face into a frown. "That's what I said."

Someone killed Digger, and Atsadi claimed he had left the criminal life. If Digger stole from the mounds, where did he take those artifacts?

"Does anyone around here buy Native American sculpture and jewelry?" I asked.

Kanuna didn't like my questioning him. He waited before answering. "We suspect Leonard Eigges. He's been known to collect Indian artifacts."

I jotted in my notepad. "Where can I find him?"

"Lives down your way, in Asheville."

"Has your department talked with Eigges?"

"His lawyers," Kanuna responded with a scowl.

Goodman slapped the desk. "Don't like lawyers?"

Kanuna bared his teeth. "Hate people who steal the old culture and hide behind lawyers."

"How ancient are the mounds?" Carla asked.

"Our ancestors assembled the structures hundreds of years ago as burial grounds or temples."

"Are there lots of mounds?" she continued.

"You find similar raised areas scattered all about Cherokee."

"And the Tribal Police Department pursues mound robbers as major criminals, right?" Goodman said.

Kanuna's face grew red. "To tribal people, it's grave robbing. Never unearth the dead—never! To archaeologists, it's like destroying ancient Greek statues."

I had what I needed. I got up. "Thank you for your assistance, Office Kanuna."

He rubbed the balm over his lips again. "I pay back Chief Deputy Goodman, who helped me in the past." Kanuna got out of his chair. "Harry, could you use some help investigating who poisoned Digger Harper?"

Goodman stood. "That I could."

The tribal officer dusted a speck off his sleeve and stared first at Goodman and then at me. "I'll help you."

Before leaving, I phoned Bruce and asked him to research Mr. Eigges. I needed to get back to the mansion and tell Roth about this collector of Indian artifacts. A new suspect. I needed to ask this Eigges about Atsadi and Digger.

Leaving the station, I shook Goodman's hand. I got into the Mustang with Carla and drove back out of Cherokee along the Oconaluftee River.

"I'm impressed," Carla said.

"How's that?" I said.

"You got the name you sought, Eigges. Now we go find him?"

"Hold on. Remember the movie, *All the President's Men*?"

"What about it?"

"First, we follow the money."

She knitted her brow. "Meaning?"

"We visit Andy Murphy first. He'll connect us to Eigges."

"What if he won't?"

I hoisted my balled-up fist. "I'll raise this. Hope Murphy doesn't sprint into it."

16

I'll always remember this case: the investigation into who killed Digger Harper. My role on Roth's team is Big Guy, the enforcer. Occasionally, I do something clever, but mostly I'm her charging rhino. In this case, the pursuing had turned upside down, with some suspects attacking me as the prey and not the hunter. I guess there has to be a first for everything.

Roth watered the plants behind her desk, her back toward me, her white hair falling straight down to her shoulders. "The tribal police believe Digger stole relics from the Cherokee burial mounds?"

I slumped in a chair before her desk. "Their Officer Kanuna thinks so."

She turned, with her dark eyes, prominent against her white hair and milky-white complexion. "Did this other activity lead to Digger's death?"

"Maybe."

"You found an electronic tracker on Atsadi's car?"

"I did."

"The tribal police planted the device?"

"That's my guess."

She tilted her head to the side. "Why?"

"They're trying to forge a chain of evidence back to some guy named Eigges."

She set her watering pot aside and remained standing, staring at me. "Do the police realize Andy Murphy gave instructions to Digger about robbing the mound?"

"They know nothing about Murphy."

"Find him," Roth said. "Track his compensation backward to Mr. Eigges."

She'd agreed with my plan, so there was no need for further discussion. I left her and spoke with Bruce, our computer expert. He located an Andy Murphy, age fifty-nine, who lived at a trailer park in West Asheville. I went to find Carla.

She peered at the computer in her office. "I'm going over your invoices for the Crown Hunt case."

"And?"

"You drink too many beers."

I grinned. "You don't do badly in that regard."

She smirked. "What's up?"

"Let's go interview that Andy Murphy guy who told Digger which burial mounds to loot?" She turned off her computer and went to get herself ready.

We got into my Mustang and drove to West Asheville. The trailer park had mobile homes spaced one after another down a tree-lined road. I parked two units away from our target on Le Vista Lane. My body still felt sore from the ambush in the woods, but I had dressed for comfort: jeans, a blue polo shirt, and a timeworn sports coat to hide my M1911 pistol in a holster on my belt. Carla had dressed both for action and a professional appearance with a black jacket, a gray blouse, black pants, and black running shoes.

At Murphy's home, I knocked on the door while Carla stood behind me. No one answered. I thumped once more.

A soft voice, barely audible, sounded behind the door. "Who's there?"

"Don Gannon. Mr. Eigges sent me."

"Who the hell are you?"

I knocked a third time. "Talk to the Sheriff or me."

The door opened. A slight man faced me. "What d'ya want?"

I shoved past him. "Thanks for the invite."

The Spartan furnishings in the first room reminded me of a motel room. The top of Murphy's head reached my chin, even with his baseball cap, with Asheville Tourists in bold letters. He frowned. "I asked what you want?"

With wide-opened eyes, he backed away from Carla and me and reached for a pack of cigs. The reek of cigarette smoke in the room stunned my sense of smell. He fired up one.

"You're Andy Murphy?" I asked.

"I am. What does Eigges want?"

I noticed the two fingernails on his left hand had yellow stains where he held his smoke. "Did you deliver Eigges' messages to Digger Harper?"

He gestured at me with his left hand. "Maybe. Why d'ya want to know?"

"Tell me ... or talk with the Sheriff's Office."

He narrowed his cloudy blue eyes and gamely puffed on his cig, a small man cringing before my bulk. "Yeah, I delivered messages to Digger,"

I grinned at Carla and turned back to Murphy. "How did you get them?" Carla pulled the sleeve of my jacket and whispered, "Be careful." I stepped in front of her.

Murphy finished his smoke and stubbed it out in a green, marble ashtray, filled with butts, ash, and stink. His eyes widened like a scared rabbit. "Went to his big house."

"Give me an address," I said.

His eyes went blank. "I'll have to find it."

My quarry slid sideways to a built-in cabinet and opened its glass-paned doors. He turned his baseball cap around, so the brim faced rearward. Next, he stood on his toes and pawed over file folders along an upper shelf. He bumped a book onto the floor and nudged the book out of his way with one of his Doc Martens boots. Then, he rummaged through the next lower bookshelf. "Here somewhere." I peeked over his shoulder. He opened folders and seemed to search old, discarded notepads and paper scraps.

When Murphy had gone down the bookshelves, he stooped to get into an open area below them, a space crammed with boxes resting on the floor. "Think I found it."

Murphy bent and wrapped his spindly arms around a large carton and strained to raise it. "Hard to lift."

I shoved him aside with my left arm. "Got it." I bent down and grabbed the box; it weighed little, mostly empty.

Behind me, Carla shouted, "Look out!"

I lunged to my right. The weighty top shelf fell and hit my head. My skull, still sore from my earlier fight, stung and throbbed, with my brain flashing bright lights. Instinct screamed, *don't black out. Get up. Move.*

I collapsed, shifting the wooden bookshelf and books off my left flank.

Through my pain and a blur, I saw Murphy reach into his Doc Martins and pull out a black, rectangular object. He popped it open, a switchblade.

I clawed for the pistol in my belt holster while Murphy, knife in hand, came at me.

The blow had dazed me. Enough to make me move in slow motion.

His yellow fingers held the knife inches from my face.

Whack!—A shower of cigarette butts, ash, and stink flew everywhere.

I held my pistol. Murphy staggered off the ground, still holding the knife.

I shouted at him, "Drop it!"

Murphy screeched, "Screw you." He limped through his kitchen and out a second door. I didn't shoot him or chase him either because I couldn't see straight. I slumped to the floor.

Carla bent down beside me and stroked my face. "There's a new cut on top of your head."

"You swing a mean ashtray."

She brushed ash off her action outfit. "Kept watching to see when he was going to sprint into your fist."

#

Carla and I were back in Roth's office when Taylor appeared in the doorway. She did her gliding walk to the front of Roth's desk and stood to begin her report, "I done finished a-searchin' fer the monkshood."

My boss glanced at me and then at her. "And the outfit?"

"A-huntin' fer monkshood, either in a garden or the woods, I disguised myself as an Appalachian Club worker."

Roth's eyes wandered from the ranger hat—a green, wide-brimmed sunhat—to the cotton gloves on her hands, and zinc oxide on her nose. "I'm guessing you dressed as a ranger."

"Yes, ma'am. I were a-classifyin' herbs and flowers—everyone I talked to wanted to help me."

Roth spoke. "Those who act suspicious are easy to identify. Those who cloak themselves in goody activities are well disguised."

Taylor had everyone's attention. "I moseyed to Old Fort on the road where the Harpers live 'n went—house by house—toward their home."

Roth nodded approval. "And your disguise worked?"

Taylor pulled off her hat, revealing her red curls, and dropped it on a chair. "Yes, ma'am. The people in the houses were a-puttin' on coats and a-diggin' in the yards with me."

"Find anything?" Carla asked.

"Didn't find monkshood. One neighbor fed me lunch in front of a warm fire."

I pictured Taylor in her ranger hat, charming the neighbors in a folksy way, moving on afterward to the next yard.

Roth tapped on her desk. "What happened at the Harper house?"

"Michael, Digger's adopted dad, answered the door," Taylor said. "I told him I were a-classifyin' plants a-growin' in our mountains. He explained I needed to jaw with his wife, Bertha. She did the family gardening, and he went to get her.

"After a spell, I faced Bertha. She'n were big with fleshy arms adorned with bracelets and fingers heaped with rings. Her'n mouth were in an oval, neither smiling nor frowning. She asked, 'What is your favorite mountain plant?'

"I reckoned Bertha done decided to test me. I replied I adored the Tall Bellflower. It has those dark blue flowers, which are flattened and a-growin' in clusters. It at the end of da bloomin' period fer this year. That big woman jawed me further about mountain flora, which questions I answered. Finally, she guided me out to her'n flower garden. No monkshood in her'n garden."

"What did you think of her?" I asked.

"Bertha a-mite ill. Everything she done irritated me," Taylor answered. "A-gussin' she'n plum mean."

Roth began tapping again. "Did you find the poison plant near their house?"

"I strolled to da next-door neighbor and got behind the Harper house. I entered a meadow and done seen purple-blue flowers. Monkshood grows in da woods behind Bertha's house."

"Well done, Taylor," Roth said.

"When I finished a-searchin' in Old Fort, I drove to Digger's house. Lilith were at home, an we jawed fer a spell."

"Had Lilith found any monkshood around Digger's house?" Carla said.

"Lilith and I walked the woods around the house a-lookin' fer it. Ain't no monkshood in the nearby woods."

"I done told Lilith I found a patch of monkshood near the Old Fort house. But why'd Digger's mother and father want to kill him? Lilith told me her fiancé didn't get along well with Bertha, but he stayed out of her way."

"Any monkshood around Hayes' shack?" Carla said.

"Mickey and I went a-searchin' around Hayes's house, but we had to avoid his'n dogs."

"Did you find monkshood in the woods in Hayes' neighborhood?" Roth said.

"No, ma'am."

"Taylor, we identified another suspect, Paul Atsadi," I said.

"Bruce done told me 'bout Atsadi," Taylor said. "I went to Cherokee and seen a mess of monkshood in the woods around Atsadi's house."

"You found the suspects who had aconite at hand," Roth said. "You did well. Can you guess who poisoned Digger?"

"No, ma'am."

Roth raised her eyebrows. "There's something fundamentally exhilarating to a detective about trying to pull all the clues together." She went into her comatose state, staring out the window for three or four minutes.

"You made four observations," Roth said. "The killer obtained the monkshood that poisoned Digger at some place other than Digger's property. Hayes doesn't have a ready source of monkshood."

She paused and continued after a moment. "The Harpers had monkshood but no apparent motive. Although Atsadi had access to monkshood, he had worked at his realtor company, forty-five miles away, when someone murdered Digger."

# # #

That evening, Carla and I ate at the Italian Kitchen restaurant, in the heart of downtown Asheville. White linen covered the tables, wood paneling overlaid the walls, and solid wood planking formed the floor. Carla and I ordered the shrimp scampi and white Chianti wine. A flood of Italian meals flowed out from the kitchen on a gale of garlic, causing my taste buds to salivate.

We were quiet at first, filling our mouths with delicious shrimp. She kept staring at the meals coming out of the kitchen. "After eating Taylor's Appalachian Mountain food, I find this eating out wakes up my taste buds. It's like stepping from a dim building into the bright sunlight."

I sampled the Chianti and smirked. "Because you're elegant and sexy, I will not tell Taylor you said that. After she recovered from her shattered heart, she would rip yours out." Taylor's ancestors, the early Scotch-Irish settlers, didn't have seafood—like shrimp—in the Appalachian Mountains. On the other hand, Taylor does fix a succulent freshwater trout.

I noticed Carla's low-cut blue dress and the downward slope of her breasts as she leaned over the table to coil the linguine on the tablespoon in her left hand, occasionally glancing up with her mischievous grin. This voluptuous, petite beauty had held my attention since the beautiful day she had come to Asheville. Later tonight, I would suggest driving up to Sunset Mountain. I envisioned parking in that short turnoff bordered by trees. We hadn't yet returned to the mansion and snuck up to Carla's room.

She finished her shrimp scampi and leaned back. "I am learning much from you ... by working on our case. You are like a brother to me."

I stopped the wine glass on its way to my mouth. *Ouch—She used the dump word.*

"I wanted to let you know I enjoy working with you." She hesitated before resuming. I realized my back had begun to sweat. "Larry Buchanan offered me a lucrative position at his company. I'm considering his offer."

Damn, I thought. *What's that snake trying to do?* "That's good news. I like having those around me succeed."

We went quiet, no more eating with gusto. We seemed like the quintessential old married couple who ran out of subjects to discuss. I too began appraising the dishes coming out of the kitchen and broke the silence. "Our visit to Murphy had its hitches. We don't know where he's hiding, but we learned he knows Eigges. What if he has tipped off Eigges?"

"I see where you're going," Carla said. "Soon, we'll rattle Eigges' cage and see what shakes loose."

"Talking of detective work, are you ready to pick up Lilith?" I asked. "We need to pay Johnny Hayes a visit."

#

As evening switched over to darkness, Carla and I taped one of the new GPS devices onto the frame of Johnny Hayes' truck. Hayes had parked his grimy black pickup truck, with a white driver-side door-panel, on the two-lane road above his shack in Asheville. Next, we snuck back to my Mustang, which I had parked at the next crossroad.

From where she had been waiting in the rear seat, Lilith asked, "Any problems?"

Carla slipped into the front passenger seat. "Nope, it's hooked up."

I settled into the driver's seat and yawned. "Ladies, let's go home."

Lilith continued as if I hadn't spoken. "How do you know if it's working?"

I turned toward Lilith. "Bruce, set up the tracker software at the mansion. He tried it out."

Carla continued without hesitation. "I wonder if they'll take the truck out tonight?"

"Let's don't leave yet," Lilith said. "We could watch for the truck?"

Good grief. I'm exhausted. "We've done enough for one day."

Carla's leather seat creaked. "Listen to Lilith. We're out here. Wouldn't hurt to see what Hayes does."

"I know Hayes poisoned Digger," Lilith said. "What he's doing now?"

Carla and Lilith had decided to play detective. But my eyelids wanted to close, my mind to shut down. "Let's get some sleep. Check out the tracking equipment tomorrow. We'll know exactly where he goes; if he goes anywhere at all."

We sat in a dark car because of a thick cloud cover. I heard the rear seat rustle as Lilith leaned forward. "Ms. Roth told you to listen. I want to watch Hayes' truck."

I rolled my eyes in the darkness. *They don't get to tell me what to do, do they?*

Carla scolded me. "I saw that. Doesn't hurt to make Lilith happy."

The women had hemmed me in and they spoke while I hunted for words, lagging them by a sentence or two. Quarreling with women took energy but giving in on the small stuff saved stamina. I would argue with a woman to take off her clothes; it wasn't worth arguing about watching a truck. "I guess we could stay a little longer—"

A clattering, black pickup truck drove through the intersection.

The ladies shifted from verbal give-and-take to full-up silence. I caught sight of a white door-panel on the pickup's side. Hayes had started to move. My silver Mustang hid in the darkness as an octopus hid in its ink. As the taillights flowed away, before Carla and Lilith would tell me to shadow Hayes, I started the engine and pulled out onto the road, trailing at a distance without switching on my lights.

Carla sucked in her breath. "Lights!"

I flicked on the headlights and hung way back, so Hayes wouldn't discover my beams in his rearview mirror. Lilith shouted from the rear. "Get closer. Don't lose him."

"I won't lose him."

Lilith leaned over the back of the driver's seat. "Closer."

"We have a tracker. Besides, he's probably driving to Morganton." I lost sight of his truck but picked him up again on I-40 going east.

Hayes pulled off the Interstate at Morganton, drove along a two-lane road, parked, and walked into the woods, trailed by his two friends, one of whom still limped. They lugged what appeared to be shovels and picks. I drove past his truck and stopped my car farther down the road. A flash of lightning lit up the horizon and thunder boomed in the distance.

"I saw train tracks to our left," Carla said.

"Hayes went in that direction," Lilith said.

He must have estimated this site to be near the X shown on Nathaniel Harper's map.

Carla stepped out of the passenger door, automatically turning on the overhead dome light. She pulled the hoodie, on her gray tracksuit, up over her head. "You think they plan to dig?"

Lilith clambered out the door behind Carla. "Why else come here?"

Before the dome light went out, Carla shrugged her shoulders. "We could make sure."

"We won't know unless we follow them," Lilith said.

My stomach flipped-flopped, the way it does when I see a calamity coming. I had to stop Carla from becoming Nancy Drew and dashing after Hayes with her new amigo, Lilith. I stepped out the driver's door and leaned over the top of the car facing the two women. "Don't do it. We don't want them—"

As my eyes adjusted to the darkness, I saw I was alone. Jeezus Cripes. These women didn't just run off? I popped my trunk and took out my dark-olive rain jacket, my heavy-duty, incandescent flashlight, and my pistol. I took off across the road in the direction Hayes and his two friends had gone. Unable to see clearly through the dark murk enclosing me, I walked at a tortoise's pace, shunning the use of my flashlights. My heart raced and thumped.

Drops of rain pelted my face. The storm had moved closer. My ears picked up the clomp of shovels somewhere ahead. I slipped through a field, sticking close to trees, until I spied the three men, illuminated by a lantern on the ground, taking turns digging. I spotted my two missing women slumped down behind a raised bank. My pulse slowed in relief. I whispered, "Carla," and she, visible in the slight glow from Hayes' lantern, turned toward me. "They're burrowing for gold."

"Probably are," I said.

Lilith whispered. "Bet they dig every night."

"Let's head back," I said softly.

"Wait," Lilith said.

"We've seen what Hayes is doing." I sensed the wind blowing stronger than it did several minutes ago. "Storm's a coming."

Storm it did, catching Carla, Lilith, and me in full flight, showering us with heavy rainfall. Water cascaded off my rain jacket and soaked my jeans. I ran fast enough to keep ahead of Hayes and slow enough to avoid pitfalls and tree branches. The wind gushed against me, slowing my progress, driving rain like darts onto my body.

We reached my vehicle, clamoring in and sloshing about, mud and water spilling over the upholstery. We had slathered my car with dampness and dirt. "I feel like I'm sitting in a darn aquarium."

"I'm all wet," Carla said.

"Who's gonna help me clean the interior?" I said.

"I will," Carla said. "Get me home."

I turned on the windshield wipers and pulled out onto the road. "Not a total waste."

"How so?" Lilith asked.

I drove away through the rain, thrilled the women had avoided trouble. "We know what they're doing and where."

17

ROTH'S MANSION, ASHEVILLE — THURSDAY

The next morning, I called a former sweetheart and well-informed reporter at the Asheville Citizen. She answered with a grating perkiness. "Good morning! Helen Fiery speaking."

"Helen, my dear. Don Gannon speaking. How are you?"

"I haven't heard from you since you took me to one of the Shindigs on the Green—three months ago."

"You looked lovely."

"You're after something."

"Helen, you misjudge me. Just wanted to hear your voice."

She carefully pronounced each word. "What. Do. You. Want?"

I brushed down my cowlick, a tad nervous. "Well, now that you mention it—"

"Go ahead!"

"Who's Leonard Eigges?"

She paused, then spoke. "What have you done for me lately?"

"Ms. Roth shared info with you about The Case of the Missing Heiress. And, I invited you to the mansion for one of Taylor's superb dinners."

"Having difficulty with the word, *lately*, are we?"

I sighed. "I'm investigating Digger Harper's death. I'll give you the scoop after I solve it."

Silence. Thirty seconds later, she finally said, "Okay, but I'll check up on your progress—a lot."

"Deal. Tell me about Mr. Leonard Eigges?"

She was in. I heard the background noise of her keystrokes as she queried the paper's database. It was amazing how women could multitask. "He's old money. Spends his time managing a sizable investment and property portfolio."

I scribbled notes. "Know anything about him collecting Indian relics?"

"My editor attended a fundraiser at his estate. The occasion showed off an impressive Native American collection."

"You got an address and number?" She gave me the information and said she would be calling to collect on our agreement.

I called Eigges' secretary and asked to talk to him. She told me he did not give interviews and hung up.

#

I called Chief Deputy Goodman, "Let's meet. Need your help."

"You got something for me?"

"I do."

"What?"

"Tell you over lunch. Meet me at the Tavern on the Square."

"You buy the beers. I'll listen."

Roth stopped me in the front hall. "Our history professor, Angela, plans to finish digging through the Harper diaries. We're meeting in my office at two o'clock this afternoon. You call Lilith, and I'll tell Carla."

After arranging with Lilith to join the afternoon meeting, I went downstairs through the garage. Outside, the rain had stopped. An overcast sky diffused the light, and the temperature continued chilly but not cold. I cleaned my car's interior, grumbling because Carla was nowhere around to help, then drove downtown and met Goodman in civilian clothes at the bar. Sitting together, we ordered lunch.

Goodman gulped the beer the bartender put in front of him. "What ya got for me?"

I reminded him of the tribal police's suspicion of Mr. Eigges.

Goodman took a second gulp of his beer and frowned. "Tell me what I don't know."

"Digger worked out the name of Mr. *X*'s intermediary, the message carrier."

Goodman stared at me and waited.

"Carla and I visited the guy."

Goodman dropped his glass down on the bar with a *whack*. "Damn, Don. You should have told me first."

The bartender placed our food on the bar. I rushed into the rest of my narrative, trying to avoid Goodman's wrath. "I tricked the intermediary into saying he worked for Eigges."

Goodman wrote in a small, spiral notepad. "Tell me the name of this go-between."

I gave him the background information on Andy Murphy and explained he had disappeared after he had walloped me on the head. "Mr. Eigges won't see me. Need your help."

Goodman chewed his burger, and next tugged on his goatee. "I'll have to tell Officer Kanuna at the Cherokee Tribal Police about this Murphy."

I took a sip of beer. "Why?"

"I cooperate with my colleagues. Something you don't seem to do."

Absorbing his rebuke, I pressed forward. "About Eigges? Probably our Mr. *X*? Will you help me get to him?"

Goodman appeared rooted in thought. "I should question him. He'll talk to me if I tell him it's a murder investigation."

"And take me along?"

"Let me talk it over with the Sheriff. I'll identify you as my confidential informant."

I bought him another beer and returned to the mansion for the two o'clock meeting.

# # #

Carla sat at her desk.

"Good afternoon, Miss Diaz."

"Feeling better, are we?" she said. "Recovered from last night's run in the rain and mud? Ready to harass the female staff?"

I eyed her curves and smiled. "I harass only slow-witted damsels."

She faked a wide-eyed look of surprise. "Quick-witted, am I?"

I gave her my best ogle, a sustained stare. "Very."

"This quick-witted female is still exploring your city. What is the big stone building on the side of the mountain to the north?"

"Has a red-tiled roof?"

"Bingo."

"That's the Rose Roof Inn. Has a restaurant on its patio—great view of the city."

She giggled. "Wish someone would escort me up there."

"I'll take you."

"Great. Let's work out a time—"

Taylor stood at the door. "Professor Lightfoot, Angela, done arrived. Ms. Roth said for you'ns to come to her office." My watch displayed two o'clock.

We gathered in Roth's office. Lilith arrived and rang the doorbell a few minutes after two. As I went to the front door to let her in, I noticed Angela had slipped away to the computer room to speak with Bruce. As a detective, I detect.

Once she had spread her journal copies on her desk, Roth launched the first question. "Did the Union Navy regroup and try to push up the James River?"

Angela explained, "The Confederates invented the torpedo; we would call it a mine today. This new technology—hidden in the water—hindered Union ships going up the river."

"The more desperate the situation, the greater the need for the simplicity of comeback," Roth said. "Where was Nathaniel Harper?"

Angela flipped through a few pages of the 1862 journal. "The midshipmen served part of the time at Fort Drewry. He worked at Drewry's Bluff, enjoying his time because the ladies came out from Richmond to picnic there."

I jerked my head in Angela's direction. "What about the Confederates? Did they ever go back downriver?"

Angela turned to one of the journals and summarized what she read, "Several Southern ships slipped through the sunken barrier. Some ran aground in the river and retreated when pounded by Union guns from the shore. Called the Battle of Trent's Reach."

"Harper was there on one of the Confederate ironclads," Lilith said.

"When was this?" I asked.

Angela glanced through the diary. "The battle took place in January 1865, shortly before Richmond fell."

"What happened to Nathaniel?" Carla said.

"The collapse of Richmond's defenses ended the need for the James River Squadron," Angela said. "Harper had to join the infantry."

"Did a final naval battle take place?" Roth asked.

Angela shook her head. "The Confederates sank their ships and retreated from Richmond."

I visualized the sailors sinking their ships and switching to being foot soldiers. "In retreat, the midshipmen and sailors marched away to the trains leaving Richmond?"

"To guard the gold train going to Danville," Angela said. "The naval men were the only combatants trained as infantry and not under General Lee."

Roth made a steeple of her fingers and pursed her lips. "Angela, you've read the journals?"

Angela bobbed her head.

"Have you found any fraud, any forgery, in Harper's diary?"

"I have not. These documents appear authentic."

Roth's face lit up as she looked at me. "I do believe we seek buried booty at the same time we seek a killer."

Writing in his journal, Nathaniel Harper had led me in his final steps through Danville, through Salisbury, and to Morganton, where he buried objects. What I still didn't know was how his adventure had any connection with Digger's death.

##

In the late afternoon, the doorbell rang. I walked to the front and opened the door. A man in unicolor garb—a light blue shirt, a dark blue tie, and a dark blue suit—stood on the steps. He had a long face and a prominent frown. "Larry Buchanan, to pick up Carla Diaz."

I recognized him from a formal dance I had attended at the country club. "I think we've met before. I'm Don Gannon."

Expressionless, he examined me as if scrutinizing a bus schedule on a kiosk. "You played football at Asheville High School and State."

We observed each other. Feeling awkward, I replied, "Did you go to school locally?"

"A private school in Washington, DC. Would you inform Carla I'm here?"

I trudged off to get Carla. I recollected Buchanan's father built up a fortune building and selling houses. After his father passed away, he'd become a wealthy man. He had a reputation as a graceless individual; at any rate, he looked down at my school.

I knocked on Carla's door and found her cheerfully dressed in a knee-length plaid skirt and a tight sweater showing her petite and busty figure.

"Buchanan's here," I said as if announcing we were serving anchovies for dinner.

Ichabod Crane took Carla out for the evening.

During the evening meal, Bruce egged me on to drop my envy of Buchanan and to woo Carla. Taylor served me and said, "You'ns better not fool around, or you'ns lose her." I was blue because of the weather, wasn't I? Carla wasn't my girl, or was she?

18

ROTH'S MANSION & DOWNTOWN ASHEVILLE — FRIDAY

Roth glared at Lilith, Carla, and me, sighed, and reluctantly put down the book she had been reading. "Report, Don."

I explained how Carla, Lilith, and I had kept tabs on Hayes as he crawled around the terminus of the 1865 train tracks in Morganton. It seemed he shoveled up the ground every night and afterward refilled those holes before driving back to his shack before dawn.

"Pinpointed a location, has he?" Roth asked.

I felt distracted, trying not to stare at her intense red lipstick, which jarred with her full-length, maroon dress with wide lapels. "Pinpointed? He's digging up an area the size of a small airport."

"Hayes is using Digger's map for hunting whatever Nathaniel Harper put in the ground," my boss said. "Does he know you're following him?"

"If Hayes knew, he'd be in my face like a cross-eyed badger."

The doorbell rang, and Roth glanced up. "That would be Angela. She seems fascinated by the Nathaniel journals."

I chuckled. "She is spending more time here than at her campus office."

I rose to leave. Roth gestured with her hand for us to remain seated. "Let's see what she has to say."

Angela entered Roth's office and greeted everyone.

Roth glanced longingly at her novel, resting nearby on her desktop. She sometimes had a lazy bent, only working when she wanted to exert herself. She had started down the slick drop into one of her slothful moods. I had the informal duty to pester her back into action when she reverted. "Boss, what do you want us to do?"

She addressed a question at Angela. "Suppose a train worker or a farmer had dug up the cache? Would we know?"

Angela gave a dismissive wave of her hand, poking out from the long sleeve of her white cotton blouse. She spoke at length. "I have been thinking about that possibility."

"And?" Roth asked.

"It would have been in the local newspapers. Libraries keep microfilm or microfiche for historical research. We need to search Morganton-area papers, scanning for an article about digging up old objects, ancient crates."

I tilted my head from side to side to see what others thought. "Digger had a procedure, including checking the library. Wouldn't he have gone to check old articles?"

Lilith rotated forward in her chair. "He was poisoned before he finished checking."

"Search the newspapers at once," Roth said.

Angela made a steeple of her fingers. "I'll begin hunting through old issues. My readings lead me to infer the amount of gold leaving Richmond may have been lower than estimated. Maybe Midshipman Harper buried something other than gold."

Lilith, sitting beside me, jerked and stiffened her posture. "My fiancé believed they buried the gold. He said if you don't know what you started with, then don't say nothing got lost."

Angela grinned, her white teeth gleaming against her ebony skin. "But, Lilith, in a hundred and thirty-five years, this lost gold hasn't surfaced. A blizzard of novels, comic books, movies, and gossip may have spun a folktale."

Lilith's face developed a red tint, and her bobbing head tossed her flaxen hair up and down as she jumped in to defend Digger. "You don't know. If a treasure hunter dug up the lost gold, they wouldn't admit it. The state or federal government would take a tax, and you'd need to labor through a mound of red tape."

Angela tilted her hand at Lilith. "No one could keep that kind of discovery secret."

Angela paused and added, "Also, the Confederate gold train paid out currencies as military payrolls. They used up the final reserves as they moved south."

Roth had been bracing her chin in her palm, but now she glanced up. "What do you mean?"

Angela flipped through her research notes. "Historical archives claim thirty-nine thousand dollars went to Southern soldiers when the gold train reached Greensboro, North Carolina. An estimated hundred and eight thousand dollars went to Confederate soldiers around the Savannah River as payment. Forty thousand dollars went for provisions in Washington, Georgia."

Lilith jumped in again. "But that doesn't mean Digger—"

"Get started checking the Morganton newspapers," Roth said.

"Okay," Angela said. "Lilith, will you help me at the library?"

Lilith waited half a minute. "Yup, sure will."

"I'll pick you up tomorrow."

"You and Carla will continue to keep an eye on Hayes' excavations," Roth said to me. "Investigate Paul Atsadi more closely. He has motive and access to monkshood."

As soon as I nodded my head, she asked, "Did others testify at Atsadi's trial? If yes, why would he attack Digger and not the other witnesses?"

"I'll ask Bruce to go over the court records again," I said.

Roth closed her eyes to think. "Have we forgotten anything? Your attention has been on Hayes seeking buried coins and Atsadi digging up Cherokee mounds. I think it possible neither path will lead us to Digger's killer."

I thought back over my clues and dead ends from the last few days. "I need to talk to Digger's father, Michael. He's been calling to check on my progress."

"Talk to him at Old Fort. Don't bring him here."

I gave a thumbs-up. "Michael Harper is long-winded. I've never met anyone else who could cram so many words into such a simple conversation. Carla and I'll go see him."

Roth dismissed me. I went to write up the meeting for my records. *Digger is dead and gone, but Lilith stands up for him. She has had a hard time in her life, but she won't stop pushing for what she believes. She's got a real drive that I'm starting to appreciate*, I thought as I walked to my office.

I drove downtown and parked in the high-rise garage near the *Citizen-Times* building. My boss wanted me to go to Malaprop's Book Store to pick up some novels. Coming out the exit on Battery Park Street, I heard my name. "Don! Wait up."

It was Helen Fiery, the newspaper reporter. I kept moving. She clicked at me in high heels, catching up with me.

I turned around. "Oh … Helen."

She, a California transplant who had kept her tan since arriving in our Eastern mountains a few years back, halted in front of me. "Where's my exclusive? Is Eigges connected to the Digger Harper death?"

We stood face-to-face on the sidewalk, with shoppers and tourists flowing around us as water whirls about a boulder in a stream. "I promised you your scoop," I said. "Don't contact Eigges."

"Why not?"

I gaped at her with an open mouth. "You'll make him cover up."

Helen glared at me. I told her, "Got to go."

She hooked my arm and held up six fingers and counted them down, one by one. "How. Is. Eigges. Connected. To. Digger?"

She had the instinct of a good reporter, always pushing. I kept my voice low, trying to reason with her, appease her. "Damn it, Helen. I'll tell you when I know."

She exhaled and rolled her eyes to the sky. "Reporters poke around. That's what I do." She pushed closer, thrusting her chest against me until she stood in my face.

As I gently pushed her away, I noticed she had a freshly-showered smell. "Soon. I promise." The people on the sidewalk slowed to stare at us.

I turned and began to walk away, but she clicked after me and gripped the sleeve of my brown sports coat. "I'll give you more time. But, you're on a short leash, Buster."

I took a deep breath and peeled her hand off my coat sleeve. "Okay. I understand. Do you know any more about Eigges?"

She gave me a tight-lipped smile, with eyes losing their flash. "He's eighty years old. Lives on a mountain just outside of town. Overlooks a sprawling forest area."

"He's wealthy," I said. "How did he make his fortune?"

"Old money."

"His family made it how?"

She brushed her long, silky hair away from her right eye. "The French Broad River powered cotton mills at one time."

"They were in textiles?"

Helen thrust her hip out provocatively. "The history of Asheville is interesting. A long time ago, there were many jobs along the river."

"And the Eigges family owned the mills?"

"They built houses up the banks for the workers; had a church for the families. Eventually, the industry went under."

"What does Mr. Eigges do today?" I asked.

"These days, he's a financial investor," Helen said.

"Anything else?"

"Three years back, two intruders got on Eigges' estate. His gardener attacked them with a machete. Cut them badly."

"Thanks for the info." I turned to leave.

She had my arm again. "I hear there's a new hottie in Roth's mansion?"

"Carla Diaz is Roth's office manager. I'm training her to help us investigate."

Helen winked. "When you get tired of her, call me." She turned and clicked away. "Ta-ta."

#

The evening was tangy and bitter: I played pool and drank beer in the game room with my two sidekicks, Mickey and Bruce, while Buchanan took Carla out again; this time to the movies. She came back late, dropping by to say goodnight and rush off to her bedroom. She seemed aloof and preoccupied.

Bruce stood against the wall. "As the poet voiced, 'Tis better to have mud wrestled and lost, than not to have mud wrestled at all.'"

Mickey drove his ball into a side pocket, stood up from the pool table, and turned to me. "My all-knowing wife says you're not ready for emotional commitments." He circled the table and bent to take his next shot. "Said you have the romantic follow-through of rock and

Carla's train is going to leave the station without you." Mickey shot and watched his ball bounce off the cushion rail.

"That's Don," Bruce said. "Either his women leave and never come back, or they return at a time and place just to embarrass him."

To distract myself, I walked to the patio doors on the outer wall and closed the drapes, ignoring the taunts of my mates.

Bruce chalked his cue stick and considered the remaining balls. "How do you feel about Buchanan having all that money?"

"Poor," I said. "Have to drown my distress in beer."

Bruce sank his ball. Mickey said, "Lucky shot."

I stood back from the table under a colorful picture of an English fox hunt. I thought about Carla. She's cute and smart. It's not my responsibility to warn Carla her escort is shallow and mean-spirited. Who knows, maybe Carla was after his money? Her dates were none of my business. There'll always be a prettier woman.

I addressed Bruce, "We're out of beer. It's your turn to go to the refrigerator." Tomorrow, I'm back on the case, finding some way to interview Eigges.

19

An Asheville Estate — Saturday

In the morning, while Carla and I had breakfast at the Genial Mushroom restaurant, I checked my answering service. Goodman wanted me to ring him. He answered on the third one.

"Harry, what you got for me?"

"Ah, it's Sleuth the Mooch. Where are you?"

"Downtown. With Carla."

"We should talk."

My meatball hoagie arrived at our table. "Did you get us in to talk with Eigges?"

"Yep. Called him this morning. He'll see me."

"How'd you get him to agree?"

"Told him I'm trying to solve a murder. I wanted to ask about his employing Paul Atsadi."

Why would Eigges discuss his involvement with Atsadi, taking funeral objects from the Cherokee reservation? "Won't he incriminate himself?"

"Told him I'm investigating a murder, not his allegedly taking objects out of graves."

"Can you do that?"

"Robbing funeral objects from tribal land falls under a 1990 federal law. He agreed to help with the murder investigation if I didn't pursue infractions under that grave-robbing protection law."

"Still don't understand why he consented to talk about Atsadi," I said.

"He hesitated at first," Goodman said. "I explained—if he didn't cooperate with me on Atsadi—I had no option but to open a full-scale investigation with the Cherokee tribal police about the grave robbing."

"What happened?"

"He talked police harassment and said he would stick the county manager on me. I talked about civic duty and keeping it simple."

"And you won the argument."

"He agreed to meet me off the record."

"Will he have a lawyer present?" I asked.

"No lawyer and I won't record our conversation," Goodman said.

I was in to see Eigges. "I am impressed by your accomplishment."

"When are you going to do some of the heavy lifting?" Goodman asked.

I acted as if I hadn't heard. "When is our appointment?"

"Two o'clock this afternoon. I'll swing by the mansion thirty minutes beforehand and pick you up."

I mouthed to Carla, "Goodman got me in to see Eigges."

"Can I come?" she asked.

"Can Carla come?" I spoke on the phone.

"Afraid not. Just me and you."

I shook my head at Carla. She pouted and mouthed, "I'm coming."

"Before we disconnect, I have something else," Goodman said. "Kanuna says Atsadi's car tracker suggests he's been driving around Cherokee. Probably showing houses. He's not going out to rob graves at night."

"Atsadi keeps saying he's changed his spots. Maybe he has?"

"Kanuna reports no phone calls between Atsadi and Eigges," Goodman said.

I took a bite of my hoagie and glanced at Carla, who continued to pout. "Good info."

"What about the guy who hit you in the head?"

"Murphy's hiding from us. Carla and I have been searching for him. We'll find him."

"Keep me informed."

When he hung up, I hesitated to meet Carla's eyes. "Sorry. Goodman can't take more than one civilian to meet Eigges."

Back at the mansion, I got ready to go with Goodman to question Eigges. I decided not to wear my belt holster with a weapon. After all, I would be with the Chief Deputy and why on earth would I need a gun?

# # #

Goodman, trusty as a well-worn pair of jeans, drove down the lane toward Roth's mansion. He stopped his white Crown Victoria in front of me. I eyed the big black letters, SHERIFF, on the side of the car. Goodman wore his cold-weather uniform, with a long-sleeved black shirt including a US flag sewn on his right pocket. When I opened the passenger door, he blocked me with his right palm. "You carrying?"

"Nope."

"Good. Told Eigges I had an assistant. Not an armed gumshoe."

I unzipped my dark-olive jacket and climbed in beside Goodman, gagging on a haze of Aqua Velva in the compartment. He drove toward Eigges' estate, a short distance away. Rolling down my window for fresh air, I felt grateful to Goodman for getting us in to see him.

Goodman paused at a stop sign. "Is this the way?"

I lifted my shoulders in a half shrug. "The way to his estate?"

"The way to Digger?"

I scratched my chin. "Don't know. Can't answer unless you tell me what you're talking about."

"The way to solve Digger's murder."

"They—Atsadi, Murphy, and Eigges—robbed Indian mounds together with Digger," I said. "Maybe they killed Digger because they had a falling out?"

He focused on his driving as if preoccupied. "Have you found that guy who smacked you on the head? What was his name, Murray or Murphy?"

I felt embarrassed and covered my eyes with my hands. "Carla and I have searched everywhere for Murphy."

Goodman clicked his tongue. "Can't track Murphy down?"

I closed my eyes and took a calming breath. "He's vanished."

He chuckled. "You'll need dumb luck to find him." He focused on his steering. "What have you found out about Eigges?"

Because Helen Fiery had told me, I knew about the man we were visiting. "He's eighty years old. Lives outside of Asheville on a mountain overlooking a big-ass forest."

We had reached Eigges' estate. Goodman drove past a wrought iron gate and down a curving asphalt road. Under a partially overcast sky, a sinuous line of gray mountains rose in the distance. I viewed a close-clipped green lawn, bordering the narrow estate road, transforming into well-kept grounds of grass and stand-alone trees. "Know what's wrong with these grounds?"

"Ain't nothing's wrong," he responded.

"Yeah. A heavenly abode."

Goodman turned the steering wheel to follow a gradual turn in the lane. "Eigges has a gardener, Palo Sanchez. He left the gate open for us."

"You know him? Because?"

"Palo's handy with a machete, as well as lawns. Savagely cut a trespasser. We've jailed the gardener a few times."

A red-brick, stately home came into view. Goodman steered his vehicle under a sunroom built out from the side of the house and over the lane. Craning my neck, I observed a massive, squarish house under mansard roofs. I counted two large, red-brick chimneys. My peripheral vision spotted a slight man, a little under average height, with white hair, pushing a wheelbarrow full of cut brush. As our police cruiser got close, I recognized Andy Murphy.

"Stop! That's Murphy—the guy who dinged my head."

The Chief Deputy jerked his Crown Victoria to a stop. Murphy raised his head and stared first at Goodman and then me. He sucked in a deep breath of surprise, dropped the wheelbarrow handles, and ran. I chased him through a labyrinth of gardens and lawns. Since I ran most mornings, I gained on him. I cornered him inside a courtyard of raked sand, enclosed by a tall wall of orange bricks. He faced me, sucking in deep pulls of air, his eyes bulging from their sockets. I rammed Murphy, shoving my shoulder into his chest and flipping him onto the ground. Remembering he had pulled a knife on me the last time we met, I patted his right foot and boot, finding his switchblade. I yanked him upright.

A voice came from behind me. "You trespass."

I whirled, holding Murphy by his sweatshirt's collar. A man, about five feet eight inches tall, husky, stared with steely eyes and held a machete pointed toward me. I had found Palo.

My hands grew cold, freezing. "This man is wanted for assault. I'm with the Buncombe County Chief Deputy Sheriff."

Machete man grinned. "You trespass."

I hesitated, my spine plunging into the chilling cold. I had never witnessed a machete in combat. My old self-defense instructor in the Military Police had seen the gruesome, sickening damage a machete could do.

Holding Murphy's collar, I turned him sideways and pushed around Palo.

He glided to block me, shifting with smooth, balanced steps, much like the movements in ballroom dance. All the time, Palo sneered and cut the air. His smirk and a thin mustache intensified his evil power.

My leg muscles tight, I yanked Murphy away from Palo. The machete man followed with gliding steps.

I shifted away from Palo again, being driven back against a high brick wall. He stalked me with choreographic steps, his right leg forward and his left leg behind the front one. Next, his right foot went to the lower left. Left foot crossed behind the right foot and went to the front. Always his weapon forward of his body.

I opened the three-inch switchblade I had taken from Murphy and kept him in front of my body. My stomach muscles tightened. Where was Goodman?

Palo's machete seemed to be about a foot and a half in length. The blade didn't have much flex. It could cut and stab.

He advanced on me, cutting the air. I stumbled back with Murphy. Palo could keep this up; he wouldn't run out of ammunition. "Put down your machete. I'm with the Deputy Chief Sheriff."

"You trespass."

Where was my backup? The chunky gardener stood in a long-sleeve, black shirt and blue jeans, holding the machete before him. My old instructor had told me there would be a moment of shock after a machete blow, followed by a bloody mess. When I shot someone with a pistol in combat, I rarely knew right away how much destruction I had done. With a machete, blood tells how much damage was done.

I kept retreating, holding the knife with its puny blade. "Goodman! Help," I shouted.

Moving stiffly, with locked legs, I had slowly backed up through the courtyard until the high brick wall blocked my way.

Only Murphy stood between Palo and me. Murphy whimpered. Palo stared at me, his machete swinging in its quick motion. "No one trespasses here."

"Freeze! Drop the machete."

Oh, hallelujah! I thought.

Palo, slicing with the long blade, swung around in a smooth step to face Goodman.

In his long-sleeve black uniform, the Chief Deputy stood firm, holding his pistol, a Glock, before him. "Stop—I will shoot."

My knees shook in relief. I held Murphy in front of me.

Palo hesitated, then dropped his machete, and kneeled.

Goodman aimed his pistol at Palo and kicked the machete out of his reach. "Don! You okay?"

I slowed my breathing in relief. "You just saved my butt."

"Didn't want to have to look at your chopped-up body."

The law took over and rambled through its procedures. Goodman got Murphy and Palo cuffed and into his Crown Victoria and he informed Eigges they had to cancel their meeting and reschedule. My clothes, drenched with sweat, stuck to me. My gut knotted like a wrung-out sweatshirt; I lashed myself for not bringing my pistol.

Because we suspected Murphy of stealing Cherokee artifacts, Goodman summoned Cherokee Tribal Police Officer Kanuna to Asheville. Goodman and Kanuna interviewed Murphy and Palo in the county jail. A lawyer, provided by Eigges, was present. Murphy argued he had struck me because he feared I would assault him, and we had to drop the charges because of the claim I had started the fighting. Palo argued he had confronted me because he thought I had trespassed, but the Sheriff's Office kept him incarcerated pending further investigation. Both Murphy and Palo denied stealing from burial mounds on the Cherokee Reservation.

# # #

Goodman drove me back to the mansion, where I changed into fresh clothes and joined Roth for lunch out on the flagstone patio. Her hands hit the wrought-iron table, shaking the plates and cups. "I'm not happy with your case."

I glanced at her. Maybe she had decided the Confederate booty did not exist. I pushed aside Taylor's cornbread salad. "Are you telling me to lay off the gold search? Focus on Digger's killer instead?"

She shook her head. "Lilith's retainer, your salary, is disappearing fast. Find the killer."

While Taylor came out from the kitchen and served bacon-potato soup and hot cocoa, I pinched my lips together. When she left, I asked, "What do you want me to do?"

"Get the killer and focus on what Nathaniel buried."

My throat tightened. "Hmm ... what can I do I'm not already doing?"

She gave a disgusted snort. "Step up surveillance on Atsadi, the ex-con, and on Murphy, the intermediary. Nail them or eliminate them." She sipped her soup.

"I'll see what I can do."

"When?"

I shifted in my wrought-iron chair. "You want surveillance and bugging on both Atsadi and Murphy?"

Roth raised her eyebrows. "ASAP."

In the garage under the mansion, I revealed our white van, the Handyman's Spy, to Carla. "We cloak our stakeout with this 1995 Ford Econoline, a cargo vehicle."

Standing at a wooden counter, Bruce soldered a battery onto a small FM transmitter and microphone. Carla watched him work at the counter, and next glanced at the van. "It's very plain. The ladders and buckets on the roof of the van seem normal." She viewed the van through its front window. "The bucket seats and the front area are typical," she said. "I see a panel—between the rear compartment and forward area—hides what's in the back of the van."

I took satisfaction in explaining the ways of the gumshoe to Carla, who, combined with her natural curiosity, picked up information easily. "The surveillance cameras mount on the ladders and rubbish on top," I said. "A monitor, inside the van, shows the camera scenes."

Carla opened the van's rear door and pointed toward the monitor inside on a counter. "There's a chair. Who operates the system?"

I raised my chin higher and grinned. "Bruce does his best work in front of a computer. He'll control the receiver to capture the signal from the bug in the subject's house."

She wrinkled her forehead. "Signal?"

"Bruce and I hide a small microphone and FM transmitter in the household. The bug is voice activated to save battery life."

Carla raised her eyebrows. "You break in?"

Was she going to raise a stink with Roth about our breaking the law? "Hmm … yeah."

She began a slow smile. "Teach me how to plant a bug."

#

To enter Atsadi's home in Cherokee, we cut out a circular section in a rear window, holding the glass pane with a suction cup. Reaching through the hole, Carla opened the window, and we entered. Half an hour later, after hiding the bug and ensuring it worked, we concealed our entry before leaving. We cleaned the glass with soap and water, applied glue along the edge of the circular glass, and let the glue set. The glass glue bonded instantly and dried crystal clear.

Carla and I fled through the brush. Entering the nearby van, Bruce gave us a thumbs up: he had heard us speak into the bug in the house. "Well done, Carla," I said. "You were magnificent. Sowed a bug."

Carla, her face flushed, danced in a small circle and flung out her arms again and again. "I did it. I did it."

Bruce and I grinned at her, sharing in her joy. "Yeah, you did it," I said.

Carla straightened her ponytail. "I guess we sometimes park the van at Murphy's trailer and sometimes at Atsadi's home?"

"Yeah," I said. "Plus, we have a second FM receiver we can take around in a car. We can't park the car long in a neighborhood. Too obvious."

"What's next?"

I rubbed my neck and glanced at the monitor and the FM receiver. I explained *next* would be the slow, boring duty of a detective. "Think of a buzzard circling high overhead, hunting for a rabbit. We watch Atsadi and Murphy and see what happens."

"We're eagles," Carla said. "Not buzzards."

What I didn't know at that point was that we were the rabbit!

20

OLD FORT & MORGANTON, NORTH CAROLINA —
SUNDAY

Carla and I sat for breakfast; she had her face in the newspaper. Taylor brought grits to the table. I lingered to savor the warm grits with cheese and butter, letting the smooth, thick mixture slide over my tongue. I gave out a contented sigh. Nothing better than living in North Carolina in the morning. Carla, hailing from Ohio, complained about the excess butter clogging her arteries. I ate in silence and reflected on our search. "Do you remember Angela's warning?" I asked. "It popped into my mind."

"What warning?" she asked, speaking from behind the paper.

"Angela told us, 'Nathaniel Harper stuck something in the ground; we just don't know what.'"

She lowered her paper to glance at me. "Someone must have known—back in the time after the Civil War—what the midshipman carried on the train."

"Who?"

She held up a finger. "What about the Harper family's oral history? You told me Michael Harper knows a lot."

I glanced across the table at Carla's ocean-blue, long-sleeved dress; the fit narrow around her waist. "Impeccable dress," I said.

She studied me. "You're not so bad yourself, Big Guy. I admire a man who dresses his age."

We raised our coffee cups to each other. "Let's drive down to Old Fort," I said. "Talk with Digger's dad."

She folded the paper. "See the professor but not the battle-ax?"

"Visit Michael. Mrs. Amiability won't tell me crap."

"Why go?"

"Roth is anxious to get her hands on any gold in the ground."

"And we talk with Michael Harper because?"

"As you suggested, his family might have an idea of what Nathaniel buried."

She nodded a slow, steady motion. "Let's go visiting."

I called Harper, and he told me to come this morning.

I pushed my Mustang five mph over the speed limit going down I-40 to Old Fort. Indian summer had dropped upon us: I felt the warm sun and viewed a clear, blue sky. Carla didn't speak, gazing intently at the deciduous trees along the highway, changing color to yellow and red and shedding their leaves. Her lips, normally curved upward in a half-moon grin, drooped in a frown.

"You're distant," I said.

She turned from watching the roadside and, after a moment, spoke, "Remember when we ate at the Italian Kitchen restaurant?"

"Wonderful shrimp scampi. What about it?"

"Remember? My dilemma?"

"Tell me again."

"Larry Buchanan … offered me a position at his company."

Buchanan again. Ugh! Why did that snob—that effete snob—keep coming up? He's a bore, egotistical. Carla and Buchanan went together like a beautiful heron and roadkill. An iciness gripped my stomach, followed by a plummeting sensation. "Hope you stay."

She gazed out her window. "It's a large jump in salary."

"Have you told Roth?"

She sighed a long, drawn-out exhale. "Let's drop it."

When we arrived at the two-story, wood Harper house in Old Fort, I parked on the street in front. Big Bertha, Michael's wife, answered the door. She waited, silent, projecting an icy expression, and blocking the doorway to us.

"Have you met Carla?" I asked.

Bertha responded coarsely, ignoring Carla. "Found Digger's killer yet?"

"Busting my tail to find out."

Bertha raised her head and glared over her nose at me. "The Sheriff's Department made any progress?"

"Don't work for the Sheriff."

Her face stayed frozen. "I guess you're here to see Michael." She opened the door all the way. "Check the den."

I led Carla back to the den, where Michael tossed the morning paper aside with a smile. Carla and I settled onto a leather couch facing him.

"Told your wife we hadn't made progress," I said. "She didn't want to talk with us."

"She's afraid you'll ask for money—investigating my son's murder. Every moment of the day, I agonize over Digger's death. I miss him with every fiber of my body. Why won't he be here to enrich me in my old age? I hope you soon—"

"You enjoy history?" I asked, interrupting him. "Trust your family's oral history?"

He held his left index finger over his mouth and slipped me a white, sealed envelope, which turned out to contain a check to investigate Digger's death. "Umm, yes. Many's the night I talked with my mother and grandmother about our Southern heritage. During cold winter evenings, we sat around the fireplace—"

I shoved in a question when Michael took a breath. "April 1865, Nathaniel Harper left objects in the ground near railroad tracks?"

"Uhh, he did. Just before he—"

"Tell us what he buried."

Michael paused a moment and then began. "My relatives often discussed the great carnage that swept our country. Our noble family always reckoned Nathaniel hid something. Back in 1865, he told my kinfolk he did. The family thought he concealed crates to use for guerilla warfare—"

"Did he bury gold?"

He pondered the question before answering in his hurried, unbroken speech. "Not sure what he concealed. When I was growing up, I heard he buried crates. No one in the family—".

"Anyone dig it up?"

Michael stared at me with a puzzled expression. "Umm, we didn't."

"But Nathaniel buried something?"

"I'm sure—as certain as I am the Boston Red Sox will not win a world series—he hid something where the tracks terminated at Morganton. He said he did, and my great-grandfather didn't lie. I know my family's history."

I was making some progress. Nathaniel buried something, but what?

Carla interrupted, "The day Digger died, he fell to the floor, knocking over a sugar bowl."

Michael gawked slack-jawed at Carla. "Umm—"

"Why did he draw a skull-and-crossbones figure in the spilled sugar?"

Michael squinted at Carla as if his vision blurred, his chin slack.

She furrowed her brow and set her jaw. "It's important. Did Digger mean his death was due to buried gold—in the way buccaneers hid treasure?"

Michael had a deer-frozen-in-headlights expression of bewilderment. "Maybe."

"How did Digger handle a crisis?" I asked.

He grimaced. "How do you mean?"

I kept pushing. "Digger was dying from poison. Was he thinking right?"

He hesitated before answering. "I never saw him panic. Over the years I grew to know my son, he thought clearly. If he were dying, he would tell us something critical."

My eyes lost focus, and I drifted off into my mind, leaving Michael to prattle on about the family he respected so much, the ancestry and the country he loved. Leaving the Old Fort house with Carla, my back slumped with frustration. Michael knew zilch about what Nathaniel Harper might have concealed in the earth.

#

Driving back toward Asheville from the east, the road rose higher and higher, revealing handsome views of magnificent mountains in the distance. Carla began chattering and admiring the vista as if determined to absorb all the beauty as she passed, happy on a bright fall morning. She looked gorgeous: smiling her wide grin, beaming with her brown eyes, and radiating joy. She had tossed off her previous despair. Occasionally, we parked along the road, while Carla viewed trees changing color and distant peaks soaring.

One pull-off along the highway lay beside a gentle slope down to a field and woods. We viewed the scenery and walked down the slope toward the meadow.

"Watch your step," I said.

"Worried about me?" Carla replied.

"Hate to see you fall on your pretty face."

"I'm shorter—more stable than you."

"You're prettier and curvier."

She raised one eyebrow. "Mr. Gannon, are you flirting?"

We had reached the bottom of the incline, walking into a field of wild asters, swelling their purple petals toward the sun in celebration of surviving another cold night. Carla walked through the flowers, which reached a height of three to four feet, stretching up to past her hips. Perspiring somewhat from the sun's warmth and my exercise, I followed her.

"Why are they still flowering?" she asked.

"They appear late in the year," I said.

"So pretty."

I felt befuddled by all I saw: the field of asters on a warm autumn day, Carla with her big smile and vivacious nature, and her pleasing, Romanesque form. She walked farther into the field, paused, and turned toward me.

I reached around her waist. She looked up at me. I bent down, held her, and kissed her.

Closing her eyes, Carla squeezed my back and kissed me in return. I felt her warmth. My heart pitter-pattered.

She stiffened, dropped her head, and pushed us apart. "No." Carla scurried through the asters back toward the path up the slope.

Shit, I thought. *First glee and now sorrow.* Why had I grabbed her? When I reached the car, Carla already sat in the passenger seat, leaning against the door.

"Carla, I'm sorry. I blew it."

She continued leaning against the door, shaking her head.

"Remember when we went to Billy's Tavern in Herndon? We connected, hit it off. I wanted to go there again."

She kept her head turned away from me.

"I was wrong."

I started the car and we drove back in silence. At the mansion, she jumped out and ran through the hallway, passing Taylor.

"Carla, what's wrong?" Taylor asked.

Carla hurried up the stairs, two at a time.

Standing in the front doorway, I struggled to endure my bottomless shame. Taylor gawked at me, shook her head, said, "You could screw up Christmas morning," and hurried after Carla.

#

That night, Bruce and I tailed Hayes' pickup. "Guy, I don't understand why we got to tail Hayes' truck," Bruce said. "Cuz we know he's going to the Morganton train tracks."

"If Hayes changes his plan, we'll know because we're behind him."

"He's not going to change plans. You tail him because you're stubborn."

"I am a careful planner."

Hayes drove to the Morganton train tracks. We stopped down the road from his parked vehicle and waited for Hayes and his two buddies to begin digging. "This is one creepy stakeout," Bruce said. "I'm in a vampire movie where the creatures haunt the night."

I yawned. "I admire you. For a computer nerd, you have big-time imagination."

He coughed. "And I'd rate you a lot higher if you'd wrap up this investigation."

"I don't know who killed Digger, but I will."

"*Phffft!*" Bruce said. "God grant I live that long."

I opened the door and got out. "Hayes has had time to start. Let's check on them."

Bruce slipped out his door. "They're pig-headed. No squirrel would keep digging so long for a lost acorn."

We crept through trees and, from behind a mound, watched Hayes. Working under lanterns, three men took turns excavating, which they had done every other night we had followed them here. They dug a big hole, didn't find what they searched for, and moved a little way off to dig again.

"Someone from the railroad has to have seen their lanterns," Bruce whispered.

I nodded even if Bruce couldn't see me in the dark. "You'd think so."

I began to backtrack off the mound. "Let's get out of here. We've seen what we see."

"Another thing," Bruce whispered. "We've been followin' Hayes. What's the link to Digger's death?"

"Lilith thinks Hayes killed Digger, and we enjoy her money."

Bruce turned his ankle in the dark, but he hopped to the two-lane road. By the time we got back to Bruce's Ford Explorer, he could barely move with his ankle sprain.

"Maybe Mickey got a lead?" Bruce asked.

While Bruce and I had spied on Hayes, Mickey had been driving the Handyman's Spy van to listen in on Atsadi and Murphy at their homes. Carla had gone off on a date with Larry Buchanan, and Roth had stayed in the mansion to drink wine and read a book.

I called Mickey. "Find out anything?"

"Nothing," Mickey said. "All quiet."

"What's Atsadi doing?

"Drives to his realtor office. Shows houses for sale."

"Murphy?"

"Lying low. Staying at home."

"Any of them making phone calls?" I asked.

"No calls between Atsadi and Murphy," Mickey said. "Or between them and Eigges."

"Keep listening to the bugs. Something will break."

"Is Hayes making progress?" Mickey asked.

"Bruce smells failure. He thinks the police are going to catch Hayes."

Neither of us spoke for a moment. "What about Eigges?" Mickey asked. "Are you going to interrogate him?"

"Goodman and I see him tomorrow at his estate.

# # #

I returned late to the mansion and went to Roth's office to report. She had almost finished her book, *The Brethren* by John Grisham, and a bottle of wine. She let me finish my report of our surveillance that night before speaking, "It's a matter of time until the police catch them?"

I yawned in my chair. "Yeah, Hayes and his lackeys are going to get caught."

She perked up in her chair. "Why haven't they found the crates?"

I cleared my throat. "Maybe Hayes dug in the wrong place, where the crates aren't."

She shook her head. "Insupportable. You told me they had dug up an area the size of a small airport."

"That's true."

She thought a moment. "Maybe Hayes is in the right place, but nothing's there anymore?"

21

An Asheville Estate — Monday

The next morning, Chief Deputy Goodman and I finally got to interview Eigges. Doused in his usual Aqua Velva, the Chief Deputy had turned on the heat in his car to ward off the nip in the air. I cracked the window to keep from gagging. He drove through the wrought iron gate of Eigges' estate, down the long asphalt driveway, under the room built out over the driveway, and parked in a circular courtyard. The large, red-brick house must have had ten thousand square feet of livable space on the inside. Responding to our loud knocks, a timid woman, wearing a black uniform with a white collar, answered the door. The maid led us into a great hall vaulting upward for three stories.

"Many walnut trees perished to build this room," Goodman said.

I studied the side panels and floor, gleaming with polish. "Do I need to remove my shoes?"

The maid led us through the house to a glassed-in patio at the rear. The enclosed area had a flagstone floor, a low stone border, wrought-iron furniture, and a magnificent, elongated view of the Blue Ridge Mountains. An old Irish Setter lay on a rug in a corner. Invited to sit, we waited for Eigges. The Setter raised its head and stared at us. I got up, went to kneel, and petted the dog. The Setter licked my hand. The dog seemed satisfied and plopped its head back on the rug. I returned to my chair.

Several more minutes passed until Eigges entered the patio. His entrance was regal, with a cigarette holder held out at a perpendicular angle to his body. He appeared younger than his age: his hair dyed brown, his posture straight, and his eyes emitted the haughty glare of the lord of the manor. "Are you Chief Deputy Goodman?"

Goodman—wearing the black, winter uniform of the Buncombe County Sheriff's Office—answered, "I am, and I'm investigating the death of Digger Harper. Let me introduce Mr. Gannon"—Goodman nodded at me—"who is assisting me in my investigation."

Eigges shook our hands and sat with a patio table between us and slowly raised his cigarette holder for a puff. "I'm here to help. My civic duty."

Goodman stroked his goatee. "Tell me about Paul Atsadi and Digger Harper."

"They did tasks for me. At first, I employed only Mr. Atsadi as a private contractor. Later I used Mr. Harper."

"What did they do?" I asked.

"They excavated Native American artifacts on private land for me. Pots, masks, and statues. You may tell me they took items from tribal land, but I never told them to do so."

As Eigges talked, I gazed through the glass framework enclosing the patio, viewing a vista first sloping down to rolling lawns and evergreen trees before rising to the mountain range in the distance. The dreams that only big money can buy.

"Both Atsadi and Digger dug at an Indian mound in Cherokee," I said. "Digger arrived first and hid when Atsadi arrived. Did you direct them to go to the same mound?"

Eigges waited a minute before answering. He fiddled with his holder to remove his finished smoke. Reaching into a pocket of his blue blazer, he pulled out a packet of cigarettes, Rothmans, and inserted another smoke. "I did not. I always engaged them separately. I directed no one to steal from tribal land." His left eye winked impulsively.

"After seeing Atsadi at the burial site," Goodman said, "Digger turned him in, informing the tribal police. Later, Digger pillaged the mound himself?"

He took time to raise the holder to his mouth and leisurely smoke. "I found out later that's what happened," Eigges said. I had a friend with a nervous tic; he perpetually blinked one eye. Our host had a similar compulsion, and he annoyed me.

"Since you could no longer use Atsadi to supply artifacts," Goodman asked, "did Digger become your only supplier?"

Eigges rubbed the side of his nose and looked straight at the Chief Deputy. "You agreed not to use my words to pursue me for allegedly taking Indian relics."

"Any involvement you tell me about tribal theft is off the record," Goodman said. "I'm interested in Atsadi's possible connection to the Harper murder."

Eigges crossed his legs and settled back in his patio chair. "With Atsadi in jail, Digger returned to the mound and brought back two clay statues, each about a foot high." He reached into another pocket of his blazer and withdrew three photographs. Goodman and I examined the pictures, which showed one sculpture of a sitting woman holding a bowl and another of a man seated.

"Can we see the objects?" I asked.

"I hesitate to hand you an actual item pilfered from a burial site. The sculptures aren't here anyway."

"These photographs are of the items both Atsadi and Digger sought?" I said.

Eigges raised his holder and took a drag. "I paid Digger in cash for the two statues."

I chuckled. "Taken from the Cherokee reservation."

"I didn't know he had taken them from the reservation."

"Digger sold you the sculptures," I said. "Did Atsadi know?"

"I don't believe so. I didn't tell him."

Goodman paused to write in his notepad. "Do you have any reason to suspect Atsadi of killing Digger?"

"No," Eigges said.

"Why do you say that?" Goodman asked.

"After Atsadi got out of jail, I talked with him. He said he had stopped taking hard drugs."

"Is he working for you again?" I asked.

"I offered Atsadi his old job. He said he no longer raided mounds."

The Irish Setter stretched and came over to me to let me scratch him. "Was he mad at you?"

Eigges shook his head. "He said he accepted blame for what happened and had started a new life."

When I had questioned Atsadi, I had seen no indication of drug use. "Did he say anything about Digger?"

Eigges took another half minute to smoke. He was irritating. "He didn't talk about Digger."

I looked at Goodman. He raised both palms to face up, which I interpreted to mean he had no further questions. "You think Atsadi was a thief stealing for drugs but not a killer?" Goodman asked.

Eigges straightened his back as if getting ready to stand. "That's what I said. Are we through?"

Goodman and I exchanged glances. "I have no more questions," he said and pushed his chair back. "If I need additional information, I'll phone."

To show he remained in command, our host went through his rigmarole of reloading his cigarette holder. "The maid will see you out."

Leaving the estate in his patrol car, Goodman and I said nothing until I broke the silence. "He confirmed both Digger and Atsadi visited the mound to steal. Do you buy that Atsadi didn't know Digger returned for the two statues? It was a double-cross."

The Chief Deputy turned sideways toward me, pondered my question, and turned his eyes back on the road. "Why lie?"

He drove into Merriman Avenue and continued south. "I believe Atsadi kicked hard drugs and is going straight. A few get to the end of their fast lane and can't remember where their old life went. Terrifies them into a rebirth."

We hadn't been able to tie Atsadi to the murder. Tonight, I would switch over to following Hayes in Morganton, trying to pick up a clue. I had agreed to take Lilith along too.

"It's pitch black," Lilith said. "How can I watch Hayes digging?"

That night, Bruce drove Lilith and me directly to Morganton, without tailing Hayes' pickup. We three sat in Bruce's Jeep, parked on the side of the road, waiting for Hayes and his two buddies. "Your eyes will adjust to the darkness," I said. "Plenty of moonlight."

Lilith's leather jacket rubbed against the Jeep's cloth seat as she turned to me, where I sat in the rear. "I want to eyeball the huge strip of ground Hayes has dug up."

My vision had begun to adapt. I now made out the shape of different trees in the woods. The road seemed deserted. A constant noise—*ch-ch* ... *ch-ch-ch*—grew in intensity.

Lilith made an *umm* sound. "I've heard those crickets for years. What are they?"

"They're katydids, bush crickets," I said. "Suppose to chirp, 'Katydid! Katydid! Katydid!' Their noise will cloak our walk through the woods to see Hayes' excavation."

"Did you see that?" Bruce asked.

I glanced outside the vehicle but saw nothing. "What?"

"Farther down the road, I saw a red glow. Cuz, someone pulled on a cigarette."

"Don't see anything now," Lilith said.

"It was there for a second," Bruce said. "Close to the road."

I stared along the road ahead of us. Several moments later, my eyes detected a mass, a form, lighter in hue. "Cars parked ahead of us. What're they doing?"

"Don't know," Bruce said. "Maybe we ought to leave?"

I saw the headlights of a vehicle roll up on the road behind us. It stopped. "Hayes and his crew have arrived." They got out of their truck and turned off their lights.

"They're going to the train tracks to search for the gold," Lilith said. "Let's go after 'em. Watch 'em."

I checked the road ahead of us. Nothing moved. "Don't like those cars being there. Let's stay here and keep an eye on them a bit longer."

"I want to see what Hayes is doing!" Lilith demanded.

I didn't think that smart. Hayes must have been the one who attacked Lilith at night and stuck her in a bag. Seeing him at the dig might traumatize her. "Wait. We're not going to screw up if we watch a little longer."

"If those vehicles are police cars, I think they plan to sweep up Hayes," Bruce said. "Cuz they'll catch us too if we go out there."

We waited. Nothing happened. The guys in the cars had fallen asleep or time had stopped. Blood flow to my rump decreased, and I shifted my weight to bring back feeling. Two white lights gleamed. Similar lights appeared in a row behind the first two—parking lights.

The lights, still in a row, moved at us. I ducked. Four white police cars, Crown Victorias, drove in single file past Bruce's Jeep. Once they reached Hayes' pickup, they stopped and doused their lights. By the moonlight, I glimpsed shapes moving into the woods in the direction of Hayes' group.

"The police have gone into the woods," Bruce said. "Should we leave?"

Lilith opened her door and stepped out. "Let's see what's going to happen." Bruce had turned off the interior lights, and our car remained in darkness. Lilith moved across the road in the direction of Hayes. I realized our roles had altered. Lilith had to lead, and I had to keep her butt out of trouble. Bruce and I followed her.

Lilith tramped through the twigs and leaves. I caught up with her and whispered, "Please let me give you a tip on quiet walking in the woods." She turned to listen. I gave her the short course: put the side of the front foot down first and next slowly lower other side and then the heel. I saw her nod. Her movement through the forest grew slower and quieter. Sweet Jeezus, Lilith and I had begun to communicate.

Ahead of us, lights glowed through the trees. We remained back in the woods and viewed the police, the diggers, and the torn-up ground. The brightness radiated from the lanterns Hayes had brought and the flashlights of the black-uniformed police officers. Hayes shouted at the officers. They tried to cuff him, but he pushed an officer away. Another officer held a TASER and shot out the twin barbed darts. Unruly muscular convulsions racked Hayes' body. The police cuffed him as he lay on the ground.

Lilith, with no love lost for Hayes, squealed, "Yes. Zap him again."

I yanked her farther back into the woods, hiding behind a downed tree trunk. "Shh. They'll hear you." The police didn't notice her outburst. They arrested the diggers and led them away. Crime scene investigators arrived to photograph Hayes' setup and document the extent of damage to the railroad grounds.

Lilith glanced under the fallen trunk to spot the police pull Hayes away, and she beamed. "Sweet, sweet." Lilith next gazed at the drawn-out region around the train tracks. "Good grief, they've shoveled up a huge area." She kept staring at the extent of the dug-up ground. "Hayes didn't unearth any gold?"

"No gold," I replied.

"Where is it?" Lilith asked.

I shook my head. "Digging is over. Nothing here."

We worked our way back to the Jeep. I sat in a rear passenger seat. "Lilith, do you still think Hayes needed to kill your fiancé?"

"Not sure anymore."

I turned toward her—plenty of room in the Jeep to shift my bulk. "Goodman said Hayes had an alibi when the killer poisoned Digger."

"World has flipped over," Bruce said from the driver's seat. "Feel it in the air. You two have started using tact to discuss things."

"When I wanna hear from you," I said to Bruce, "I'll tell you."

"I'm just saying you're not screwing up as much. Can't you take a compliment?"

"If Hayes didn't kill Digger, who did?" Lilith asked. No one answered as Bruce drove back to Asheville. What we couldn't possibly have known was that our client would later provide the key clue.

22

ROTH'S MANSION & CHEROKEE — TUESDAY

I had been sitting on my bed for five minutes, putting off going downstairs. Squeezing my eyes shut, tightly, I remembered my awkward embrace of Carla, berating myself for my impulsive grab and kiss. I prayed Carla would forgive me. Bruce, in similar circumstances, would drink himself into a stupor; each of us handles our anxiety differently. Finally, I crept downstairs to face my rebukes.

The women ate at the mansion's breakfast table. When I entered the room, their full-on information exchange braked to a screeching halt. Taylor frowned; Carla gave me an annoyed glare and turned to her plate without a word; Roth said, "Good morning, Don."

I lowered my head, grunted a greeting, "Morning," and sat beside my boss.

The women resumed their previous discussions. Needing to break in, I waited for a gap in their back-and-forth. No opening. When I sensed a letup, I drove in. "I don't have a plate." All three stopped and stared: I must have shouted. Taylor pulled a plate from a cupboard and put it in front of me, without a word. *Thump!*

Taylor tightened her lips and stared at me every time she served the table, chastising me for my misconduct with Carla.

After breakfast, I took my coffee to Roth's office, where she had taken a seat at her desk to continue reading The *Brethren* novel. Intermittently, she lowered her book a little to peer at me, almost immediately raising her book again. She was on a fence with her staff, having to soothe the women without ridiculing me. Ultimately, she lowered her novel.

"You've provoked the women."

"Don't want to talk about it."

"Taylor told me your misdeeds—several times."

"What do I do?"

She lowered her book onto the desk. "Grow up."

I took a deep breath. "What do you mean, 'grow up'?"

She grinned, a silly smirk. "You're too shy with Carla. If you think she's your soulmate, tell her. What works out works out."

"I'm too timid?"

"A confident woman panics a shy man."

She went back to her reading but—after a moment—turned back to me. "And disregard any advice Bruce gives you about women."

Wanting my counseling session to end, I got up to leave. As I reached the door, Roth asked, "She kissed you back?"

"She did."

My boss wrinkled her forehead. "Maybe she can't make up her mind."

Roth had summoned the professor, Angela Lightfoot, for an all-hands meeting at the mansion. As we gathered before Roth's desk, Carla was polite but standoffish. She looked foxy in a pink turtleneck sweater and a below-the-knees white skirt. A few minutes later, Lilith and Angela arrived, and Taylor served coffee and tea, giving me a cup without dropping it on me. She remembered I took my drink black. Maybe she had decided to allow me back into the mansion.

Angela sipped her coffee and began without preamble. "Lilith tells me Hayes dug up Morganton but can't find Confederate gold."

Roth jerked her head up. "You found something, didn't you?"

"Railroad workers found a cache of decaying wooden crates. They stumbled on it"—she hesitated for professorial effect—"back in March of 1923."

Heat flushed through my body. "We're just now finding this out?"

My boss made a curt nod toward Angela. "And?"

Angela shook her head. "Retrieved rusted guns, rotted ammunition barrels, but no gold."

My boss raised her eyes to the drum chandelier with a white fabric shade in the middle of the ceiling. Roth's current expression was a lopsided grin. "We're about a century late and a fortune short."

Angela handed out sheets of papers from her briefcase. "I made copies of the newspaper article."

Roth grabbed copies. "What are you showing us?"

"Read the left column on the third page."

I read the specified page among her copies of the old articles. Angela had uncovered the story at the Morganton library. The article declared railway workers had found hidden crates near train tracks.

I twisted my college ring on my left hand. "No gold—but revolvers and rifles from the Civil War period. What do you think?"

"They found what Nathaniel Harper buried back in April 1865," Angela said.

Roth sighed. "Weapons to unleash guerilla warfare."

Lilith jabbed her finger at Angela's article. "The piece includes a diagram showing where they found the cache."

My mind compared the newspaper's diagram to Nathanial's map. "The workers found the crates near the *X* mark on the map he drew."

"It's not likely two separate caches were buried in Morganton along the train tracks," Angela said.

Lilith started crying, holding her hands to the sides of her face. "Poor Digger. He searched for something found seventy-seven years before."

My muscles quivered. "Don't understand why Digger hadn't checked this out."

My throat contracted at Lilith's weeping. We waited, remaining quiet to respect Lilith's feelings. I didn't see the gold map as a motive to kill Digger. Hayes wouldn't have murdered Digger for a map he already had. Now, Angela and Lilith found Nathaniel Harper hadn't buried gold at all. Where did those coins go? Maybe Angela was right: The Confederates paid out the reserves as their forces retreated south in April 1865, the final month of the war.

Roth sipped her coffee and set down her cup. "Tell me about finding weapons and barrels. How many in the discovery party?"

Angela took the question. "A work crew—eight to twelve men."

Roth glared at Angela and hummed a tune to herself. Roth had told me humming helped her concentrate. "Why were they digging?"

"They were reworking the ballast under the rails and sleepers," Angela said.

Carla looked puzzled. "Sleepers?"

Roth answered. "The wood supports under the rails."

I pressed Angela. "How did they stumble on the hiding place?"

Angela held her remaining paper clippings. "The crew had to shore up the track foundation. They dug down and happened into what Harper had put in the ground."

Roth rubbed her nose. "Suppose this crew had found gold."

Angela shook her head. "But they didn't."

Roth shot back. "But if they had, what prevented them from concealing it?"

Angela held up a palm. "The paper maintained there was a large crowd, including railroad officials."

"Your point?" Roth asked.

"Difficult to hide a huge cache of gold in a mob."

"But did you investigate the possibility?"

"I found the cache had been a hot topic in Morganton."

"And."

"People would have known if the railroad men had suddenly grown rich."

Roth nodded and pushed the intercom on her desk. "Taylor, bring the bottle of Biltmore Estate Merlot and glasses.

She leaned back in her chair and glared at each of us. "We aren't solving our case."

My boss must've been stung that there was no gold. "We're following every lead."

"We're charging after a trio of county nitwits and tracking a tomb robber," Roth muttered to herself. "None of our suspects has a good reason to kill Digger. All our suspects seem to have alibis for the morning he died."

Taylor arrived with the Merlot bottle and glasses. Roth poured and began to quaff her first glass. It was early, and I stayed with my coffee. No one else wanted another drink.

I broke the silence. "What do you want us to do?"

Roth lowered her glass. "Digger must have done or seen something to cause his poisoning. What was—?"

I interrupted. "How do you know?"

Roth plunked her glass down on the desk. "Ugh! Don't start some serial-killer nonsense. Search for cause and effect."

Roth hummed a quiet tune and paused to study each of us. "During the last month, what did Digger do differently? What seemed odd?"

Silence settled. I recognized the tune as the old Otis Redding song, "Sittin' on the Dock of the Bay."

"What sort of different?" I asked.

Roth continued to hum and wiped up spilled merlot with a napkin. "An investigation is like a jigsaw puzzle. Say I have four pieces

I am trying to force together, but they don't fit. Say something about the color of the pieces isn't right."

I understood. "We need to go back and systematically redo our investigation."

Carla seemed mesmerized by my boss. "Is that how a P. I. works?"

Roth shook her head. "Usually, the criminal makes a mistake by sheer stupidity or says the wrong thing during an interview or gets caught in a forensic follow-up or an eyewitness saw something. In our case, we have none of those."

Carla's eyes had grown wide. "No, we don't."

Roth continued. "I want to backtrack over the period before the crime."

She took a sip of her wine and twisted to Lilith. "You know how your fiancé spent his last month?"

"*My* last month with Digger."

"Was he angry about some slight or did he argue with someone? Go back and search for a rare event."

Lilith adjusted her black-rimmed glasses on her nose. "Me?"

Roth pointed at her. "Especially you. You spent the most time with him."

Roth turned to Angela. "Go over Digger's journals again."

Angela laid her paper clippings on her lap. "You mean Nathaniel's journals?"

Roth shook her head. "The journals Digger kept. Search especially for any mention of a skull and crossbones."

My boss poured another glass of merlot. "Why did Digger draw that symbol in the spilled sugar? Who gained by murdering Digger?"

Roth drives me daffy with her brusqueness, her tendency to read trashy novels instead of working the case, and her insistence I tell her word for word what I do outside the mansion. Don't know what a genius is, but she reminds me of a maze puzzle: a single path leads through the maze to the exit. Somehow, she avoids the blind-alley pathways and takes the successful route to the exit. Just as a mother, she always knows the answer. Christ, I left home to experience the world but wound up working for my frigging mother anyway.

# # #

Bruce and I listened to the bug in Atsadi's bungalow. A wispy sprinkle had been falling since dusk, followed by a mist which began with darkness. We had positioned the Handyman's Spy van, Roth's 1995 Ford Econoline, on a nearby shoulder of the road. Bruce listened through the headphone, and then slipped one of the headphone cushions off his ear. "I heard Angela met with Roth and you."

"A lengthy discussion."

"Any progress?"

I shifted in my chair. "All happy investigations resemble one another, but each of my inquiries is unhappy in its way."

Bruce chuckled. "So, progress is slow."

"I frown a lot."

"What did you learn this morning?" Bruce asked.

I told Bruce what happened.

Bruce shook his head. "No gold. Not good. You've failed Roth."

"Well, nobody's flawless." On the monitor, I inspected the camera views outside the van. One camera showed a light on in Atsadi's house, but nothing moved.

"How is Carla working out?"

"She's quick-witted."

"But does she help you?"

I nodded. "Takes to detecting."

Bruce took a moment to listen to his headphone and settled back in his folding chair. "Taylor told me you put a big hug on Carla. Heard there was a disagreement between your lustful will and her unresponsive won't."

"Don't want to talk about it."

"Larry Buchanan is putting a full-court press on Carla, while you pounce on her like a vulture out of the blue."

"Don't want to talk about it."

"Must confuse the poor woman."

I didn't answer him.

Bruce widened his smile to show me all his teeth. "Where's she tonight?"

"Buchanan picked her up earlier. Third night in a row."

"Hmm, lost love. You're back to drinking beer with Mickey and me."

I rubbed my neck and checked the monitor with the camera views. "The light went out in Atsadi's house."

Bruce checked his written notes. "He's showing a house tomorrow. Guess he's gone to bed."

I felt sleepy. Being on stakeout will do that. "Do we drive over to Murphy's trailer house? Listen in on him?"

Bruce took off his headphones. "I'm tired of listening to bugs. Let's pick up spying again tomorrow?"

I flicked off the monitor and the outdoor cameras. "Call it a night. Tomorrow, we're hunting for a new lead to the killer."

I could see Roth wouldn't get her Confederate gold, and Lilith's money would only last so long. Couldn't begin to imagine when Roth would cut her losses and pull out of our search for Digger's assassin.

23

Burke County Jail — Wednesday

I sat frozen, not able to believe what had taken place.

Earlier this morning, I had been happy, hadn't foreseen the falling guillotine. Earlier, I had jogged, showered, dressed, and arrived downstairs to find Roth gazing through the kitchen door out to the patio and saying, "Nice day." I had viewed the sky, a clear azure common to Asheville, not a true sign of the storm about to impact me. "We're having breakfast on the terrace," she said. The terrace stood to one side of the patio, an elongated roof over the gray flagstone. Roth had had the wrought-iron tables pushed into a row. Taylor served a breakfast of scrambled eggs, grits, bacon, and coffee. Roth and her staff gathered under the terrace roof to devour the meal and read the paper.

The table teemed with activity: Mickey snatched the sports page from Bruce, and I reached over the table for the grits as Taylor set down a pitcher of fresh iced tea.

"Yo' great breakfast, Taylor," Bruce said.

She smiled and said, "Priciatcha."

Bruce had raised his eyebrows at her husband, Mickey.

"She said 'I appreciate you.'"

Mickey lunged for more eggs and studied the people at the table. "Where's Carla?"

Lowering her paper, Roth glanced around the table. After a few beats, she turned to me. "Carla resigned."

My breathing stiffened as when a loved one has flown away, froze as I had missed a golden opportunity. Carla had fled.

The news shattered not only me. Roth's announcement came as a surprise to everyone. "Why?" Taylor asked, standing in the doorway back to the kitchen. "Where she a-goin'?"

"She's taken a job with Larry Buchanan," Roth said.

Taylor put down an empty plate. "Can't you'ns pay her more?"

Roth shook her head. "Buchanan gave her a lofty salary increase."

By chance, Carla took that moment to join us. She got a hug from Taylor. I lowered my head to the flagstone with a sheepish expression. Carla answered Taylor's question about where she'd stay.

"I'm moving to a furnished apartment. I'll miss you."

"Sorry, buddy," Bruce whispered to me.

#

I stood in the front hallway of the mansion, with my rear end propped against a table along the wall. Carla waited outside in the driveway, surrounded by three suitcases and a black shoulder bag. She wore a blue trench coat hitting at her upper thigh, her glossy, brown ponytail lying on the collar; the view caused my stomach to tremble. A yellow taxi drove down the lane and took Carla away. My soul crossed into a dark night. I leaned against the table—no motivation to move.

"Don?"

Roth stood behind me. I hadn't heard her. She took my arm. "Let's go for a walk?"

Afterward, I moped at my desk, passing the time by acting as if I studied papers, but wafting.

Roth, without the veil she usually wore and with her straight, white hair to her shoulder, stopped at my office door. "Hayes is in a Morganton jail."

I glanced up. "So?"

"Go talk with him?"

She wanted me to drop in on the guy who had tried to turn his dogs loose on me. "Hayes won't see me."

She checked her wristwatch. "Talk Goodman into questioning him and tag along."

Goodman agreed to drive me to the Burke County Jail in his Crown Victoria, an hour-long trip. A large parking lot surrounded the jail, a two-story structure with the prison on the first floor. We passed family members of the inmates waiting in a visitation line. Once inside, we went across a large, drab room filled with some twenty tables. It smelled like stifling air and sweaty feet. I followed a detention officer and Goodman past inmates dressed in orange and down a corridor. "Is this a contact visitation?"

Goodman nodded. "Contact. There'll be a table between us."

"Single room or open court?"

"Closed room."

The detention officer led us into a room with a single table in the middle and four chairs. We sat at the table on one side of the room.

Hayes, wearing an orange boiler suit and accompanied by a guard, entered through a door opposite from us. The guard sat Hayes down on their side of the room and shackled his prisoner's arms through a bar mounted on the table. Hayes' lips curled into a sneer. "Welcome to camp. Where's my inmate package?"

"Didn't bring anything," Goodman said.

Hayes scowled, puckering his brow. "If you want to talk with me, bring cigs next time."

"Didn't know you smoked," I said.

Hayes gave me a stink-eye stare. "They're for my dogs."

"You have dogs in jail?"

"Means his buddies," Goodman said.

"What do you want?"

I held up copies of the Morganton newspaper articles to the detention officer, who nodded his head; I gave them to Hayes. "I have an unpleasant surprise for you."

Hayes ran his palm over his crew cut. "You plan to stay awhile?"

Hayes bent over the papers and read. He slammed the table. "Damn! All the time, it wasn't there."

Silence. I peered around at the prison setting, taking it in.

Hayes raised his head. "Finders keepers and losers weepers. But sometimes, you're the loser." He leaned backward, frowning at the pages. "Damn."

Hayes stopped staring daggers at us. He seemed in a mood to talk. I let the silence slide by for a few beats. "Who poisoned Digger?"

Hayes raised his eyes and leaned forward. "Not me. The crazy woman—Lilith—accused me."

Goodman rested his body, stroking his goatee. "Did you steal Digger's map?"

"I did. But he had the original."

I rose out of my chair and leaned across the table. "Did you kill him to get the gold?" The guard, standing behind Hayes, shook his head at me and raised his hand to get me back in my chair.

Hayes spread his arms out to his sides and widened his eyes in a doe-eyed expression. "Digger had a frigging worthless map." He stopped and snorted. "Turned out none of us would have gold."

"You didn't answer my question."

"I didn't kill him. We were chasing gold at the end of a rainbow. Almost always, it's a wild-goose chase."

"Your alibi?" I asked.

"When?"

"The morning someone killed Digger," I said.

"We played cards and drank," Hayes said. "Started the night before. Drank to exhaustion the next day."

I stared at Goodman, not sure what to ask next.

Hayes pushed his wire-rimmed glasses atop his head and studied us. "Get the charges against me dropped."

Goodman gave Hayes a steely stare. "Why would I do that?"

"Help you get the killer."

My heart raced, but I remembered Hayes was a con man. "Do you know their identity?"

"Maybe."

Goodman snickered. "You tell us, and I'll consider helping you."

Hayes pursed his lips. "Digger was my friend."

Goodman and I waited.

"I'll help you catch his killer if I can."

Hayes was a con man, but I thought he spoke the truth. I wished Carla had been with me. She read people better than I did. I passed Hayes my card.

Goodman pushed his chair back and rose to leave. "We'll take you up on that."

# # #

After the dual excitement—of Carla resigning and Hayes talking with me at his jail—passed, I withdrew to my office and brooded over Carla breaking away. Lilith called to interrupt my moping. She wanted to brainstorm with me about capturing Digger's murderer. I agreed; I had grown to value her strong-minded approach to uncovering Digger's assassin. She asked to join me at the mansion. I told her, "Come on over now."

About the time I expected she would arrive, I put on my dark-olive rain jacket and walked outside to the driveway. She drove up on her navy-blue Vespa and greeted me with, "Why isn't Carla with you?"

All I could manage was a bitter smile. "Carla's gone. She resigned."

Lilith's mouth fell open. "She's smart. Worked well with you."

Lilith hung her helmet on her scooter but kept her brown leather jacket. We stood outside in the balmy October day to discuss the case. Lilith summarized her uneasiness. "I am confused and disappointed. They—Ms. Roth and Chief Deputy Goodman—don't believe Hayes poisoned Digger."

She paused, her face appearing puffy, her eyes red. "If not he, then who? The guy who just got out of jail, Atsadi, couldn't have murdered my fiancé. He was miles away at the time of the poisoning."

I didn't interrupt but listened.

"I need to talk with someone to vent my anguish."

Roth must have seen us talking. She burst out the front door and joined us, walking down the front steps to the driveway. Her often eccentric clothing made perfect sense today: it would keep her warm. She dressed in a black long-sleeved tunic dropping to the ground, a black wool scarf covering her hair and wrapping around her collar, and sunglasses. Her garb reminded me of an empress in a science fiction extravaganza. "Good to see you, Lilith."

Lilith greeted Roth and described how she had driven to the mansion to discuss the case and her worries.

Roth viewed Lilith with a slight grin, maybe showing encouragement for her. "How can I help?"

"I need someone to listen."

"Doesn't Don listen?"

Lilith lowered her head and said to me, "You're a man. You don't listen."

I took a moment to reflect, turning to view the stone steps rising to the mansion's front door. I recalled Roth told me not to argue with Lilith. "No offense."

Roth answered her. "I'm fine with standing and talking to you."

"Thank you," Lilith said.

Roth pinched the bridge of her nose. "What do you think?"

Lilith wiped her eyes. "About what?"

"Our next step?"

Lilith glanced at Roth and then at me. "There's no gold. Nothing to reveal who killed Digger."

"Do you agree?" Roth asked me. "On the morning Digger died, the man Digger helped put in jail was in Cherokee?"

I believed Goodman had vetted Atsadi's whereabouts. "Seems to have an alibi."

Turning toward Lilith, Roth said, "Think. Work it out."

Lilith continued to wipe her face. Their brainstorming needed a new approach. Roth began a fresh tactic. "You knew Digger how long?"

"About three years."

"When did the attacks begin?"

Lilith thought for several seconds. "Somebody fired at Digger two and a half weeks ago."

Roth laid a forefinger across her lips. "Before that … how often did violence occur?"

I leaned back and listened to Roth and Lilith confer.

"Never before."

Roth shifted her feet. "What did your fiancé do on a normal day?"

"Talked to people. Read in the library. He explored old houses."

I thought about the timing of the attacks. "Digger went through his parents' attic. When?"

Lilith took off her plastic-framed glasses. "Seven and a half weeks ago."

"Shortly before the attacks?"

"Yes."

Roth regarded me. "Hmm. What do you think?"

"Something changed seven and a half weeks ago," I said.

Lilith rearranged her glasses on her face. "My fiancé got excited—found these old Nathaniel documents."

"At first, you thought the map was important," Roth said.

Lilith corrected her. "Digger did."

Roth rubbed her chin. "But, we know the cache was ancient guns and gunpowder—already dug up."

We stared at each other until I stated the obvious. "Digger found something else in the attic."

Lilith's eyes lost focus. She mumbled to herself. "What was in the attic other than the map?"

Roth snapped her fingers. "What else did your fiancé discover?"

Information gushed from Lilith. "Digger found old family photographs—of Harpers from the late 1800s and the early 1900s. Of Michael and Bertha Harper. Michael's old army uniform was in a trunk. Old family mementos, children's toys, and pendants."

"What else was noteworthy?" Roth said.

"Nothing. Digger removed lots of stuff to his house."

I thought about the items Lilith had recalled. "Let's ask why your fiancé drew a skull and crossbones in the sugar pile?"

"I thought he meant buried treasure," Lilith said.

The three of us paused and stared. Presently, Lilith said, "What do you think the symbol means?"

"Don't know," I said.

"What should I do?" Lilith asked.

Roth rubbed her hands together. "Lilith, I think you're making progress."

Lilith appeared puzzled. "But I don't know what Digger meant by the symbol."

Roth turned back toward the mansion's front door. "Go back over all the things your fiancé found in the attic?"

Lilith shook her head up and down. "Sure."

"Interpret the symbol differently," I said. "Aim to link it to an item in the attic."

24

WEST ASHEVILLE — THURSDAY

A phone rang somewhere. I woke to find my earphones were on my ears; I had fallen asleep listening to a recorded mystery book. The clock on the dresser read twelve something. My hand bumped against the phone in the dark. "Hello."

"This is Bruce. I'm in the van."

"Where?"

"Murphy's trailer."

"What's up?"

"Palo Sanchez, the machete man, is in the trailer."

"You're listening to the bug?"

"Palo drinking and getting loud."

"Good. Has he let slip something about Digger's death?"

"No. But he might get violent."

I thought about waking up Mickey but remembered he had a surveillance gig tonight. "I'm coming."

I disconnected and phoned Roth. "Yes."

"It's me. Don."

"Yes."

"Bruce called. The machete man's at Murphy's trailer."

"Set the alarm system when you leave."

I cautioned Roth, "Keep your Mossberg 500 shotgun close," and left to help Bruce.

# # #

I parked my Mustang off on the shoulder and walked to the white van. I had put on a black, leather bomber jacket and blue jeans over my pajamas. My pistol lay snug in a holster on my belt. I tapped the side of the vehicle, pulled open one of the two rear cargo doors, and entered the van.

Bruce, with white earphones placed amidst the corkscrews of his hairstyle, turned from the console controlling the outside cameras and the listening device. "Listen to this." He switched the bug's output from the earphones to speakers.

"—keep your mouth shut," Palo said.

"But I took the relics," Murphy said.

Slosh! Slosh! Slosh! "Palo's been pouring the whiskey all night," Bruce said.

"Heard it from Mr. Eigges … Goodman's after Harper's killer," Palo said.

"That Gannon guy—" Murphy said.

Smack! "Ouch! Stop that." Murphy said.

"Palo's been hitting Murphy a lot," Bruce said.

"Fool! Goodman not interested in you," Palo said.

Smash! "What was that?" I asked.

"Sounds like a glass bottle breaking." Bruce switched the bug's audio back to his earphones and turned to me. "Palo and Murphy argue and drink."

I sat in the van's second chair. "Audio is strong. They're close to the bug."

Bruce didn't hear me. He had his earphones over both ears.

I tried talking to Bruce again. "Murphy's nervous."

"He afraid of going to jail."

"Because he received the stolen relics?" I asked.

"He's afraid Goodman will charge him for Digger's murder," Bruce said.

I glanced at the monitor showing the external camera views around the van. The neighborhood had little illumination from streetlamps, but the moon was bright. Nothing moved outside. "What about Palo?"

Bruce had his left ear snug against one of the earphones and the right ear free to listen to me. "Palo's been telling Murphy not to worry. To keep his mouth shut."

"Palo's drunk."

Bruce nodded. "He finished the whiskey. Switched to rum."

I raised my eyebrows. "What do they say about Digger?"

"Puzzled about his death."

"They said that before."

Bruce twisted to me and raised his eyebrows. "They don't know we're listening."

Maybe they didn't kill Digger. "Switch back to the speakers."

"—the rum," Palo said.

"Yeah, tastes good," Murphy said.

"Things continue taste good if keep mouth shut," Palo said.

"I'll talk before going to jail," Murphy said.

"Shut your mouth," Palo said.

Aieee!—"Put that machete away," Murphy said.

Sounds of a struggle and a table and a large solid object falling over. Shrieks from Murphy. Bruce and I hesitated. If we let Palo chop Murphy, his wounds would be on us. If we rushed to subdue Palo, we would be confirming we unlawfully wired Murphy's trailer. Over the sound of the struggle, I heard Murphy say, "What the hell is that?"

"Stomp it," Palo said. The transmission stopped.

Bruce turned from the console with wild eyes. "They found the bug."

Bruce and I stared at one another. "What if they come looking for us?"

Bruce fiddled with the monitor. "They won't. They're drunk and it's dark outside."

I wasn't so sure. Our van stood out on a mostly empty street. After all, Palo had sounded nuts and violent. "Turn off the electronics and let's leave."

I scanned the camera views, searching for any light or movement. Several minutes passed. Bruce worked with the console controls and turned to me. "Not a peep. Bug's dead."

"Let's go!" I said. "You're taking too long."

Bruce kept working at the console. "Just a minute."

One of the views, on the monitor on the counter in front of Bruce, had flickered. Palo stood in a sweatshirt with a hoodie, baggy pants, and holding a long object. He stared at the van. He must have run out onto the street and spotted our van. Palo was at the van.

I jumped for the rear doors and shouted at Bruce. "Go." He scrambled for the opening into the van's front compartment.

We had taken too much time and I didn't get to the rear doors in time.

Palo yanked a rear door open and stepped up, climbing into the van with the night a backdrop to his ghastly machete. He looked scary and nimble.

I heard Bruce drop into the driver's seat, heard him turn the key in the dash, and felt him jam the accelerator down. The van jumped forward. While trying to get my pistol out of my belt holster, I tumbled rearward inside the van.

Palo kept his equilibrium by grabbing a rear panel door and halting his fall rearward out of the van.

Bruce hit the brakes, stopping the vehicle.

Falling now toward the front, I flung out my arms to cushion my tumble and landed on the floor under the counter supporting the console.

Palo hung on to the door; his eyes fastened on me.

My body jerked with fright. My right hand searched for my pistol under my bomber jacket. My left hand bumped against a hard cylinder.

Palo rushed at me, raising the machete above his right shoulder.

I jerked the cylinder, a red fire extinguisher, up and in front of my head. The fingers on my other hand felt my pistol under my jacket but couldn't grab it. Palo sliced with his machete, hitting the extinguisher, striking the edge of the counter, and brushing my left cheek.

I pulled out the pin at the top of the extinguisher and compressed the lever; a torrent of white foam hit Palo in his face. He backed away and rubbed the sleeve of his left arm over his eyes. Then he searched for me.

The cut wasn't painful for a second, but next, I experienced agony and the sticky feeling of flowing blood. My fingers found the pistol in the belt holster. My eyes were on Palo.

Palo stood hunched over, holding the machete in his right hand. I faced him with my M1911 in my right hand. We stood close; if he sliced, I couldn't react quick enough to avoid another wound.

"Got a gun."

Palo said nothing.

"Get down. On the floor."

In a swift movement, Palo shifted the machete to his left hand. He had put me in danger. With a single stroke, he could cut and disable my right arm.

Pow! I shot him in his left shoulder.

The machete dropped. Palo held his upper arm. Bruce phoned 911. I pushed Palo onto a chair. From my MP experience in Iraq, I judged his rate of bleeding as steady but not excessive.

"Sheriff's Office and EMS on the way," Bruce said. He had his pistol pointed at Palo.

I touched my face. My hand came away bright red. "Call Roth."

"I did. She's sending Mickey."

Mickey arrived and went with me to Murphy's trailer. He opened his door. A blow had bruised the area around one of his eyes. "Palo's crazy. He tried to kill me."

I glanced at the overturned furniture and the general mess in the living area. "Palo's got his troubles."

"Your face is cut. Bleeding."

"Get me a clean towel."

While Murphy went for a towel, I pointed to the area where Carla and I had planted the bug. "Mickey, help me recover our eavesdropping device."

Mickey pushed a couch aside, and I shook out a blanket. No small device with wires. I turned a hassock upright, finding the smashed metal and wires. "Got it." As Murphy returned with a ragged towel, I concealed the crushed bug with the sole of my shoe.

"I need protection," Murphy said.

I pressed the towel against my face. "You need to talk to Goodman."

Mickey looked through the blinds of the trailer window. "Flashing lights. Authorities here."

Murphy glanced out the window. I picked up the flattened bug and slipped it into Mickey's hand. "Lose it."

The three of us walked out to the van and the emergency vehicle. The paramedic and technician had Palo on a gurney and were taking him to Memorial Mission. A fire engine, with medical support capability, drove up. The empty street had become packed. Goodman had arrived and started interrogating Bruce. The Chief Deputy spun and got in my face before he realized I dripped blood. He pulled back and said, "Someone help this man."

I shook my head. "I'm okay. It's a scratch."

Goodman rotated his vehicle's side mirror up. "Take a look at yourself."

My left-side face was red with a gaping cut. My right-side face was a pallid white. I appeared ghastly. My knees began to bend. My vision blurred with bright lines. Goodman had his arms around me to hold me up.

# # #

In the interview room at the County Courthouse, Tribal Police Officer Kanuna and Chief Deputy Goodman faced Murphy across a metal table. I listened behind a one-way viewing mirror on the wall. A bowl-shaped overhead lamp of separate lights illuminated the room. The walls were gray up to a height of three feet, and the rest of the wall and ceiling were a cream color.

Goodman had a folder in front of him on the table. "Did you carry Eigges' written orders to steal?"

"I did," Murphy said.

Goodman continued. "Did you deliver orders to Digger Harper?"

"If I tell you true, will you help me?"

Goodman exchanged glances with Kanuna. "Help you how?"

Murphy had a distant, empty stare. "Protect me from Palo. And reduce my tribal sentence for stealing Cherokee relics."

"I've charged Palo with aggravated assault," Goodman said. "He's accused of intent to commit bodily harm and doing the same."

Murphy blinked his eyes at Goodman. "Where is he?"

"In the hospital. Getting his left arm repaired."

"What about Gannon?" Murphy said.

Goodman pointed to his face. "Got twenty-four stitches to close a four-inch cut."

"Deep cut?"

Goodman shook his head. "Cut wasn't that deep."

Kanuna crossed his arms. "Palo's not a problem just now. Finding two missing Cherokee statues is."

Murphy grasped his hands on his chest. "You help me. I'll help you get them back."

"Did you give the man and woman statues to Eigges?" Kanuna asked.

Murphy nodded his head. "Been in his manor. Know where he keeps them."

Kanuna and Goodman exchanged gazes again. The tribal police officer turned back to Murphy. "You'd be willing to sign an affidavit stating Eigges took ownership of the two statues?"

"Yeah. And I took pictures of those statues—where Eigges exhibits them."

"With an affidavit, we can get a wiretap and search warrant," Kanuna said.

"What do I get?" Murphy said.

Kanuna taps on the table. "Deliver solid info for an affidavit."

Murphy stared with an open mouth.

"An affidavit that gets us a search warrant."

Murphy leaned forward at the desk. "And?"

Kanuna continued. "And we'll do our best to get your charges dismissed."

Officer Kanuna, Goodman, and I gathered in the Chief Deputy's Office. "You get the warrant," Kanuna said, "and we'll hit the estate."

Goodman shook his finger at Kanuna. "Hold on."

"What do you mean?"

"What about my murder case?"

"What about it?"

Goodman rolled his eyes at the ceiling. "He stole the statues. Did he have Digger killed?"

"How do I know?" Kanuna said.

Goodman switched from eye-rolling to spreading his hands out in reconciliation. "We don't know. We tap Eigges' phones."

Kanuna frowned. "Murphy knows where he keeps the statues. We raid at once."

Goodman grew red in his face. "Eigges doesn't know Murphy is cooperating with us. Those two statues aren't going anywhere."

If I supported Goodman in this intercounty fight, Kanuna would be outraged at me. If I sided with Kanuna, Goodman would be livid with me. If they asked for my opinion, my winning effort would be to act dim-witted. I sat there with my bandaged face and acted the Sphinx.

Kanuna threw up his hands. "Okay. Okay. We'll tap his phone as soon as we get a warrant."

Goodman pointed his finger at Kanuna. "And do the raid later."

"And do the raid later."

I slipped out, leaving them to argue the fine points.

First, Carla leaves. Next, Palo slices my face. What more could go wrong?

25

DIGGER'S HOUSE — FRIDAY

I went through the mansion's main hall and down the stairs to the lowest level where I had parked my 1999 Ford Mustang. As I got in the driver's seat, I had no idea today's simple undertaking with Lilith would flush out a killer in full savagery.

A drizzle had begun when my vehicle pulled into the gravel lane to Digger's house, the structure of weathered wood siding and a metal roof. I took the flagstone walkway to the covered porch and knocked. Lilith, in a long-sleeved, white sweatshirt and blue jeans, opened the door. She had a pale complexion as if suffering from nausea.

I sighed. "Are you okay?"

"A little morning sickness."

"Why don't we skip this morning?"

She held the door open for me. "I'm fine. I'm not that far along."

Cardboard boxes littered the living room. "These cartons hold things from the Harper attic?"

She plopped in a chair next to a box. "No. These cartons contain every item Digger found lately, all intermingled without organization."

Lilith had reminded me Digger worked fulltime at treasure hunting. "Where did he look for treasure the past few months?"

She placed a finger on her chin and took a moment. "He went through an old house, a lady, a hoarder, had in West Asheville." She thought some more. "He also explored a ramshackle church in Hendersonville."

"Will there be lots of boxes to search?"

Lilith chuckled. "Lots."

She hesitated, laid back in her chair as if she wanted to rest a minute before rummaging through the cartons.

"You seem depressed," I said.

Lilith nodded. "On Digger's death, I vowed I'd find his killer. When I returned to his house, I felt despondent."

"You're down because Digger died?"

She shook her head. "Our search for the shit who poisoned my fiancé is taking too long."

It was a natural thing she felt low. She had sacrificed: paid a large fee to Roth Security and searched long hours for a lead; nevertheless, she ended each day facing disappointment. "We'll keep investigating," I said.

She began to cry. "I return to this house and want to fix a rum and regular Coke, and sit in the living room, gazing at a photograph of Digger. I can't drink because I'm pregnant. So futile."

"Don't despair. It'll only make you miserable. Roth always solves things in the end."

There was nothing else to do, I thought, but struggle on, looking for a clue to the killer. I rose and peeked in the box beside my chair. It contained items Digger brought to this home—from the Old Fort attic and the other sites he searched. Carla and I went through all the documents and objects in each box we searched.

Lilith sat with her legs doubled up under her body, and her sweatshirt spread over them. "Just a month ago, I snuggled with Digger and viewed these items: photographs, letters, porcelain figures, and brooches." Now she reviewed them again, maybe feeling the loss of someone who should have been here with her but wasn't. Lilith inspected every photograph and each page of the journals without spotting the symbol her fiancé sketched in the sugar pile. I began pawing through another carton. I surveyed everything in that carton and raised my head.

Lilith had stopped burrowing and stared off into the distance. "Roth was right. I can remember an image. Digger showed it to me."

I sat on the floor. "Remember what?"

She had pressed her fists to her cheeks. "It's a symbol, twisted by memory. A memory is flitting about in my head, never motionless."

Lilith had started to recognize something. She had, so far, failed to bring that shadow vision into bright light. She needed to do something else, I thought, and let her subconscious search her memory cells. "Keep plowing through the boxes."

She unfolded herself from her sweatshirt and began digging in a box. "When I find the symbol, I'll know it."

She took each object in her hands, studied it, and put it in a pile next to the box. When she finished, she scooped the pile back into the box. "Digger got excited about finding another item," she said. "What was it?"

I helped plunk the discarded things back in her empty carton. "Take your time."

Lilith froze her reach into a box. "I recall. It's a locket—no, a pendant." She parked herself on the floor and covered her eyes with both hands. "A pendant burrowed into a jumble of small things at the bottom of a box."

A broad smile cropped up on her face as when a first grader learns recess has arrived. Going carton by carton, Lilith stacked all the larger items—photographs, letters, and journals—in a pile. Next, she sorted through the jumble at the bottom of the boxes. I patiently straightened up behind her as she worked through the bottom layers. Kneeling, she groped through the clutter at the bottom of each carton.

"*Aha!*—I found it."

She pulled a knickknack out of the carton. An odd-looking object with a skull and crossbones emblazoned on its surface.

I sucked in a swift breath and went motionless. "What is it?"

Lilith stared at the thing with her mouth open and handed it to me. Turning the tarnished ornament in my fingers, I judged it old, but not Civil War old. The object was metal, in the shape of a skull with holes at the eyes and mouth, a skull in front of two crossbones. Though heavily discolored, the metal appeared to be silver. Why would Digger think this object important—drawing its design in the sugar as his final act? Roth had somehow figured Digger had been trying to draw attention to an object.

# # #

At her desk in the mansion, Roth had studied the pendant under a magnifying glass for several minutes. Lilith and I had been quiet as church parishioners at service. Roth put down the object and began a slight smile that built into a wide grin. "Well done, Lilith."

"Thank you, ma'am. What is it?"

"I may know. I want to discuss my suspicion with our professor, Angela."

I brushed my cowlick in my nervous tic. "Can't you give us a hint?"

Roth gave a dismissive wave of her hand. "When I'm sure."

She glanced at Lilith. "You unsure of where Digger got it?"

Lilith shook her head. "Maybe Harper's attic. Not certain."

Roth tapped on her desk. Next, she pushed the intercom button and instructed Bruce to come to her office. He arrived at the door. "Yeah, Boss."

Once Bruce had been seated, and Roth had shown the pendant to him, she said, "Make photographs and distribute to everyone."

Bruce wrote in his notepad and nodded at Roth.

"Also, can you find out if we have data on this item? If not, can you search for some information?"

"Yeah, Boss."

Roth glanced at each of us in turn. "We'll get together tomorrow. Find out what you can. I'll ask Angela to come."

#

Later, the sky bared a weightless gray, continuing the drizzle, spreading gloom over the mansion's back lawn. I missed Carla. My cheerlessness matched the dreariness. I leaned back in my chair and propped my feet on the window's ledge behind my desk. Where had Digger found his pendant? When the phone rang, I ignored it for three rings, dropped my feet off the ledge, and answered. "Gannon."

"Goodman here."

"Morning, Chief Deputy," I said.

"Can you come to the County Courthouse?"

My body didn't want to budge. I wanted to stay in my cocoon. "Why?"

"I'm meeting with Tribal Office Kanuna."

Working on the case would keep me from moping. "Be there in twenty minutes."

"We'll be waiting."

Before leaving, I walked into Roth's office. I guessed she was busy studying the pendant. At the back of the room, she read a book at her desk. "Boss, I'm off to see Chief Deputy Goodman."

She raised her eyebrows and said, "Hmm," before returning to her reading. I could see the book cover. The title read *Dark Desires of the Heart* and displayed a lusty woman clutched in the arms of a bare-chested man with ponderous pecs. I had caught Roth reading a trashy novel. I felt embarrassed and left the room without comment.

Fifteen minutes later, I pulled into the Biltmore Avenue Garage. Rushing out the parking structure, I noticed a dark blue sedan with Cherokee Indian Police on its side. I hurried through the drizzle toward two striking buildings standing off by themselves. The courthouse, a seventeen-story building of brick and ashlar veneer, stood to my left. The city hall, eight stories with an octagonal roof of terra cotta red tiles, rose to my right. I entered the building on the left and took the elevator to the upper floors.

A Sheriff's deputy escorted me to a conference room where Goodman, in a long-sleeve dark-blue uniform, and Joseph Kanuna, in a long-sleeve dark-blue uniform with a tint of gray, sat at a table. Goodman smiled and pointed me to a chair. Officer Kanuna bobbed his head a tad. I didn't know why, but he disliked me. I settled back to see what we would discuss. The room had a free flow of air. I detected Goodman's aftershave, but the scent didn't overpower.

Goodman's pressed his lips together in a straight line and spoke to Kanuna. "We can't succeed if you play loose cannon."

Kanuna responded in a low voice. "We raid the moment Eigges confirms he stole the statues and stores them where Murphy says they are."

Goodman shook his head. "We've been over this before. What are our two objectives?"

Kanuna rolled his eyes. They did that a lot. "Arrest Mr. Eigges in possession of irreplaceable tribal objects—"

"And?"

Kanuna paused and stared at Goodman. "Did Eigges have Digger killed?"

"Have to solve Harper's death. We're in Asheville, not Cherokee."

Kanuna didn't respond.

Goodman slapped the table with an open palm. "We only raid after we meet both goals."

Why was I here? The two policemen did all the talking. I chose to wait, listen, and say nothing.

Kanuna brushed over his short hair with his fingers. "You and Gannon already met Eigges once?"

"We did."

"You discussed Digger with Eigges?"

Goodman summarized. "He told us Digger stole for him."

"Did Eigges know who killed Digger?" Kanuna said.

"Told us he didn't know," Goodman said.

The conference room went silent.

Kanuna glanced at me and turned to Goodman. "You accused me of not working with you. Gannon's the loose cannon."

Goodman stroked his goatee and stared at Kanuna. "Your point?"

"When we hit Eigges' estate, we don't take Gannon."

"Gannon found Murphy, Eigges' go-between."

"So what?" Kanuna said.

"Gannon discovered your cooperating witness, Murphy."

Kanuna twisted his mouth into a frown. "Yes, but—"

"Murphy confirmed he saw two stolen, Indian figures at Eigges' estate." Goodman had become irritated, pointing at Kanuna. "Because of Gannon the cannon, we got the foundation for a warrant."

I didn't say anything. Just smiled at the tribal officer. Goodman praised me for watching Murphy, but Roth thought of it first. I planted an illegal bug at Murphy's trailer house, but no one caught me. Always be thankful for a little luck.

Goodman kept pulling on his goatee. "Remember we agreed? Together, we decide when we raid the estate?"

Kanuna grimaced and nodded. "I agreed."

Goodman beamed. "Great."

Kanuna rubbed his hair again. "What's next?"

"I go to the District Attorney. Get them to get a search warrant from a judge."

"We have probable cause."

Goodman gave the thumbs-up sign. "Murphy took snaps of the stolen pieces."

Kanuna appeared pleased. "We tap Eigges' phones."

"Learn all we can. Finally, we raid his estate."

Kanuna leaned toward Goodman. "I'm still uncomfortable with Gannon."

Goodman raised both arms above his shoulders. "We're here because he found Murphy."

Kanuna kept up his tirade. "You need to keep an eye on Gannon."

Goodman leaned back in his chair, his stomach straining against his shirt. "I told you I would."

I smiled at the tribal officer. Tried to win him over.

Kanuna switched from his perpetual frown to a sneer. "He will behave or else."

Goodman went back to rubbing his goatee. "What do you mean?"

Kanuna sneered at me. "Gannon entered the home of a tribal member without approval. He assaulted Atsadi."

Oops! I had been right to dislike Kanuna.

"If he screws up our wiretap with one of his battering-ram inquiries, I'll slap his ass in Tribal Court."

I turned my overpowering doe-eyed expression on him. He scowled back—no sense of empathy.

Goodman interrupted Kanuna. "I get it. You're uncomfortable with Gannon. Move on."

We broke up. Goodman went to see the District Attorney to initiate the request for the search warrant. I still didn't know why Goodman invited me to this get-together.

# # #

Much later that night, I took a shower and put on pajamas. It had already been a sixteen-hour day. Just before I hit the bed, I checked my voice mail. Lilith had called and left a message. "Don, I know it's late, but I drove around on my Vespa. Had a hunch. I solved the ornament with the skull and crossbones on it. It wasn't Nathaniel's map that killed Digger. I know that now. Call me first thing in the morning."

I was so sleepy. I put off calling her until the next morning.

26

DIGGER'S HOUSE — SATURDAY

In the morning, I kept phoning Lilith, but she didn't answer. My worry pushed me to drive to Digger's house. The rear door was open. Her body sprawled, prone in a doorway, half was lying in the kitchen and half on the porch. Her throat, clammy to my fingers, had no pulse.

I sat on the floor, remaining back from the pool of brown blood that stretched from her torso and lower limbs. The pool didn't seem too big, but she didn't move. Her flaxen hair shrouded her face. My nose ran, and my energy drained away. I had grown fond of Lilith; she had been smart in her way, determined as a mule, but loyal. My heart would miss her. If only I had called her back before going to sleep.

I reported the homicide to Goodman. Waiting for him to arrive, I reported to Roth. She didn't speak at first. "Why the devil would someone kill her?"

Unable to view Lilith any longer, I stepped to the small front porch holding my mobile phone. "Her death must be tied to the pendant."

"But we're holding the pendant here at the mansion."

"Maybe Lilith held something back from us?"

"Or maybe she went off, investigating by herself last night," Roth said.

The Chief Deputy arrived with his deputies. "Boss, Goodman just got here."

He strode past me to study Lilith's body. "A humble and devoted person. I liked her." He glanced at me. "You touch her?"

"Felt her throat. No pulse."

"That's all?"

"Didn't disturb your crime scene."

"Let's wait outside." Goodman led me out to the porch and pulled out his notepad. "Tell me about your last contact with her."

I explained how Lilith found the pendant.

"Let me see this thing."

"Roth has it."

"I need to see it."

I got a photograph of the pendant out of my car and gave the sheet to Goodman. He examined the photo and put it on a clipboard he carried.

"And?"

"Lilith thought Digger drew the pendant in the sugar pile to clue us to his killer."

"What else?"

"Lilith said to call her this morning."

"And?"

"No answer."

Goodman didn't respond but gazed at the white bandage on my face. "How're your stitches coming?"

"Keeping them dry. The cut itches."

The forensic group, dressed like a bug-spraying team in company uniforms, arrived. After a glance about, they investigated the area around the back porch. We waited for the medical examiner to come and remove Lilith's body. Goodman looked the thinker with his white mustache and goatee, dark eyebrows, and drawn-out stares. He got people to respect him and confide in him. We stood together in the parking area.

A forensic tech arrived with a handful of evidence bags. "Found three 9mm shells."

Goodman considered the three shells. "Might be from the pistol used to attack Digger."

"Maybe," the tech said. "The lab techs will compare markings on the shell casings."

"Fingerprints on the shells?" Goodman asked.

The tech crossed his fingers. "The laboratory can only try."

Another deputy appeared next to us. "Get the shells to the laboratory," Goodman said. "Did the killer use the same P239 here and in the Harper shooting?"

Goodman's deputy paused in his uniform of black shirt and trousers. "Anything else, Chief?"

"Check where some people were this morning."

"Who?"

Goodman held up three fingers and counted them down. "Johnny Hayes and his two sidekicks, Paul Atsadi in Cherokee, and Leonard Eigges."

Goodman and I walked to the rear of the house. The deputies had circled the porch with yellow tape. My phone rang. It was Roth. "What do you know?"

I whispered, "It's Roth," to Goodman. "The forensic team is still in the house."

Goodman tapped my arm. "I want to see the pendant."

I spoke to Roth. "The Chief Deputy wants to study the pendant."

She waited for a moment. "When will Goodman finish an initial assessment?"

Goodman must have heard her. "Have something in an hour."

"Meet us at the mansion in two hours?" I said to him.

Goodman bobbed his head in agreement.

#

Harry Goodman came around to the mansion in the afternoon. Roth wore a full-length, satin dress in black, a bulky sweater in dark gray, and her alabaster white hair long. She sat at her desk with her hands clenched into fists. "I blame myself for Lilith's death. I didn't see it coming."

Sitting at her desk, she put her hands behind her head. "Mr. Hayes and his sidekicks were located where this morning?"

"They had been released from Blake County jail."

"I asked what they were doing?"

"Claimed they hung out at Hayes' shack in the morning."

"Who else?"

"Palo and Murphy were in jail."

Roth leaned back in her chair and looked sideways at the blaze in the fireplace. Except for the sound of the burning logs, silence permeated the room. "What about Mr. Atsadi?"

"The Cherokee tribal police are checking, Ms. Roth."

Roth twisted a thatch of her hair. "Tell me about Leonard Eigges."

Goodman leaned back in his chair. "He was at his estate."

Roth stared intently at me before rotating her face to Goodman. "The shell casings?"

Goodman had his notepad out on his lap. "The lab found the same markings on the shells left at the attack on Digger and those left at the murder of Lilith."

"I think you told me the shooter used a semi-automatic pistol?"

"I told you the pistol is a P239."

She covered her eyes with a hand. "We're closing in on the killer, but, oh God, we lost Lilith."

Roth dropped her hand. "Can you recreate what happened?"

Goodman patted his notepad. "I think I can."

Goodman began his review, sometimes reading from his notes. "In the morning, Lilith turned on the propane gas heater for added warmth."

I remembered the early morning. "It was chilly."

"She walked Digger's Border Terrier along the bank going down to the French Broad River. We know because the ground was damp, a little muddy."

Roth had formed her hands into a steeple. "Your team studied the footprints. Did she meet anyone?"

"No one. Back in the kitchen, Lilith deleted any messages on the phone, and fixed an English muffin and coffee."

I interrupted. "Lilith wasn't at the kitchen table when I found her."

Goodman glanced at the notepad to refresh his memory. "We think she put on her jacket and moved out to the screen porch off the kitchen, at the rear of the house." Goodman glanced to Roth. "Maybe she was uncomfortable eating in the room where her fiancé died."

"What happened next?" Roth asked.

"Lilith didn't towel off the terrier's feet. The dog scampered around the porch, putting down prints, pressing his nose against the screen."

"Some scent or noise spooked the dog?" I asked.

Goodman crossed his legs in front of himself. "Here's what I think. Lilith sat in her Adirondack chair, while a murderer crept up to the porch."

Roth took in a deep breath. "Explain."

"The shooter walked through the woods and sneaked under the porch. I saw footprints. Appeared to be made by rubber boots, garden-type footgear."

I leaned forward in my chair. "I imagine the terrier went bonkers."

"We studied muddy dog prints and a bulge on the screen. The Border Terrier must have bounded to the porch screen over the intruder, repeatedly leaping against the wire mesh."

If I had called Lilith as soon as I got up, maybe she would have left for the mansion and saved herself. But I hadn't been there to help her. "The agitated dog alerted her?"

Goodman's expression displayed gloom. "Over the yelping of the dog, I'm guessing she heard a scraping noise. I found someone pushed an object—like a gun barrel—against the aluminum mesh of the porch screen."

Goodman raised his chin and stroked his goatee. "First shot! It went through the screen and killed the dog."

Digger's dog was affectionate and loyal. The shooter had heartlessly snuffed out his life to get a clearer shot at Lilith. "What was Lilith doing?"

"I'm guessing Lilith jerked upright in the Adirondack chair," Goodman said.

Roth interrupted. "Why do you think that?"

"We found an overturned tray beside her chair. She must have felt vulnerable, her leg muscles hoisting her up, driven by an impulse to get off the porch."

Goodman stopped and lowered his head. "Lilith dashed for the kitchen. Second shot! Another hole in the screen showed the shooter fired again."

I imagined Lilith dashing toward the kitchen. Her concentration must have been on the doorway leading back into the house. "That shot struck her?"

"We think that bullet hit her in the side."

"Did it knock her down?" I asked.

Goodman nodded. "Lilith fell, and her body crushed some cereal boxes on the floor. She got up and tried to get into the kitchen."

"The shooter fired again?" Roth asked.

"Third shot! Caught Lilith in the back and knocked her on her face. Her body wound up in the doorway into the kitchen."

I had found Lilith in her final position. "What was the trauma?"

Goodman shook his head. "I have to wait for the autopsy. Death was rapid. I estimate the torso shot penetrated the aortic, which wound has a high mortality rate."

"Where did the shooter go inside the house?" I asked.

"Based on grimy footprints, the perpetrator stopped at the body, before stepping over it and going through the kitchen to enter the living room."

"Could you tell why?" I asked.

"The footprints led to the backpack and leather coat of the deceased," Goodman said. "The killer searched for something."

Goodman smirked. "What do you think the perp scanned for?"

I gave him a thumbs-up. "A pendant with a skull and crossbones."

Goodman nodded. "The pendant Roth had at the mansion."

Roth watched Goodman. "You have anything else?"

Goodman glanced down at his hands. "The laboratory pulled fingerprints off the shell casings at the Lilith shooting. The prints of Hayes, his two sidekicks, Atsadi, Palo, and Murphy don't match those on the spent casings."

Staring at Goodman, Roth again formed her hands into a steeple. "Are you saying we have the fingerprints of the killer, but we don't know whose they are?"

He paused a moment. "We have the prints of the person who loaded the P239's magazine. We haven't been able to match those prints to a person."

Harry stood up and put on his coat to leave. "I'll let you know what we find about Mr. Atsadi's alibi. Don, stay in touch."

After the Chief Deputy left, I asked Roth what she wanted to do. "We've pretty much spent the retainer Lilith gave us. Michael Harper sent us some funding, but Bertha watches him."

"And?"

"Do we save money by cutting back on our investigative effort and letting Goodman solve the case?"

My boss moped and slumped; consequently, I judged she wasn't in the mood to worry about her company's reserves. "We're going to find the spineless bastard who killed our client. Cinch up your safety belt; it's going to be a violent hunt!"

She stared through me with unblinking eyes. She was tough, relentless, smart, and Roth was my hero. "Finding the culprit will be difficult," I said.

She glared at me. "Finding a way is only difficult until it's not."

# # #

I couldn't find my appetite at dinner, picking at the country ham, lying under red-eye gravy and over white grits. Lilith was gone; the Medical Examiner's Office had her lifeless body. She wouldn't deliver a child. Carla had moved out of the mansion and started working for Larry Buchanan's company. My world hung bleak, shrouding even our kitchen-breakfast room in the gloom. Staring into the plate before me, I wasn't conscious of Roth until the chair beside me skidded on the floor, and she sat down.

"Despair is a downer. It dulls our wits into apathy."

"Just thinking," I said.

"You lost two important people. Do something."

"There's nothing I can do."

"Find the killer. I will not advise you on how to approach Miss Carla Diaz."

Taylor leaned over my shoulder to fill my iced tea glass; consequently, she heard the end of Roth's sentence.

"He idn't ready fer a bond," Taylor said. "Didn't pay no heed to Carla. Darn fool."

Our forthright cook returned to the stove, and my boss continued talking.

"Lose the gloom. Tomorrow, we'll get Angela here and investigate the pendant."

"You aren't going to advise me on Carla?" I asked.

Roth busied herself with her meal and ignored my question. I finished breakfast and left the table.

Behind me, Roth said in a low voice, "When the man is ready, the woman will appear."

My boss—she of the crusty exterior—hid a heart with a romantic outlook on life. I was now positive a breakout would come through the pendant, and we would solve the enigma.

27

Downtown Asheville — Sunday

I finished breakfast and read the morning paper in Roth's office, hearing the occasional click of her coffee cup settling into its saucer, when my mobile phone rang.

"Is this Gannon?"

I had heard the voice before, but I couldn't identify the speaker, who spoke with a gruff, red-neck accent.

"I'm Gannon. Who's this?"

"Johnny Hayes."

A call from Hayes was one of the last things I expected. But I had given him my phone number when Goodman took me to visit him in jail. "I heard you got out of the Morganton jail."

"Got out on bail."

"How can I help you?"

Across the room, Roth put down her section of the paper, looked at me, and raised an eyebrow. I cupped the phone's handset and mouthed, "Johnny Hayes."

"You'll want to hear the stuff I know," Hayes said.

"So, tell me."

"We need to meet."

What could he know I didn't? I tried to think. My nostrils caught the slightly fishy scent of Taylor's deep frying in the kitchen. She was setting up to deep fry hush puppies. Whatever I did, I needed to get back in time for her lunch. "Where?"

"Naughty Hops Pub."

"I'm leaving now," I said.

Half an hour later, I met Hayes inside the pub, with its musty cigarette smell. Under the high ceiling, he was seated at a black wood table and a black chair with a metal frame, working his way through a flight of beers. We both dwarfed the chairs.

"I'll tell you things 'bout Digger an' Lilith," Hayes said. "You buy da beers."

I got the waitress' attention and ordered beers for Hayes and me. He seemed bigger than life, using an outdoor voice easily rising over the drone of the pub. His natural expression came with squinted eyes as if always angry.

I sipped the beer and put the glass down on the cardboard coaster. "Okay. Lower the audio level."

Hayes grew quieter.

"Tell me about Lilith?"

"I was sad 'bout her death—liked Lilith even if she were tough on me. She made Digger happy."

Hayes drank his beer and looked into my eyes, maybe judging how I took his words. For my part, I judged he was honest with me: He regretted someone shot Lilith and wanted to punish her killer. "Liked Digger too," he said.

He continued, still searching my eyes. "I heard everyone thought I killed Digger for Confederate gold. Not true."

"Heard you and Digger fought," I said.

"He and I argued about hunting treasure. But we got along."

"Why are we talking?"

He punched the air and grinned. "I know something you don't know."

"You want to help find Digger & Lilith's killer?"

"Yep."

"You believe you know who killed Digger and Lilith?"

"I might."

"Who?"

"Look at his family," Hayes said.

He startled me. "Digger's family?"

"Digger and the wife of his adopting father didn't get along."

Now we both finished our beer and studied the eyes of the other. More patrons had entered, and the cold bar began to warm. A young waitress in black passed our table. Hayes and I held up our empty glasses. "I'll bring new ones, honey," she said.

"Bertha Harper is no prize"—Hayes' accusation had thrown me off balance, and I had to think what I was saying—"but I can't see her killing Digger."

Hayes grinned once more, choosing not to reply at first. "Digger and I would get drunk together. He told me the old woman hated him and often had rows with him."

"Many families argue."

"Digger moved out of the Harper's Old Fort house to escape Bertha."

"Not liking doesn't mean Bertha killed Digger."

Hayes gave me a knowing grin. "Wait, there's more."

I cocked my head and frowned. "Yeah. What?"

"My pal, Joey, was at Digger's funeral—you've seen him, short guy with tattoos, always wearing a baseball cap."

"I remember him," I said. "And?"

"Joey recognized the mother, Bertha."

"He knew her from where?"

Hayes leaned closer to me. "Joey was getting a tattoo at his usual parlor. And this old woman came in to have a tattoo removed."

Hayes gave me the knowing grin again. "At the burial, Joey realizes the old woman at the tattoo parlor was Digger's mother."

Where was this going? I began to listen carefully. "Yeah. What happened?"

"She's loud and demanding."

"I know. Bertha has an even temper. Always bad."

"So, Joey looks to see what Bertha wants."

I said nothing. Hayes paused for what appeared to be a dramatic effect. Our waitress returned with a tray and our beers. The background hum of voices grew louder.

"She wanted a tattoo removed from the inside of her left arm."

My head jerked back. Was Hayes pulling my leg? "What kind of tattoo?"

"The tattoo was just a letter, no diagram or design, placed on the inside of the arm under her left shoulder."

"The tattooist removed Bertha's letter?" I asked.

"Yep," Hayes replied.

"What letter?"

"Joey didn't remember."

"Why is this important?"

"The old woman removed the letter just after Digger told me he had a big argument with her."

"You remembered this?"

"See, I'm not as dumb as people think."

After thinking a moment, another thought popped into my head. "I didn't realize tattoo shops removed tattoos."

"Joey's tattoo parlor applies them and can remove them with lasers."

"This letter," I said, "was it ornate or a bright color?"

"Joey told me it was a plain, black letter."

"Which tattoo parlor?"

"The one on Coxe Avenue."

"Anything else?"

After hesitating, Hayes repeated, "If you want the murderer, look to the family."

I mulled over what Hayes told me. I didn't fully comprehend the tattoo's meaning, but I realized we needed to be questioning Digger's adopted parents. I thought Hayes had earned a break from me.

"I'll check her out."

"You do, an' you'll get justice for Digger and Lilith."

Hayes and I finished another round of beers. When I paid and left, he stayed and continued drinking.

###

As I reached the sidewalk my phone rang. It was Goodman. He had acted quickly. A judge had issued a search warrant Friday afternoon. He told me the phone company had set up a wiretap at the Eigges' estate that evening, and he and Kanuna had listened in on several conversations. If they'd recorded an admission of Digger or Lilith's murder, they would bust the investigation wide open.

Goodman invited me to go over to the County Courthouse to read the transcripts of the conversations. I agreed and headed on over. Mostly, Eigges discussed financial dealing with his clients. He guided staff in purchasing stolen Native American relics, for which Kanuna must have been pleased to hear. No one discussed Digger or Lilith. My effort here was a waste of time.

###

Having returned to the mansion, I got together with Roth and Bruce in my office, recounting Hayes' account of the tattoos on Bertha's arm and the allegation of frequent quarrels between Digger and her.

Before my boss could speak, Bruce butted in. "I've noticed many of your interrogations occur at a purveyor of alcoholic spirits."

"They're drinking to help me interrogate them. Many of my suspects get drunk and reverse their earlier memory loss."

Roth frowned, locking onto our eyes with what I termed her "teacher's stare," before leading the talk back to the main topic. "Mr. Hayes advocates we focus on Michael and Bertha Harper in our hunt. Do you concur?"

My feeling toward Bertha was more dislike than suspicion. "I agree."

"Me too," Bruce said.

Roth settled back in her chair and pointed to the house phone on my desk. "Don, see if you can get Goodman."

Locating him in his office, I put him on speakerphone.

"Mr. Goodman, did you find any reason to suspect Michael or Bertha Harper of Digger's murder?" Roth asked.

"No," Goodman said. "We looked—didn't find a motive."

"Johnny Hayes met with Don earlier today, and he maintained Bertha often quarreled with Digger."

"I didn't know that. Who told Hayes about their quarreling?"

"Hayes maintained Digger complained to him over beers."

"I'll have our deputies do a deeper look at the Harpers—their personal history. Other than Hayes, do you have important intelligence on Mr. and Mrs. Harper?"

"I'll let Bruce answer that question," Roth said.

"I've looked through public records for the past twenty or thirty years," Bruce said. "Nothing on Mr. and Mrs. Harper. I'll continue searching."

"There's something else Hayes revealed to me," I said to Goodman. "Shortly after one of Bertha and Digger's arguments, she had a tattooed letter—yes, I said tattooed—removed by laser from the inside of her left arm."

"What am I supposed to do with that?" Goodman asked.

"We're looking for any connection between murder, arm tattoos, and a skull and crossbones," my boss said.

"Interesting, but I can't help you. If that's all, I need to get back to work here at the Sheriff's Office."

Goodman disconnected the call. Bruce and I waited for Roth to speak.

"Maybe Goodman will find something we don't know about the Harpers."

"What do we do?" Bruce asked.

"I want Don to follow up with Atsadi and Eigges. I want you, Bruce, to keep doing background checks on the Harpers."

"Goodman and Kanuna are biting at the bit to raid Eigges' estate," I said. "It'll happen soon."

Roth pursed her lips. "Go with them. Keep searching for a link to Digger's death."

Bruce and I nodded in agreement and got up to leave the meeting.

Behind me, I heard my boss mumble to herself. "I'm going to call Angela—ask her to search for a historical connection between tattoos and skulls and crossbones."

#

After the day ended, my partners, Bruce and Mickey, and I watched college basketball in the mansion's media room and sucked beers. The outside, seen through the windows along the walls, was an opaque black. The overhead chandelier stayed off, and illumination came from the TV mounted on a wall. We reclined on one of the couches with our feet on the coffee table. The door opened, saturating the room with light from the hall. Roth and Angela stood in the hall.

Roth scanned the room, her expression stern. "Angela is here. We intend to search for Digger and Lilith's killer."

My two partners and I stared at Roth. The game continued playing.

Her face stayed grim. "Were the game turned off, we could all gather together."

I hurried to the light switch and flipped it on. Bruce grabbed the remote and killed the game.

"Gratifying. Don, would you bring another couch to the coffee table for Angela and me?"

Roth, in a burgundy tunic, and Angela, in a black dress with a beige jacket, sat on the second couch. Roth pulled a small, dark-blue bag out of her tunic and unfolded it on the coffee table. The pendant. Its dimensions appeared roughly one and a fourth inch by one and a fourth inch. The figure on the pendant was a skull with two bones—like femur bones—crossed behind. Holes formed the eyes and mouth.

Roth turned sideways to the professor, Angela. "What is it? Is it early American?"

"In Colonial times, jewelry was both no-frills and an indicator of social rank," Angela said. "The American jewelry trade slowly grew from small shops to large plants and from hand worked to mechanical creation."

Roth pursed her lips. "Is this piece from mid-eighteen hundred? Could it be connected to Nathaniel Harper?"

Angela gave a half shrug. "By then, American jewelers furnished many objects, including silver medals."

Roth spread her arms wide. "Does this piece fit in Harper's time frame?"

Angela shook her head. "I don't know. It doesn't feel right."

The pendant had a silver finish on a metal base. My notion focused on the medical bracelets warning the wearer has a disease like diabetes, epilepsy, or asthma. "Maybe it's a medical alert bracelet. It's so tarnished I can't tell what the metal is."

"What kind of disease would a skull and crossbones symbolize?" Bruce asked.

I threw my hands in the air. "I don't know. I'll investigate medical bracelets."

"I'll research at the library," Angela said.

Roth held up a finger. "I have a pawnbroker friend. I'm going to ask him what the object is. He may know, or he'll know an expert."

Roth turned to leave the media room. I heard her mutter under her breath, "So, we ram forward, our chest in opposition to the wind, our questions like tentacles pulling back answers from the past."

I was puzzled. But with that, I left the room. If we were going to break down the skull and crossbones enigma, Roth would pull it out of us.

28

AN ASHEVILLE ESTATE — MONDAY

My frustration had been growing; I'd had trouble sleeping: I couldn't find a medical alert bracelet with a skull and crossbones on its front surface. I had been at my desk searching the Internet since 4 am; my next step would be to phone and talk to live individuals. I strolled past Roth's office. She was at her desk with the phone stuck on her ear and hummed Otis Redding's "Sittin' On the Dock of the Bay."

Delores Claire, a nurse I had dated, responded to my phone call with a blistering rebuke. I didn't remember our relationship had ended dreadfully. She slammed the phone down when I asked, "Know anything about a medical bracelet with a skull-and-crossbones symbol?"

When Goodman came at eight o'clock to pick me up in front of the mansion, I had not an inkling where the bracelet originated.

#

Goodman and Kanuna had finally agreed to serve the search warrant at Eigges' home. At nine o'clock in the morning outside the estate, the sun had exposed its glow. Tribal Officer Kanuna and I sat in the back seat of Goodman's Crown Victoria. Kanuna fussed about his chapped lips and rubbed lip balm on them. Goodman sat in the front with a Buncombe County Sheriff's deputy. Our search force consisted of four squad cars, a truck, two tribal police officers, ten Sheriff's deputies, and me. After sitting in the car for a while, my sense of smell had grown accustomed to Goodman's Aqua Velva and I no longer noticed it. We waited far enough away from the estate so they wouldn't spot us from the manor house. The outside felt chilly; our vehicles had their engines running and heaters blowing warm air. A few smokers stood outside the vehicles and took drags on their fags.

I coughed to get Goodman's attention. "The phone tap turned up nothing about Digger or Lilith's death?"

Goodman turned to glance into the rear seat. "Not a peep."

Kanuna stirred beside me. "They plan to remove the two clay statues."

"We have to move this morning," Goodman said.

I checked my watch. "Almost nine-thirty."

Goodman and his deputy got on their police radios and passed the word: "We're starting the raid." Goodman's Crown Victoria, with lights flashing and siren sounding, led and stopped before the metal gate, which was closed and locked. He pushed the gate's intercom button and said, "Police! Search warrant! Open the gate!"

The sun's rays began to spread over the far mountains. After a few minutes waiting, Goodman talked with his deputy, and next spoke over the radio to the task force. "No response. We're not getting in nicely. Bring up the truck."

Goodman backed up his squad car and pulled to the side of the road. The truck, with a push bumper fitted to the chassis of the truck, gathered speed and rammed through the gate. All our vehicles swarmed down the asphalt lane to the red-brick manor. Goodman and Kanuna led the way to the front door. In response to their hammering with the door knocker, the maid, in her black uniform, opened the door. The search team surged through the doorway and rushed to their prearranged locations throughout the house.

Goodman and I hurried through the entry hall and into the dining room. We collided with Eigges in a Jacquard hooded robe, a fabric with an elaborately woven pattern. The color was gold and black, with a hooded neckline and open front. He pulled his cigarette holder and box of blue Rothmans out of a pocket in his robe. "What a beautiful morning. Stunning. On a daybreak like this, my father blew his brains away when the cotton mills failed."

Goodman and I gazed at Eigges while he inserted a cigarette in his holder. After a moment, the Chief Deputy handed him the papers. "This is a search warrant to enter your house."

Kanuna and a tribal police officer pushed past us and examined the bookcase along one wall. Murphy had told us a section opened into a large room where Eigges hid many of the stolen Native American relics.

Eigges took a puff on his cigarette and read the papers. "Why are you here?"

Goodman pulled on his goatee and watched Eigges. "We have a reasonable belief you stole Cherokee Indian artifacts and hold them in your house."

"Why are you here, Chief Deputy Goodman? You aren't in charge of catching robbers plundering Cherokee burial sites."

"The tribal police arrested Atsadi at an Indian mound in Cherokee," I said.

Eigges sat in a chair, settled back, and crossed his legs. "We went over that. I always engaged them separately for a legal task."

Goodman sat opposite Eigges. "It's not legal to dig on the reservation."

Eigges pointed his cigarette holder at Goodman. "I already told you. I never told them to dig on the reservation."

Along the wall, Kanuna and the tribal officer patiently pulled, pushed, and tried to turn sections of the bookcase.

I pulled up a chair, placed it across from Eigges, and sat. "With Atsadi in jail, Digger returned to the mound and brought back two clay statues, each about a foot high."

Eigges left eyelid twitched. "I never ordered such an activity."

I noticed Eigges glance sideways at Kanuna, who seemed to be stymied by the bookcase. "Digger acted on your instructions."

"Who told you such a lie?"

"Your agent, Murphy. He confessed he carried the statues to you."

Eigges' eyelid resumed jerking. "You have no proof. There are no statues here."

Kanuna turned a knob, and a section of the bookcase swung into the dining room, opening a portal into the hidden room. Our Laird pursed his lips. Kanuna entered the hidden room.

Before I passed through the bookcase, I smiled at Eigges. "That's life. Someone's big success is always offset by another's dismal failure."

Kanuna had switched on lights in the room and put on surgical-type gloves. The other Cherokee tribal officer took photographs. I stepped inside and touched nothing, just observed. The search warrant had come in time. I saw one sculpture of a sitting woman holding a bowl and another of a man seated. The female wore an enfolded skirt, and the male seemed without garments. Their hair was highly crafted. Other relics lay on shelves. I saw an ornate brown-and-cream woven basket. Next to the basket sat a carved pottery plate.

Eigges waited outside the hidden room and talked with Goodman. "I prefer not to discuss Indian artifacts until my lawyers are here with me." He inserted a fresh, blue Rothman into his cigarette holder. "As to the killing you are investigating, I had no reason to harm Mr. Harper."

I entered the dining room again and observed Eigges' eye stayed steady, without blinking. I wanted to hear his story.

Eigges continued talking to Goodman. "Digger knew Murphy was my agent, but he had no proof I commissioned a crime."

Goodman stroked his mustache. "Did Digger make an effort to profit—to blackmail you, for example?"

Eigges shook his head and grinned. "Even if he made threats, I would frame him for going onto the reservation and desecrating the tombs."

Goodman didn't speak; he seemed to be reflecting.

Eigges held up his forefinger. "I had nothing to gain by murder."

Goodman remained mute. He glanced at me. I shrugged. Eigges had a point.

Holding his cigarette holder in his fingers, Eigges held out both hands to Goodman. "I am long in the tooth. Why would I risk going to jail for the rest of my life, for Digger's murder?"

Goodman kept talking with Eigges. They went over Eigges' calendar and established he was in New York when an assassin shot at Digger, and he was in Europe when someone killed Lilith. The deputies searched the manor house; they located rifles, shotguns, and pistols, but couldn't find a P239. "So, who killed Digger?" Goodman asked.

Eigges glanced nervously at Tribal Officer Kanuna coming out of the hidden room. "I don't know. I didn't do it."

Taking the time to rub lip balm on his lips, Kanuna stopped before Eigges, who stood. "Leonard Eigges I am placing you under arrest on suspicion of stealing Cherokee artifacts. I am taking you in for questioning and arraignment."

Eigges said he would speak to Kanuna only in the presence of his lawyers. Kanuna read the Miranda rights to his suspect and escorted him to lockup in Cherokee.

# # #

By late afternoon, the Chief Deputy had fallen under the surge of paperwork, having no time to drive me back to the mansion. "Damn it. Sit tight. I'll get to you."

Eventually Bruce came and got me. Finally back in my office, I took a bottle of Yuengling beer from the refrigerator and settled at my desk to continue my search for an explanation of the skull-and-crossbones symbol.

My boss had entered my office and stood at my bookcases to the right of the door, polishing around books. She stood around five feet eight inches tall and weighed something like a hundred and fifty pounds, but her toes touched the floor before her heels, and she would suddenly appear without a sound. Recently she had taken to wiping down the furniture with a soft white cloth, some obsessive-compulsive behavior. "Good afternoon."

Roth had pitched her unruffled voice a little higher than customary. Right away, I had an idea she had found the link to the pendant. "You know."

Her face displayed a triumphant grin. "My guy in the pawnshop figured it out."

"How?"

"He had seen it before and had sold them."

She had me in suspense. "What is it?"

"Umm." She seemed positive she knew the connection and planned to build up to an unveiling. I inclined the back of my chair rearward.

Roth moved closer to my desk. "The Skull and Crossbones symbol has meant many things over time."

"We know that."

"Pirates, for example, but we don't have pirates. Some Spanish churches put the symbol over the doorway going out to a burial area."

"Move on. What is it?"

"My expert knew—"

I rocked my chair forward to full-upright and waited for the completion.

"Another meaning of the emblem is—"

"What?"

"The Death's Head symbol was used by the SS in World War II."

"And?"

"I think Digger was signaling us to look for a Nazi connection."

My mind hesitated, digesting what Roth had said. "Is your expert positive or making a wild guess?"

"100% Positive."

"What's it called again? The Death's Head?"

"The Germans called the symbol Totenkopf."

I realized I was staring at the small light globe on my office ceiling and I was talking. "Where did Digger get the Totenkopf? Why did he draw it in the sugar pile?"

Prodded by Roth's finding, my mind conjured up old photographs of SS officers with an eagle and skull and crossbones on their brimmed hats. "World War II and the SS. The only person I can think of is Michael Harper."

Roth sat down at my desk. "Do you think he poisoned his adopted son?"

"Michael's not a killer. He would have to be furious to off another human."

Roth pressed her fingers to her lips. "Angela will know the history of World War II or she'll know someone who does. Let's get her involved."

Roth talked with Angela on the phone and then hung up. "She'll talk with her experts and then discuss World War II with us."

"You've solved the crime."

She favored me with another aphorism. "The good ends fortunately, and the bad miserably. That's what detectives do."

29

RIVERSIDE CEMETERY, ASHEVILLE — TUESDAY

I said my goodbyes to Lilith on a cold day in a constant drizzle. At Riverside Cemetery, Bruce, four other pallbearers, and I lifted her casket, carrying it by its handles toward a hole in the ground sheltered by a raised canvas awning. Uniformly clothed in dark coats, mourners lined our path to the grave, all protected from the rain by a canopy of open black umbrellas. We silent six repeated a process, I thought, performed ad infinitum. I recalled ancient frescos showing coffins carried by Egyptians clothed in simple white loincloth. As we somberly bore the coffin, we wore black: long overcoats, classic men's fur caps, and leather gloves.

Carefully watching my feet to balance on a slight incline, I wondered if it all began with the Egyptians. Weren't they the ones who buried the deceased so their souls wouldn't return to haunt the living? Lilith would haunt me until I caught her killer. Having set the casket on a low wooden framework, Bruce and I stepped away and stood beside our boss.

Earlier, Mickey had driven Roth, Taylor, Bruce, and me to the church. On this day, one of her rare outings from the mansion, my boss wore a full-length black coat with hood, a coat reminiscent of the garment worn by cloister monks. Entering the nave and finding a seat among the pews, I spoke a sad greeting to Goodman and Angela Lightfoot. Before the funeral service, I spotted Carla with Larry Buchanan among the grievers on the rear benches. I guess I stared at Carla because she glanced in my direction, paused, and turned away, expressionless. Buchanan, staring straight ahead, sat in a stiff, erect posture with a slight standoff distance from Carla.

I noticed them again as the graveside eulogy ended. Carla and Buchanan stood together, distant from any group. Taylor walked to Carla.

Mostly, Taylor and Carla conversed; Buchanan appeared aloof and awkward: staying apart, saying nothing after initially greeting Taylor. He gazed in the direction of bare trees and gravestones and the occasional vault. After a while, he spoke to Carla, taking her arm and leaving together.

When we got into Mickey's Ford Explorer to leave, I turned and mouthed a silent farewell to Lilith. She never gave up. You couldn't take the dogfight out of that woman. As Mickey drove slowly along the curbless, asphalt road out of the cemetery, Roth turned to Taylor in the second row of seats.

"Is Carla happy in her new job?"

"She seemed distant." Taylor had hesitated in her response, perhaps pondering how to organize her feelings. Roth waited with her eyes focused on Taylor.

"Thing is, Carla say she a-goin' to marry that Buchanan fellow. He done propose to her."

Taylor's pronouncement left us in stony silence. A chill engulfed my arms and torso like a sudden rush of blizzard wind; I felt Carla's being receding, vanishing into a distant, remote place.

Roth didn't respond at first. She appeared to be considering something. "How is Mr. Buchanan responding? Is he overjoyed?"

"I think he's a-feelin' distant. He actin' aloof—an not goofy with happiness."

Roth moved her head slowly to stare forward and out the windshield. "You realize what you're saying?"

"Carla got herself a man with all the sensitivities of a watermelon."

We journeyed along in near silence, listening to the click of the windshield wipers and the hum of the tires. At the same time, I thought about Carla and her rush down a different path. I became melancholy and found myself fighting sadness.

#

A small refrigerator nestled under the desk in my office. Roth must have known I had it. A great detective noticed minor things. She had never said anything to me about it. I took a Fat Tire Amber Ale out of the fridge, and contemplated, and felt a buzz. I thought about what I had found. Hayes was a red-neck oaf, but I saw little reason for him to kill Digger. Eigges was an effete snob, but I saw little reason for him to kill Digger.

I took a swig and gazed out the windows at the gray drizzle. Where did Digger pick up the Totenkopf? Michael was involved in WWII but served in the US Army, not the SS. Bertha had been in Germany but was female; couldn't be in the SS. Think! Had I missed a suspect?

I reached down to the fridge and opened another ale. What had Hayes blathered about a tattoo? On Bertha's arm as in a concentration camp, but she hadn't been there. She was German and didn't belong to a religion the Nazis oppressed. I could ask Angela; WWII counted as history; our historian could answer questions about the past. Wouldn't hurt to ask her. I grabbed a six-pack and glanced up and down the hallway; no Roth in sight.

I found Bruce typing at his keyboard in the computer room. "I need help catching Lilith's assassin."

He spun around. "How?"

"Talk to Angela."

Bruce powered down his computer and grabbed a six-pack out of a cupboard. "I'll drive."

The Asheville campus of the UNC overflowed with trees. Bruce drove his Jeep into a parking garage, and we walked to Angela's office with the ales under my coat. Her office door was open, and she worked on her laptop. She turned with a smile. She observed me for a moment. "You look like you're healing well."

I started to rub my face but stopped. "We want to talk."

She moved to her conference table. "Let's talk."

I wasn't sure how to begin. "Does a link exist between the SS and tattoos."

She took a moment to ponder. "Why?"

"Because Hayes said Bertha Harper had a letter tattooed on her arm."

"Yes there is."

Bruce glanced from Angela to me. "Does that mean she was in a concentration camp?"

She shook her head. "Concentration camp tattoos are numerical. But you say Bertha's tattoo was a letter." Angela patted her afro. "I researched the SS last night."

"And," I said.

"There is a possible connection between a letter tattoo and the SS."

I took a sip of ale. "What is it?"

"Blood."

"Blood?"

"For efficiency, the SS tattooed the blood type of each Waffen-SS member on the left arm."

"Left arm?"

"A small black ink tattoo located on the underside of the left arm, usually near the armpit."

Bruce and I sipped ale and gawked at each other.

"In an SS hospital, the medical team immediately knew the patient's blood type," Angela said.

Bruce scratched his chin, thinking. "Everyone in the SS had the tattoo?"

"In theory, the SS blood group tattoo was applied to all Waffen-SS members."

But Bertha was a female. "All SS members were males, right?"

"My readings suggest SS soldiers got the tattoo. But others treated at SS hospitals might have gotten the tattoo."

Bruce bent forward and put his arms on the table. "Don't you find this hard to believe?"

Angela acted surprised. "What don't you believe?"

Bruce sipped his beer. "Want a beer?"

Angela shook her head.

"We're in the mountains of North Carolina, fifty-five years after the war."

"And?"

Bruce settled backward in his chair. "Getting involved with the SS and arm tattoos is impractical, smoke and mirrors."

Angela folded her arms. "Why?"

Bruce held up a forefinger. "Other armies in the war used dog tags."

Angela frowned. "But other armies could have tattooed their soldiers."

Bruce sipped his beer. "They didn't. Dog tags have lots of room for information."

"So there were two methods."

Bruce set down his beer can. "I just find it hard to believe we're getting involved with SS tattoos."

Angela stood and went to her desk. "You could be right. I don't know. I think we should consider Bertha had a tattoo for blood type."

Angela phoned the mansion. "Ms. Roth, I'm going to put you on speakerphone."

After Bruce and Angela explained her thesis tying together the SS and tattoos, my boss replied, "Gratifying."

I took another sip. A job well done. "What do we do now?"

"Let's meet in my office tomorrow," Roth said. "Angela, please join us and tell us all you know about the connection with the SS."

#

When the drizzle died away and the afternoon temperature rose to a comfortable level, the Asheville citizenry came out for the *Drum Circle*. Bruce, Taylor, Mickey, and I attended the festivities to bond as a group, limber up and relax, and mull over our sleuthing puzzles. By six o'clock, I saw happy people beating about twenty drums—mostly hand drums—and a tambourine, sitting and swaying on the brick walls at Pritchard Park. Gathered around the drummers, we swayed along with a large crowd, a diverse crowd of different genders, ages, and nationalities.

"I keep forgetting you have no sense of rhythm," Bruce said.

I stuck out my tongue at him. "I know, I know. Can't dance and can't jump because I'm white."

"Was thinking that, but I didn't want to say it."

I continued to dance to the pulsating rhythm of the drums, an African rhythm. "I am giving this my full effort, and that is my triumph."

"You look like a goof."

From the nearby fire station, two trucks left with sirens blaring. A late-arriving man with a drum walked up to the wall searching for a seat.

"Look," Taylor said. "There's Carla and Larry."

Following Taylor, we looped around the pulsating people, like ants moving about their nest. Carla and Taylor had their heads close, chattering and exchanging information. I nodded to Buchanan, who nodded back after a pause. Presently, Carla and I swayed near each other. "I like the drum circle," Carla said, "it's so disorganized and uncomplicated." She pointed toward the drummers, allowing me to observe a diamond engagement ring on her left hand.

"I know," I replied. "The drummers appear to have no voice instructions about what to play or when to start."

"When do they stop?"

"Maybe a couple of drummers get tired and quit, and that starts the stop."

Larry appeared beside Carla. "This is noisy and seedy. Let's head out for our dinner at the Country Club. Our kind of people will be there."

"The Country Club is nice, but I want to spend time with the folks here," Carla said.

"I am getting a headache from all this drumming. We need to go now."

We said goodbye as Carla and Larry left. Bruce and I watched them leave. "I wonder if Buchanan manages to discover a little sorrow in whatever makes the rest of us happy," Bruce said. "At first, I thought he disliked me because of my race."

I butted in. "No, Buchanan dislikes most of us regardless of national origin."

Returning to the swaying people around the drum circle, I realized I felt lonely amid the throng. I felt sorry for Carla and myself—and sorry for Buchanan. I looked forward to Roth's strategy session tomorrow. I wanted to get back to finding the killer.

30

ROTH'S MANSION, ASHEVILLE — WEDNESDAY

B y late morning, Angela arrived at the mansion, appearing confident and carrying a case holding papers and spiral notebooks. Once Roth, Bruce, and I assembled in Roth's office, our historian began her report.

"I have more information about Bertha and Germany."

I had agonized over various interpretations of the tattoo and the pendant; furthermore, how had the two led to Digger's and now probably Lilith's deaths? I spoke to my unease. "In the attic of the Old Fort House, Digger may have found the pendant adorned with a skull and crossbones. Correct?"

Angela bobbed her head. "But Lilith wasn't positive he found it there."

I paused to form my question succinctly and not drift. "World War II ended fifty-five years ago, and Michael and Bertha lived at that time."

"Yes."

"Michael fought in Europe as a US foot soldier—certainly not a member of the Waffen-SS."

Angela tugged at her earlobe. "Agreed."

I continued my thought. "The SS filled their ranks with men. Bertha is female so she wouldn't have been SS."

Our history professor said nothing, pausing as if in a history class mentoring students. Finally, she said. "Ask the question differently: Did the SS use female front-line troopers?"

"No."

"Did the SS use female guards?"

I hadn't expected that question. "Don't know. I guess they did."

"The Waffen-SS sent their members, all males, to fight on the front lines. SS camps had female and male guards."

I thought about Angela's question. "What kind of guards?"

"From what I've read, the SS guards acted like hard-nosed, hateful terrors with fierce attack dogs."

Roth pinched the bridge of her nose. "You think Bertha guarded a concentration camp?"

Our history professor pulled papers from her research files. "I suspect so."

"Why?"

"I found Fürstenberg, Bertha's birth town, is the town across the lake from Ravensbrück."

I stared at Bruce with my dumbfounded expression. "Ravensbrück?"

"One of the first Nazi camps for women."

"What do you know about this camp?" Roth asked.

As Angela told the Ravensbrück story, she picked through her research papers. "The Waffen-SS started the camp around 1934 by purchasing land across a lake from a small town called Fürstenberg."

"Where Bertha lived as a young woman," Bruce said.

I tried to orient myself in time. "Hitler had taken control of Germany?"

"They bought the land a year after Hitler became chancellor of Germany. A large group of women—almost nine hundred—arrived at the site in 1939, just before the start of WWII."

Listening to Angela, I realized I held my breath. She sought to tie the pendant back to a ghastly time in the human experience.

Bruce interrupted. "Were these Jewish women?"

"Not necessarily. The first women prisoners were German." Angela turned to one of her spiral notebooks. "The Nazis imprisoned this early group because these women opposed Hitler. They formed a hodgepodge of communists, Jehovah's Witnesses—considering Hitler the Antichrist—prostitutes, criminals, mentally disabled individuals, and Gypsies."

"When it started, it was a prison?" I asked.

"The Nazis initially set up Ravensbrück as a slave labor camp," our professor said. "A German electrical company built a factory adjoining Ravensbrück. The prisoners marched to the factory to build electrical components."

A corporation used prisoners for cheap labor.

Angela kept reading from her spiral notebook. "Other prisoners cut down trees, built barracks, and made roads through the compound. Prisoners fabricated prison outfits and uniforms for the *Wehrmacht*."

And Bertha Harper was born in Furstenberg, just across the lake from the concentration camp. Was this a coincidence or a link?

Angela frowned. "My hunch is that Bertha Harper, born Bertha Reinhardt, answered a newspaper advertisement and enrolled at the camp as an overseer."

"How many prisoners did the camp hold?" Roth asked. "If a small slave labor camp, couldn't you find the names of the guards?"

Angela paged through her spiral notebook. "Ravensbruck housed roughly ten thousand females by 1942 and fifty thousand by 1945. Broken down by national origin, Poland, Russia, and Germany provided the majority of the women at the site. The camp held large numbers of prisoners and changed constantly."

"What about the guards?" I asked. "I assume you're saying the SS used female guards to secure the women captives."

"Males made up the top SS administrators at Ravensbrück," Angela said. "Otherwise, women overseers controlled the prisoners."

I held up a forefinger. "These were the guards who did not belong to the SS?"

"These women were civilian employees of the SS."

I had visited the Holocaust Museum in Washington, DC, and seen pictures from the concentration camps, but I didn't remember this prison. "Were the prisons in Germany less cruel than elsewhere?"

Angela went through her spiral notebooks. "In the years from 1939 to 1945, this German prison grew more horrifying. Early in 1945, the Nazis built a gas chamber at Ravensbrück and slew five to six thousand women in this facility."

Bruce emitted a groan. "Did others die?"

"From 1939 to 1945, about 130,000 women arrived at the prison, and some 90,000 perished."

Mostly, the room was silent, a silence broken by the occasional popping noise at the end of the room from the fireplace hearth near Roth's desk. I didn't know about Ravensbrück because I generally disliked talking or reading about this inhumanity toward other human beings. "How did women die?"

"They died from hunger, illness, and the brutality of the Nazis, including viciousness of the female overseers. The Nazi terror ended in April 1945 when Soviet troops reached that part of Germany."

Angela stopped speaking, maybe pausing to consider the actuality of what she described. After a minute, Roth inquired, "What did your readings reveal about the nature of the women guards?"

The professor paused a moment, appearing to consider what my boss had asked. "Well, the Nazis often recruited young women guards from poor or middle-class families."

"The SS took care of their camp guards?" Bruce asked.

Angela glanced at him. "A camp overseer received good pay and comfortable living quarters, with maid service and cooking provided by the prisoners."

"Did they have uniforms like any prison guards?" I asked.

"The jailers wore uniforms: field-grey jacket, culottes-type skirt, two uniforms, two pairs of boots, a pair of gloves, stockings, blouses, and a field cap."

Roth spoke up. "Did the uniform include the emblem of the death's head?"

"Not the female guard uniform."

"I assume a newly hired female went through training at Ravensbrück," Roth said.

"Yes. Given time, most young recruits grew used to the SS thinking, they would obey all orders, even the most horrible. The young guard came to believe her task as important to the Nazis as fighting in battle."

"You mentioned viciousness by the women overseer," Roth said. "Exactly what kind of conduct are we talking about?"

"You really don't want to know, do you?"

Roth scowled. "Maybe you could give us brief examples of the behavior of the female guards."

Angela opened her research journal and searched her notes. "Brief examples … hmm … one overseer beat, shot, and whipped women prisoners in her charge. Another used her German Shepherd to attack the prisoners. Still, another slit the throat of a captive with a sharpened shovel blade."

"What happened to the camp jailers at the end of the war?" I asked.

"When the war was over, the Soviet army captured many of the guards at Ravensbrück. In trials at the end of the war, the Allied courts sentenced the female guards more harshly than the male guards."

What Angela was saying had come a long way from Nathaniel Harper and his last train to Danville. I was curious and interrupted. "Some of the guards got away, right?"

"In the confusion at the war's end, some female overseers exchanged their uniform for civilian clothing and slipped back into the general population."

My boss cut in. "So our working hypothesis is Bertha slipped out of the concentration site in 1945 and took cover in her hometown of Furstenberg?"

Angela nodded. "So in all probability, shortly after the war ended, Bertha met and married an American soldier named Michael Harper. When she immigrated to the U.S. with him, she would not have revealed she had been an overseer at a concentration camp."

"What about the blood-type tattoo spotted on Bertha's upper arm?" I asked. "Would she have received a tattoo as a civilian jailer?"

"No," our historian answered. "But she might have been treated in an SS hospital and gotten the tattoo there."

I understood where Angela was going. "From what you've told us, I am guessing a prison guard might have adored the SS and wanted to carry a death's head pendant."

"I am estimating, but I think it possible."

Roth took her time before continuing. "You have a hypothesis about Bertha's guilt matching what we know. You have instinct; bring me proof."

Maybe Bertha was just a nasty piece of work but not a war criminal? "How did she get into the US without immigration identifying her wartime activity?"

Angela gave a dismissive wave of her hand. "Just after WWII, the US didn't have immediate availability to all records. Bertha might have got lost in the crowd and later entered the US without getting caught."

I felt perplexed. I found Bertha to be obnoxious, but I lacked the will to judge her the monster described by Angela.

Bruce broke in. "If she was a Nazi concentration camp guard and entered the country illegally, then she could be deported immediately? Right?"

Roth held up her hands. "What would have motivated Bertha to poison Digger?"

I pictured Digger in the Harper attic going through all those dusty boxes. "Digger found the Totenkopf. Somehow he discovered Bertha's tie to the pendant and maybe he showed it to her."

"She must have figured it would be just a matter of time until Digger said something to his adopted father," Roth said. "At best she would have faced a number of awkward questions."

And Digger's fate was sealed. "What do we do now?"

Roth went back to pinching her nose and staring at the trees beyond the mansion. "This is awkward. We have an instinct about Bertha. Chief Deputy Goodman will tell us he doesn't have reasonable grounds for suspecting Bertha committed a crime."

"Take her fingerprints and compare with those on the shell casings," Bruce said.

Roth shook her head. "Goodman has to be careful. A citizen's rights include the right to remain silent and the right to be free from unreasonable searches." Roth went quiet and stared at the forest again. "We need to talk with Chief Deputy Goodman. I think the state and federal authorities are best suited to dig into Bertha's past, going back fifty-five plus years."

#

Before we broke from our meeting, Roth confirmed I would initiate our talk with Goodman. She also directed me to bring her proof of Bertha's guilt. I had to obtain Bertha's fingerprints somehow; maybe from the surface of a throwaway drink container.

I had organized our three findings to convey to Goodman. First, Digger drew a Totenkopf in the sugar. Goodman might believe that. Second, Hayes alleged Bertha had eradicated a tattoo of a letter from under her arm. I can hear him say, "Nonsense." Third, Bertha's birth town is across the lake from Ravensbrück, a WWII prison camp. Goodman would utter "Complete buncombe."

Back in my office, my brain thrashed to concoct a scheme to get Bertha's fingerprints. My body rested in my recliner chair, and my feet nestled on the ledge under the windows behind my desk. What would be a dependable surface to secure Bertha's fingerprints? I imagined her holding a wine glass or an aluminum soda can.

I envisioned three approaches to pick up Big Bertha's fingerprints on a throwaway beverage container. First was breaking into the Harper's trashcans, but the courts might toss the prints because we entered property illegally. The first approach was out. The second was following Bertha throughout the day to recover any container she tossed, but that would take time because many shops serve drinks in containers other than glass or aluminum. This second approach could take too long a time.

I concentrated on the scene outside the window; some of the leaves had started their fall. My brain birthed a third approach, which might not work, but even if it crashed, it would be amusing and quick. Bertha is a miser, so use her weakness to get her to the mansion. We'd ask Michael to drive to Asheville. When he's on the way, we'd phone Bertha and ask if Michael remembered to bring the cash to pay us to hunt Digger's killer. Wild grizzlies wouldn't keep her away from the mansion.

My right leg had fallen asleep, and I dropped my feet back on the floor. Ahh, the feeling came back. Yeah, Bertha shows up and roars at Roth to unhand her money; in reply, Roth acts meek and accepts her punishment. Big Bertha is rude, but Roth asks her to have a glass of wine while Roth goes to get the check Michael had given us. Bertha puts her fingers all over the wine glass and—

A voice burst forth out of thin air. "Snooty fox to see you'ns." I rotated my chair. Taylor stood in the doorway. "Seed her'ns bloomers through her dress."

Helen Fiery, my favorite reporter, materialized behind Taylor. As Taylor moved back into the hall, Helen jutted out her hip and filled the doorway, a bright smile on her face and unblinking, predatory eyes. She nodded a dismissal at Taylor.

Behind Helen's back, Taylor stuck out her tongue and mouthed, "Hussy."

Helen had on a tight-fitting, tan-and-white print dress, revealing the faint outline of her panties, inflating—no, I meant *inflaming*—me with a famished craving for soft, tan human flesh.

She brushed silky-smooth, brown hair away from her right eye. "Thanks for the exclusive on the Eigges case."

"You wrote a good article."

"I did, didn't I?"

She entered my office. She had a navy-blue tote bag, complete with two wine bottles, two glasses, and a corkscrew. She had shut the office door.

"You owe me for your exclusive," I said.

To make room for the wine bottles and glasses, Helen removed a picture frame and an inbox from the top of my desk. "Ixnay. Take me out again, and I could owe you."

As my brain fried with lust, it tried to warn me, *Get her out of here—act grown up.*

I brushed my cowlick back while I considered what she had said. "What's with the wine bottles?"

"To celebrate my newspaper article about Mr. Eigges."

"Nice of you."

"And another event."

"What's that?"

"Now that your ladylove has flown the mansion, maybe I can help?" She poured wine into a glass and handed it to me. Next, she sat and crossed her legs, pulling the hem of the print dress way up her thighs.

Staring at her thighs, I sipped the wine. "I like it."

Helen grinned a wicked smile. "The wine store recommended a Cabernet Sauvignon."

The wine had a slight taste of cherries. "What do you know about war criminals?"

She stared and kept drinking. "A little."

"What government agency handles this?"

"Like a spy in the US?"

I emptied my glass. "Uh, huh."

Helen had moved her chair around my desk to where I sat. She refilled my glass and patted my leg. "Department of Justice."

Her tan-and-white dress had a print from Greek mythology. As she got closer, I distinguished fairies and nymphs in a forest among scantily clad women in linen cloaks and tree fronds. "Do you have a contact in Washington?"

She continued to rub my leg, but her unrelenting eyes studied me. "Why?"

My wine had vanished. I held out my glass for a refill. "No reason."

She shoved her long brown hair away from her eye. Next, she pulled her hem up to hip level and sat in my lap. "I don't believe you."

My fingers fumbled the glass, but I snagged it again with a wild grab. My heart raced. Her long hair covered my face, churning and shifting like the soft stream of a warm morning shower. I held onto a firm thigh and snuck a glance at the door. Oh Jeezus, the door stayed shut. I gulped wine and pushed papers off my desk. "Need a contact at the U.S. Department of Justice."

Helen emptied the second bottle in our wine glasses. "How come?"

My glass was empty in two mighty slugs. I grasped my laptop and laid it on the floor. "If I solve a crime, I'll give you an exclusive."

Helen slid off my lap and got on top of the desk, lying on her back, pulling me after her by my shirt. Her underwear had gone missing. Her print dress bunched at her torso. My heart thumped. Lust raged through my being. I jumped on the desk—and Helen. "*Aah!*" I said.

The top straps on her print dress fell away. She had marvelous breasts, round, equally full at the top and the bottom. We began a roll in the hay. The desk rocked. "*Mmmmh,*" she said.

I had the sensation of warmth and began to sweat. Helen emitted a floral and fruity aroma. *Please don't let anyone enter the room! Please!* Her moan grew noisier.

My being needed to mate with her body, to caress it. When I glanced away at the door, a rational thought slipped through my crushing lust: Roth told me to *grow up*. Was I failing her trust? "*MMMMH!*" Helen groaned loudly. The entire mansion would hear her.

I pressed my palm over her mouth.

"*MMMMH!*" she said.

I slowed.

"DON'T STOP!" she shouted.

I pushed the flat of my hand into her mouth. "Be quiet."

The desk rocked.

"*Aaaah!*" I said in a loud voice.

My hand stung. I spun off Helen and saw my blood everywhere. She had bitten deep into my hand.

Bruce knocked at the door. "Don! Everything okay?"

"We're fine."

Helen and I composed and arranged ourselves. When Helen left, the hall was empty. My hand bled like a leaky faucet. I phoned Bruce. "Need to see a doc."

"See you at my Jeep."

Bruce waited in his Jeep, parked in the basement garage. With a towel wrapped around my hand, I closed the passenger-side door. "You got-a understand," he said, "dat Helen are a does-not-play-well-with-others type of girl."

"Let's go. To the Doc."

And so, I would see about my hand and then seek Bertha's fingerprints. Growing up would take a little longer.

31

DOWNTOWN ASHEVILLE — THURSDAY

I exited my bedroom, moving rapidly through the stairs to the first floor, across the hallway to the basement, and down to the Mustang. As I drove out of the garage, I had a fluttery sensation in my stomach, edgy about my ability to persuade Goodman to believe me. I had set up a lunch meeting with the Chief Deputy at the Tavern on the Square, a location becoming our favorite watering hole to reminisce and unravel a knotty case. As I walked toward the tavern, my body shivered from the cold wind on Pack's Square gusting from various directions. My thoughts also blew in different directions, deliberations hunting for a way to tell Goodman about Death's Heads, a concentration camp, and their connection to our two deaths.

I wasn't like Roth: calm, adept at reading an individual's intentions, and able to step over pitfalls; on the contrary, I often acted without thinking and startled people. As a younger man, I struggled with this flaw of firing off my mouth before thinking about what I wanted to hit. I planned to do things differently today. Entering the pub, I settled on a strategy: My approach would be to let Goodman talk, and I would broach the SS theory only after the Chief Deputy explained he had garnered no other good suspects. When he admitted his flop, I would put forth this difficult-to-swallow hypothesis about Bertha and the SS. Hot diggity! I was growing up.

Goodman sat at a table in the center of the big room. He wore civilian clothes with his trench coat hanging over a spare chair. After grabbing a chair and greeting him, I realized a waitress had appeared beside me.

I smiled at her. "I'll have a Green Man IPA."

Goodman grinned at both the waitress and me. "Please put all the beers on Mr. Gannon's tab."

He studied my bandaged face and then my bound-up hand. "What happened to your hand?"

I think I blushed. "Don't want to talk about it."

He looked at me with goggle-eyes. "A woman?"

"Let's drop it."

Goodman raised his eyebrow. "Try feeding her chocolate, instead of your hand."

Glancing across at Goodman, I sniffed his familiar Aqua Velva aftershave. "What's new on Atsadi?"

"At the time somebody shot Lilith, he was at breakfast."

"You sure?"

"The tribal police interviewed everyone at that breakfast. Atsadi was far away in Cherokee when Lilith died."

The number of suspects just shrank further, leaving Bertha almost alone. Goodman gulped his beer and I sipped my brew. I followed with a question. "Do the tribal police think Atsadi is innocent of both murders?"

"Yes."

"Why?"

"Office Kanuna pointed out other witnesses beside Digger testified—three to four years ago—against Atsadi. Kanuna reminded me no one had attacked those other witnesses."

"He's off the hook?"

Goodman nodded. "The Cherokee police think he wants to go straight."

I saw my opening. "So, you're out of suspects?"

"I haven't given up. We're still going over the results from the crime lab."

I lowered my head to admire the color of the beer in my glass. I liked the beverages made by The Green Man Brewery, which recently had begun operations in Asheville. Raising my head, I locked eyes with Goodman; at the same time, he waited for me to speak. My opening had arrived.

"You recall Johnny Hayes said Bertha Harper had a tattoo removed from her arm?"

Goodman flinched. "Yep."

"You remember the skull and crossbones in the sugar pile on the floor?"

Goodman nodded.

"By linking the two, I believe Roth solved our case."

Goodman turned to signal our server to bring more beers. "What link?"

"Bertha was born in Germany just after World War I ended, in a town near where an SS concentration camp was later built. The SS used the death's head symbol and tattooed their members with their blood type. Bertha had a pendant with the death's head and a tattoo on her arm."

The Chief Deputy froze, interrupting me not one iota. I continued. "We believe Bertha guarded an SS concentration camp, in the process being tattooed and obtaining an SS Death's Head pendant. Digger found the pendant in the Old Fort attic and later confronted her. She killed him to prevent her being exposed and deported."

Goodman continued his freeze, still as a portrait on a wall, seemingly unable to believe what he had heard, startled into muteness.

I waited.

Finally, he roused himself and spoke. "You have a tattoo, a skull and crossbones, and the coincidence of being born near a concentration camp, which are circumstantial suppositions—not rock-hard evidence."

I waited, saying nothing. He searched around the tavern as if to confirm no one listened to our conversation.

Goodman stroked his white mustache. "Then again, I'm hunting for a suspect."

I thought I had his attention. I wasn't sure. "Do you know of any fact making our SS assumption wrong?"

Goodman held up a forefinger. "We don't know if Bertha has—or had—a tattoo under her arm."

I slowed the discussion by sipping my beer. "Hmm, does the Sheriff's Office have experience in handling war criminals hiding in the US?"

"Our office hasn't had that sort of a deportation case. I have read about former Nazis being deported from the US by the Justice Department."

"Could you help us confirm or disprove Bertha guarded a camp in Germany?"

Goodman picked up a napkin to dab at the liquid on the table, drank his beer, and stared out the continuous row of windows along the side of the building facing Pack Square. "The Sheriff's Office has no idea about wartime activities."

"Will you help?"

"We'd need to ask the feds to investigate."

He would help us explore Bertha's wartime activity. Above all else, Goodman did his job well. At the core of his character, he had to catch the guilty perpetrator.

I waited a few seconds so as not to push him. "You'll help us confirm or eliminate an SS connection?"

"I'm not convinced, but—for due diligence—I shall ask for a wartime check on Bertha."

Our search was in its home stretch.

Goodman continued. "That war is now—let me think—fifty-five years in the past. We'll get our answer faster if we work through the Attorney General's Office in Raleigh."

He looked past me in the direction of the tavern's entrance and groaned. Turning, I saw his boss, the Buncombe County Sheriff, approaching. He was a tall man, wearing a stiff black uniform and peering at me through thick-lensed glasses.

"How is the hot-shot detective?" the Sheriff asked.

Staring at me through his coke-glass lenses, I recalled once when I observed a goldfish in a fishbowl. Based on my past encounters with the Sheriff, I knew he enjoyed bullying and shaming any lower-ranking individual.

"I've meant to ask you—how do you keep that black uniform so wrinkle-free?"

"What difference does it make to you, smart mouth?"

"You misunderstand. I am in awe. When I work, I get so many creases in my suit."

He turned toward his Chief Deputy and said, "I told you not to hang out with this parasite. He's looking for the Sheriff's Office to give him free information."

"Sheriff, I agree he's a derelict," Goodman said. "I talk to all of them, my confidential informants."

"Yeah, well, okay." Turning from Goodman, the Sheriff pointed his finger at me. "You stay away from my officers." With that directive, he turned and left.

"Why can't you make nice to him?" Goodman asked.

"Sort of like kissing a toad, isn't it?"

#

I drove back to the mansion and found Roth reading at her desk; I sat in front of her. She ignored me and continued reading. I cleared my throat, progressing from a murmur to a loud rumble. She read.

"Ready to report," I said.

She regarded me, pressed her lips into a straight line, and put her book, *The Brethren*, down. She had almost finished it.

"Good read?" I asked.

"I found no good guys in this book."

Roth read lots of different books.

"What kind of guys were they?"

She squeezed the tip of her nose. "The title is about three scoundrels, judges serving time in a federal prison in Florida. Their chief activity, behind bars and using a magazine ad, is running a blackmail scheme in which they scam wealthy, gay men."

I leaned back in my chair. "Was the book dark?"

"It's gloomy about the future of American elections. Money swings the voting and subverts the natural nomination and electoral process. The money men can dictate their chosen candidate will be the next President." She sighed and turned to me. "Report."

I began recalling. "Chief Deputy Goodman thinks our supposition—that Bertha worked for the SS—may be nonsense. Despite his doubt, thinking we are off base, he is sending requests through Raleigh to explore Bertha's activities in Germany during World War II."

Roth pushed a swatch of her white hair back under the black veil and followed up with a Goodman question. "Did he confirm Bertha had a tattoo removed?"

"Nope."

Roth pushed a button of the intercom on her desk. "Bruce, would you come to my office?"

A minute later, Bruce arrived. "Yes, Boss."

"Go to the tattoo parlor Bertha used. Employ your ingenuity to confirm she had a letter tattoo removed from her arm."

Bruce nodded and glanced at me. "Did Hayes tell you which tattoo parlor?

"On Coxe Avenue."

Bruce left the room.

"Did he finish checking Atsadi's alibi?"

"Atsadi attended a breakfast sales meeting in Cherokee at the time Lilith was shot."

Roth picked up her book, paused, and set the book back on the desk. "All roads lead to Bertha: she has a source of monkshood plants, supposedly argued with Digger, and possibly served as a camp guard for the SS. We have motive and means, but we need proof." She picked up her book and continued reading.

"What do I tell Angela?" I asked.

"What do you mean?" Roth asked.

"Professor Lightfoot rooted out two key facts: railroad men found the old cache in Morganton, and the Death's Head and tattoo are connected."

My boss nodded. "Tell Angela to submit her bill. I hope she will work with us in future cases."

"Will do, Boss."

Roth turned a page. "If we had Bertha's fingerprints, we could hurry Goodman along."

"Yeah."

She kept reading; she was running out of pages. "Start your plot to get the old witch's fingerprints on a wine glass."

"I have to get Michael to come here."

She finished the last page of *The Brethren* and put it down. "Do it."

We turned as Taylor rapped on the door into Roth's office. Assuming they wanted to discuss tomorrow's meals, I bent over my desk to organize the notes from my meeting with Goodman.

"Don, you'n wants to hear what I a-goin' to say."

When Roth and I faced Taylor, she began, "Carla called me. Her voice kept a-breakin' an she cried. Her'n fiancé, Larry Buchanan, doesn't hold her and can't seem to feel fondness—she feels she done make a mistake in accepting his marriage proposal."

"Has she returned his ring?" Roth asked.

"Not yet, but surely she's a-goin' to do that."

Roth pinched the bridge of her nose. "I feel sad for Buchanan. He's got the wealth but not the heart, the sensitivity."

After Taylor went back to the kitchen, I phoned the Harper home.

"Hello. Michael Harper speaking. A sad day in Old—"

"This is Don Gannon. Need to talk with you."

He paused for a moment. "I've wanted to see you. Poor dear Lilith. Such suffering! My son gone. Poor Lilith and her pregnancy vanished. Misfortune crashes down—"

I heard him take a breath. "Need to talk. Would you come to Roth's mansion in Asheville?"

Michael continued in his booming voice. "What have you found out? First, beloved Digger perishes, and then Lilith is murdered while trying to—"

He hadn't answered my question. It was grueling to pin him down because he rambled. "Mr. Harper! Can you get together with us tomorrow? Yes or no?"

His rumbling continued, unabated. "What do you think? Hayes did it? Lilith always accused him. When she came the night before she died, I wasn't able to listen to her explain her latest suspicions."

I needed a moment to grasp what Michael had said. Roth had heard him; her eyes locked on mine. I broke into his soliloquy. "Did you say—the night before the killer shot her—Lilith rode her Vespa out to Old Fort?"

Michael heard me. He hesitated before continuing. "Lilith visited us here in the house, the night before. I didn't talk much with her; I was leaving for a church service. She talked with Bertha. When I got back, Lilith had gone. We didn't see her—"

Now I knew where Lilith went after she found the pendant: gone to see Bertha. "You need to meet Roth in Asheville. Tell us what Lilith said. We'll compare what you know with what Roth and I know."

Michael didn't speak. That was unusual. He might have sensed I was suspicious of his wife. "Let me fetch my wife to the phone. She'll tell you what Lilith said."

No. No. Don't get Bertha. "We want to talk to you alone. Not your wife. Can you come tomorrow?"

Michael waited before answering. He must have figured something was wrong. "My regular luncheon group meets tomorrow. Bunch of old friends."

"Reschedule, Michael. We need to meet. The sooner, the better."

"Why is it so important I come now?"

I suspected he had decided to come. "We're close to solving the crime."

"Is that the only reason?"

"We're running out of funds. Bring money."

"What's the address?"

"2050 Deerhaven Lane in Asheville."

"I'll be there."

"Better not tell your wife. She won't want to spend her money to solve the crime."

I had spun the web for tomorrow. If that didn't succeed, there were more extreme measures I would take. I went to wipe the wine glasses clear.

32

DOWNTOWN ASHEVILLE — FRIDAY

Goodman tramped through the entrance into the Naughty Hops Pub looking every bit the cop: eyes sweeping the patrons at the tables and bar, body moving forward at a measured pace, and wearing—as part of his civilian clothes—a tan trench coat. He had called me to set up a meeting downtown, choosing a bar other than the Tavern on the Square to decrease the likelihood of running into the Sheriff. He walked over to my two-person table toward the rear and sat down. The corners of his lips stretched back and up, a movement driving his white Vandyke beard higher and into his mustache. A stunning grin. I reckoned he had almost reached his personal goal, closing this dual murder case. Looked like a cop, thought like a cop.

His aftershave was like cigarette smoke; it overwhelmed every other scent in the room. He had pulled a chair over to where we sat and dropped his trench coat on it. His flannel shirt looked old and a little small. Not wealthy but a good detective. Once he had a beer, I asked, "So, what've you got?"

"I've been interviewing Michael and Bertha Harper."

"And?"

"Michael has alibis for the mornings of the two killings."

Wanting to hear more detail, I raised my eyebrows and waited.

The Chief Deputy sipped his beer and continued. "You've met Michael, old and retired. Many mornings, he has breakfast with other retirees at a diner in Old Fort. The mornings of the slayings, he was busy yacking with his fellow old men."

"So, he's not the killer?"

"No. He's not."

We were silent, pelted by the constant hubbub of the tipsy beer drinkers surrounding us. Goodman coughed and wrinkled his nose, apparently feeling what he was about to say was significant.

"Bertha told me she often takes walks in the woods in the morning—by herself."

"Was she walking the mornings of the killings?"

Goodman nodded. "Also, she walked in the woods the morning someone shot at Digger."

I slapped my forehead. "She did it."

Goodman grinned. "Bertha denied she ever argued with Digger. A neighbor, the woman who lives to the right of the Harper's house, overheard them arguing, quarreling loudly. The timing of that argument would be about the time someone poisoned Digger."

I pumped my fist in the air. "She did it. I know she did."

Harry grinned again and looked away, viewing the cooks around the stoves at the rear of the pub. "I like you, kid—you give a hoot. You're a little impulsive just now. When Roth is finished training you up, you're going to be one of the best."

That hushed me. I think I reddened. We ordered additional beers. I missed Lilith. She had pushed so hard to find who did the crime. If she had lived, she would be so pleased. Goodman pursed his lips and seemed to be thinking.

274

He continued talking. "Raleigh contacted the Justice Department about Bertha."

"And?"

"If it turns out Bertha was—or is suspected of—being a camp guard during the war, I'll have enough to get a warrant to search the Old Fort home."

"And take her fingerprints."

He nodded.

One way or another, we were going to get Bertha's prints soon. When we departed the bar, the Chief Deputy promised to call me when he heard from the Justice Department.

#

Roth, Bruce, and I spent a quiet evening watching TV in the media room, with its oak-paneled floor, beige wallpaper, windows on two walls, and a couch and chairs in red and beige. Elsewhere, Mickey worked on a stakeout in Johnson City, Tennessee, and Taylor cooked in the kitchen. Bruce and I sprawled on the couch, and my boss sat in a chair.

Bruce reported on his trip to the tattoo parlor. "I drove to Old Fort and parked across from the Harper home. With my long-distance lens, I snapped pictures of Bertha."

I uncrossed my legs and strengthened my back on the couch. "Did the laser operator at the tattoo parlor identify her?"

"He did. He removed a black-colored letter from the underside of Bertha's arm."

The evidence against Bertha was pilling up. "He's positive?"

"Positive. The tattoo guy said it took two treatments to remove the letter."

"Well done," Roth said.

Bruce turned to me. "Roth told me you met with Goodman today."

"Yeah."

"Progress?"

"Goodman's closing in. He's waiting for the feds to dig into Bertha's wartime activities."

Bruce looked askance at me—his mischievous grin. "Guy, how did it feel?"

I rolled my eyes at the ceiling. "What does *it* mean?"

"The shame."

"What shame?"

"Guy, you got the Boss and Professor Lightfoot to solve *your* case."

That wasn't fair. My boss is smarter than most people, and Angela, the professor, is no slouch. "I've read Sherlock Holmes, and I'm not him. The strength of our team is each detective. My strength is the team."

Bruce grinned. "Like a Russian doll hidden within another doll, you be slippery."

"Will you two stop prattling?" Roth said. "I can't hear the news." She sipped her wine and studied the TV broadcast.

I realized I had seen the newscast previously. "I find the TV news starting to be repetitive."

Bruce turned toward me, thought a moment, and then responded. "I read an article stating younger viewers are abandoning TV news, turning to the Internet."

The screen switched to local news. "We have an update on the death of Asheville resident Digger Harper, a victim of poison in his home. Anita Ramsey reporting. Anita?"

The display changed, and a smiling redhead with blue eyes and light freckles appeared. Under the screen appeared the words, Chief Deputy Goodman Asks for Federal Government Help. Anita explained,

"The Buncombe County Sheriff's Office is asking the Department of Justice for help. Chief Deputy Harry Goodman is seeking information for an unspecified suspect. Goodman stated the Sheriff's Office is following up on a lead from the public."

Roth glanced at me and bobbed her head in approval. "Events are moving faster than we realized."

The TV changed back to national reporting. I heard the house phone ringing and started to answer it, but it stopped.

Then, my boss began a harangue on one of her favorite subjects: the distressing decrease in value of news broadcasting. "Quality news programming is the best way to keep me watching. I'll leave the newscast if I see a dependence on gimmicks—fluff, rating stunts, and extravagant promotion."

I enjoyed hearing what Roth and Bruce had to say. She read a lot, and Bruce always wandered the Internet. "The best way to keep me viewing is to cover a broad range of issues and topics."

Bruce put his feet up on the coffee table. "Local news seems to be getting shallower. I see more recycled material without a local reporter."

Taylor entered the media room. I observed the inner corners of her eyebrows drawn in and up, together with her outer lips angled down; indeed, she wasn't happy. Bruce muted the sound from the TV. We waited for the bad news.

"I was a-talkin' with Carla. She done returned her ring to Buchanan."

Roth frowned. "Not exactly a surprise. What is she going to do now?"

"She not a-sayin'—she don't know."

"Poor child," Roth said. "As a young girl, I read fairy tales, with a choice of toads or princes. Carla missed her prince."

Taylor glared at me and said, "Didn't have to be. Reckon the closest thing we'ns got to a prince went missing."

33

ROTH'S MANSION, ASHEVILLE — SATURDAY

It was the day we had arranged to bag Bertha's fingerprints on a wine glass, and my breathing kept accelerating. Anxiety had me. Of course, Goodman would print Bertha should he charge her as a suspect. But Roth had grown impatient and wanted proof now that we had tracked down the killer. I changed between sitting on the credenza to the side of the front door and standing to scan the lane reaching to the mansion. No one was on that narrow road. The weather had turned gorgeous: temperature in the mid-60s Fahrenheit, clear sky, and no rain. I knew I shouldn't worry about Michael's arrival; it was going to turn out okey dokey. Now was the time when Michael went to meet his regular exercise group; Bertha wouldn't be suspicious that Michael had gone out.

A car appeared at the start of the lane. It got closer; it was red. It parked in front of the mansion; a Honda Accord. Michael got out. I had forgotten how much he was a dead ringer for a college professor with his gray hair, wire-rim glasses, tweed coat, and gray slacks.

I led Michael through the mansion and got him seated with Roth and Bruce on the wrought-iron furniture at the patio. Taylor spread lunch on the table. Michael started lecturing on the early history of Asheville. I slipped away to my office.

She answered on the fifth ring. "Who is this?"

"Mrs. Harper, this is Don Gannon. I need to talk with Michael."

"What do you want?"

"Has Michael left? Did he bring the money?"

She remained silent for a few seconds. "What money?"

I matched her silence and then resumed. "He's paying Roth to catch Digger's killer."

She shouted, "*Verdammt.*"

My stomach churned. I was close to reeling her in. Be careful.

"Put him on the phone."

"He's not here yet."

Bertha fumed in her raised voice. "I told him, 'No payment.' We give nothing."

"Ms. Harper, I better let you and Michael talk that out."

"Don't hang up on me."

"I'm going. Michael will be here soon."

Now came the sticking instant. Bertha was a strong woman. Would she insist upon coming?

"Give me your address. I am going to put a stop to this nonsense."

"Address? It's 2050 Deerhaven Lane in Asheville."

"I'm coming."

The line went silent.

It would take half an hour for Bertha to drive from Old Fort to the mansion. I had time to walk to the patio at the rear of the house. Michael had launched into a detailed description of Stoneman's raid into North Carolina in April 1865. Roth feigned interest. Bruce saw me and—when Michael glanced away—rolled his eyes upwards; not a history major. Taylor served iced tea. Michael would keep everyone busy until his wife arrived.

I went to the front door and waited for Bertha. She arrived, parked beside Michael's Honda, and stormed to the front door, muttering to herself the entire time. I estimated she—wearing a smoky gray shirt, a maroon long-sleeve shirt with rolled up sleeves, and a wide brim brown hat—had left her gardening to come.

"Welcome to Roth's mansion."

She shoved through the doorway. "Where's my husband?"

I escorted her out to the patio. Taylor was serving a cheese dish and small sandwiches.

Bertha stood over Michael and screamed down at him. "I told you not to pay for anything."

Michael took off his wire-rim glasses and seemed crestfallen. I had never seen him silent, but now he had clammed up. Bertha turned on Roth. "I want my money back. Here and now!" My boss stood, folded her hands in front, bowed her head a little, and stayed silent. Bertha continued to badger Roth and her husband.

When Bertha's complexion simmered down from a bright red, Roth said, "I'm so sorry. Let me return everything."

Bertha looked over her nose at Roth but seemed to settle down.

Roth brushed her palms together. "Don't think bad of me. Sit for a sandwich. I'll go get Michael's check."

Taylor pulled back a wrought iron chair for Bertha. She sat.

Roth returned with Michael's check, which she handed to Bertha. "I hope you don't think badly of me."

Taylor cleaned away the detritus from the table.

Roth held the plate of sandwiches out to Bertha. "Don didn't tell me you didn't approve the payment." She scowled at me.

Taylor returned with red wine and glasses. Bertha took a glass and held it for Taylor to pour the liquid.

Roth continued explaining to Bertha about me. "So hard to get good help these days."

Bertha nodded at my boss. "Be fair, they say. But if you're fair, they rob you blind." She sipped her wine and nibbled a sandwich.

While Bertha and Roth talked, Taylor continued to serve Michael, Bruce, and me. Then, she would pick up dishes and glasses and layout clean ones. She remained in motion, circling the patio tables. She put down a fresh wine glass for Bertha and gathered up the used one by the stem. Taylor returned to the kitchen with a tray of plates and glasses.

Bruce got up and left. After a while, he returned, caught Roth's eyes, and jerked his thumb upward. We had a clean set of Bertha's prints.

Shortly after that, Michael and Bertha returned to Old Fort.

Tomorrow the die would be cast. It would be a long night. For some, longer than they realized.

34

DOWNTOWN ASHEVILLE — SUNDAY

Early the next morning, hurrying through the open space of the Pack Square Park, I headed for the Buncombe County Sheriff's Office and Goodman. I found him in his office.

He put aside some paper forms and faced me. "Tell me you haven't done something illegal."

I grinned at him. "I've got some prints. Do they match the ones on the spent shells from the P239?" I handed him two sheets of paper with Bertha's prints.

"Whose are they?"

I winked at Goodman. "They're from a private investigation. Can't tell you."

He winked back. "That's okay. I think I know."

Goodman picked up his phone and summoned a technician who came and took the sheets. Goodman and I relaxed and waited.

I rubbed my hands together. "Walking through the Square, I had to enjoy the architecture of the two buildings, the courthouse and the city hall."

Goodman leaned back in his chair. "Asheville built some marvelous buildings, and then the Depression descended as a terminal cloak."

He checked his watch. "Asheville never took those old buildings down. They're still standing."

Where was that technician? How long did it take to check ten prints?

Goodman rubbed his goatee and chin. "Did you ever see the castle?"

I shook my head. "Castle?"

"Seely's Castle."

"Where?"

"Constructed about 1912 on ten acres at the top of Sunset Mountain. It was like an English castle. Made of granite from local quarries."

Where was that technician? "Big castle?"

"Big."

"Like to see it."

He shook his head. "Can't see it today. A private group owns it."

The technician returned. "The unknown prints match those on the spent shells at the murder scene."

I now knew Bertha loaded the pistol that fired shots at Digger and killed Lilith. "You're positive?"

The technician handed Bertha's prints back to Goodman. "Positive. See the ridges recurve back on themselves to form a loop shape. Both samples divide into loops pointing toward the radius bone, or thumb." The technician spent another five minutes comparing the two sets of fingerprints. He was a geek, as careful as a brown bear going through a trash can. He departed with a silly, contented grin plastered on his face.

Goodman and I stared at each other. He knew exactly his next step: ransack the Old Fort house and uncover that P239.

35

OLD FORT, NORTH CAROLINA — MONDAY

I jogged at sunrise with Bruce, finishing five miles later with a shower at the mansion. Roth joined us at the breakfast table. Taylor served a fancy cheese grits casserole, fried eggs, and coffee.

Bruce sipped his usual black brew. "Heard from Goodman?"

I swallowed a bite of the casserole. "Not yet."

Bruce heaped casserole onto his plate. "Probably takes a while."

Roth lowered her section of the Asheville paper "Surprisingly, he expects a quick response."

I glanced over at her. "Why?"

"Most of those old records are now in computer databases. And the former Soviet Union made available their files—on German participants in the war."

While he chewed on the casserole, Bruce continued thinking about the case. "Does Goodman have enough evidence to charge Bertha Harper?"

"A Justice Department finding," I said, "like Bertha entered the country illegally—would give Goodman justification for a search warrant."

Roth, who had been listening to Bruce and me, interjected her thoughts. "With a court search warrant, the Chief Deputy can take

Bertha's fingerprints. Her prints will match the prints on the spent shell casings from the bullets that killed Lilith."

Bruce nodded at my boss. "We wait."

"Soon," Roth replied. She took a bite of casserole and continued. "Unless she cuts and runs, we've got her."

# # #

I was at my desk filling out expense reports when Goodman called. "The Justice Department determined Bertha lied on her application for citizenship."

Goodman had come through for us. "What's your next step?"

"Interview her."

"Did she work for the SS at the Ravensbrück camp?"

"The German government says Bertha Reinhardt was an SS camp guard."

I interrupted him. "You have a warrant to search the Harper house?"

"Picking it up now. The Old Fort Police and our Sheriff's Office will swarm the Harper's house and grounds—early this afternoon."

When he had called, I didn't know if he phoned to update me as a courtesy or to invite me along with him. I wanted to go with him. "Can I tag along?"

"I want you there in case I have questions. Please bring Professor Lightfoot with you, if you can."

"Why Angela?"

"I might want her to examine any World War II documents found at the Old Fort house."

I wanted to be clear. "You're saying I can enter the house with you?"

Goodman responded at once. "You'll have to wait outside while the officers go in. I'll come get you after we finish our search."

#

Angela and I left my Mustang parked at an old service station east of Asheville. We climbed into the backseat of Goodman's Ford Crown Victoria. He drove toward Old Fort. "Between our deputies and the Old Fort police officers, we'll have a goodly force searching the house and surrounding grounds."

"Do you know if they're home?" Professor Lightfoot asked.

Goodman glanced at Angela through his rearview mirror. "They are."

He drove a while before continuing. "When the deputies enter the house, I want Don and you to stand back. After the house is secured, I'll bring you in, so you can observe and help me with questions."

Goodman drove on in silence, stroking his white goatee with his left hand and steering with his right, perhaps reviewing his plan for serving the warrant and searching the Harper house.

Angela broke the silence. "I see cars up ahead."

Along the secondary road leading to the old Harper home, a line of police vehicles parked on the shoulder of the road. Goodman smiled. "For once, we're ready and on time. I see my deputies and the police officers smoking and waiting close to their cars."

Goodman pulled up next to the Old Fort Police Chief's vehicle, rolled down a window, and said, "Chief, are you ready to move in?"

"Ready. You lead."

Encircled by the noise of many engines, I felt Goodman start his vehicle down the road toward Harper's dwelling. Behind us, the waiting deputies and police officers ran to their cars and followed. Warmth spread through my body, a wave of contentment. We neared our goal, catching Digger and Lilith's killer.

Parking on the lawn and roadside around the house, the swarm of cars disgorged deputies, some in uniform and others in white overalls.

As we all got out of the car, turning to Angela and me, Goodman said, "Park yourselves here."

Angela and I viewed the house, watched the deputies going through the yard and into the structure, and observed the trees behind the house, most shedding leaves. The sky showed a translucent blue vastness. The deputies who searched outdoors would stay dry. After a while, Angela gave me a wide smile of white teeth highlighted by her cocoa-colored skin. "You solved this case quickly, didn't you?"

Quick was the wrong word. I had wasted time chasing my tail with Hayes and Eigges. "With lots of help from Roth and you."

"Is your boss always that quick-witted?"

I glanced at her and dipped my head once in confirmation.

"You like her, don't you?"

Angela's question made me uneasy. Roth's my boss; I didn't see what like or dislike had to do with anything. "Sometimes she's cranky … and other times she goes out of her way to encourage me."

Angela stared at me with narrowed eyelids, paused, and turned to take in the house. "What does Goodman hope to find?"

"A P239 pistol," I said. "He'll also be searching for papers and photographs tying Bertha back to her job as an SS guard."

"What are the deputies doing behind the house?"

"They'll take soil samples from her garden. Try to prove she left that same dirt at Digger's house the morning she shot Lilith."

Angela nodded, I smiled, and we returned to watching the house, waiting for Goodman to fetch us. Finally, carrying several evidence bags, he appeared at the door of the house and made haste to where we stood. Angela fidgeted and appeared eager to question Goodman. "Did you find a P239?"

"We found it in Bertha's bedroom. Michael says it isn't his."

She should have tossed the pistol in the river. "Have you taken her prints?"

"We will when we arraign her."

Angela shrugged. "Then it's over."

Goodman held out a few evidence envelopes with photographs inside. "Maybe. Tell me if this is what I think it is."

Angela and I gathered around the Chief Deputy. He spread out the transparent evidence bags on the hood of his white vehicle. "We found four photographs at the bottom of Bertha's jewelry case. They're old."

The first photograph showed three smiling women in skirts and short-sleeved shirts, seated in a rowboat with a large body of water in the background. The woman in the middle might have been a young Bertha. The Chief Deputy showed us someone had written on the back. Before speaking, Professor Lightfoot turned the photograph over a few times. "The writing is in German. I'll try to translate. 'Other guards and me rowing out on Lake Schwedtsee—June 1943.'"

Angela raised her head to ensure we followed her. "Lake Schwedtsee is the body of water situated next to the Ravensbrück concentration camp."

He seemed to think about what Angela said and pushed a second picture toward her. It showed a woman, who resembled Bertha, in a black cape, boots, gray jacket and skirt, and a black two-cornered cap beside a German Shepherd. Angela translated German on the other side: "Me with my guard dog."

The third photograph showed a young Bertha—in black jacket and skirt, gloves, and two-cornered cap—giving a Nazi salute to an SS commandant. On the back of the photograph, someone wrote, "I succeed. I am an SS guard."

A final snapshot showed smiling SS soldiers and women guards in gray jackets and skirts. On the backside of the photograph, someone wrote, "Fellow guards and SS soldiers on holiday."

I thumped the hood with my thumb. "These photographs prove she guarded the Ravensbrück camp. Why didn't she destroy them?"

Goodman grimaced. "Sentimental importance would be my guess. The holiday photograph shows the Death's Head pendant on her jacket."

The evidence against Bertha was stacking up. "Was there a tattoo on her left arm?"

"A female deputy found no tattoo, but Bertha's arm showed slight scarring and faint residual ink under the skin."

"And?"

"I arrested Bertha for the murder of Digger Harper and Lilith Johnson."

"Did Michael Harper know?" I asked.

"About his wife?" Goodman asked.

"Yeah."

"I don't think so."

"Why do you say that?"

"When I arrested her, he seemed shocked and disoriented."

I brushed my cowlick. "What did you tell Michael?"

"I explained what we knew about Bertha's past."

Poor Michael. His adopted son is dead, and now his wife turns out to have been an SS guard. And he is Jewish and hated the Nazis. "How did Michael take it?"

Goodman shook his head. "He began to shake and shout hateful obscenities at his wife."

It sounded like Michael had lost control.

"Did you separate them," Angela asked.

"I assigned a deputy to stay with Michael and calm him down."

As we walked across the road to the Harper house, Goodman said, "As you know, I expect the rifling on the bullets our laboratory fires from the P239 will match the rifling on the bullets fired at Digger Harper and Lilith Johnson."

Ahead of us, I saw the top of Bertha's white hair in the back seat of a police car parked near the front door of the old house.

Bertha sat quietly in the police car, her chin up, lips compressed in a straight line, eyes staring out the front of the vehicle. A deputy, smoking a cigarette, watched her from outside the vehicle.

Walking back to their cars, their search over, other deputies lugged equipment to their vehicles and began to disperse.

"Wait here," Goodman said to Angela and me. He wrote in his notepad to describe the photographs.

"She seems defiant," Angela said, "as if she can get out of being convicted."

I mused, "Bertha is a snake, a copperhead. She's evil."

Angela shook her head. "Yes, but can she evade the charges?"

"I don't see how. Goodman has the motive, means, opportunity, and a smoking pistol."

Waiting for Goodman to return to his car, I phoned my boss. "The Sheriff's deputies found the P239, and they'll take her fingerprints. Goodman has Bertha in custody."

"Gratifying," Roth said. "She may avoid deportation by spending the remainder of her life in prison."

"The deputies also found photographs of Bertha taken at Ravensbrück during the war. She was there—"

Angela pulled on my shoulder. I turned my head toward the house. Angela pointed at the car holding Bertha.

Suddenly, there was Michael Harper, his salt-and-pepper hair and wire-rim glasses evident, closing in on the vehicle, with a deputy chasing him.

I turned to Goodman standing next to me. "I thought you said you separated Michael from his wife?"

Goodman said, "Oh good grief," and scurried to intercept Michael and the deputy.

Michael carried an object.

The chasing deputy gained on Michael but reached the car in which Bertha sat after Michael got there.

The deputy standing beside the car holding Bertha reached for his sidearm.

Blum!

It was a gun blast, its loud reverberation echoing back from the surrounding contour of the ground. Deputies now surrounded the car.

"What was that noise?" my boss asked.

"Boss, I'll call you back. Someone fired a shotgun."

Angela stayed right beside me. I made out a crowd of deputies around the police car Bertha was in; furthermore, several had grabbed Michael Harper and pushed him back through the front door of the house.

As the crowd moved back from the vehicle, I noticed what appeared to be a sack of clothes and small shards of glass spread over the backseat in the Sheriff's car. An officer stood nearby holding a shotgun, a Remington 870. The object I had first seen on the wall in the Old Fort House.

Goodman appeared, his face a mask of horror. He shouted at his deputy. "I told you to hold the old man, not give him a gun."

"He was sick," the deputy said. "He went to the bathroom."

Goodman's face was blood red. "You had to stay with him. That old building is a connecting warren of rooms."

Beside me, Angela stared with brows raised, and her eyelids opened with the white showing above and below. She held her hand over her mouth and pointed at the sack of clothes and blood. "Is that Bertha?"

"Yeah, that's her."

I held Angela's shoulders as she threw up. A young deputy, eyeing the ground and backseat area to avoid stepping in blood and flesh, brought a blanket and covered the body. I shook my head. Michael had closed the case: Bertha would never harm anyone again.

36

ROTH'S MANSION, ASHEVILLE — TUESDAY

Bruce pounced on me when I entered the kitchen-dining room. "Your cowlick is standing straight up." He grinned at me, glancing up from the breakfast table. "You need to go back upstairs, apply another glob of styling gel."

I grinned back. "You should talk. Your corkscrew curls are more like corkscrew frizzes."

Taylor stood at the stove. "Donnell, I'm a-lookin' at your cowlick, and I think it's cute. Sit in your cheer and I'll bring your coffee."

Roth cleared her throat and gazed up from the morning paper. "Taylor, we've discussed your using that word. Please say *chair*."

"Yes, ma'am."

Across the table from me, Mickey spoke up. "Asheville paper reports the Sheriff's Office solved the murders. Sheriff Bradford took complete credit."

On the table to my left, Taylor set down a cup of coffee, dark roast, smelling of cinnamon. I picked up on the discussion of who did what to close the Digger case. "Goodman did the smart investigative work for the Sheriff's Office. However, his investigation ended with his deputy letting Michael Harper grab the hunting shotgun."

"Yeah," Bruce said. "That mishap gave Goodman a black eye."

Roth, in a long maroon tunic over a gray dress and a black headscarf over her white shoulder-length hair, spoke up. "I want to talk with Chief Deputy Goodman. To thank him for sharing information and working with us on the case."

Over the rattling of the newspaper and the verbal chatter at the table, I heard the doorbell ring, followed by Taylor shouting, "I've got it."

Returning, she said, "Someone to see us." Looking around, I found Carla standing in the doorway to the kitchen/dining room. She wore her blue trench coat, tailored with a cinched waist and dropping to her upper thigh. She didn't remove her coat, signaling she wouldn't be staying long. Flashing her big smile, Carla stood with chin up and bright eyes. The breakfast table grew quiet as she entered and said, "Hello, everybody."

We greeted her in a chorus, followed by quiet again.

"I want to say goodbye. I've only known you for a short time, but I'm fond of you."

Roth folded her section of the paper and set it on the table. "You're smart. You were working well with Don."

"Ms. Roth, thank you for treating me kindly and for allowing me to work here." The small dynamo with the ponytail seemed confident and pleased, with the corners of her lips lifted and wrinkles forming at the corner of her eyes.

Roth rose, spread her arms to Carla, and hugged her. "I enjoyed having you here. You fitted well in our team, and you have a knack for investigative work." My boss broke off, and next continued. "You called off your engagement with Mr. Buchanan?"

"I broke it off."

"I see," Roth said. "Ended your engagement and your work with his company?"

"Both."

Roth took in a deep breath. "You got engaged two weeks after meeting Buchanan."

"And I returned the engagement ring after another seven days."

Roth shrugged. "Women do that sometimes. Where are you going now?"

"I am leaving Asheville to visit my parents in Ohio."

Roth nodded. "You can always return, Carla. Your former job will be here for you."

Carla smiled and ran her hand through her ponytail. "Thank you, Ms. Roth. For now, it's time for me to leave Asheville, time to think."

Carla walked to our table, kissed me on my cheek, and returned to the door, where she turned back to Roth. "I'm glad I came. Congratulations on solving the case. Goodbye." She left.

I sat at the edge of the table near the hallway. I heard the lyrics of her song as she sang softly:

It's time to say so long

So long brings me sorrow

What should I have done? Should I have grabbed her at the table, like when I kissed her in the field? She is special; I wanted her to stay. Maybe she'll return, but she's leaving for now. What can I do? Won't forget her?

Taylor returned from watching Carla drive away and turned on me, with her brows lowered and drawn together and her eyes bulging. "Donnell, what is wrong with you? Why didn't you kiss her back? She's the best thing in your life." She stamped out of the room. I guess breakfast had finished.

"I think I agree with our red-headed cook," Bruce commented. "Cowlick, you missed your opportunity." Bruce left the room.

Roth considered me, pursed her lips, and said, "You may yet get a second chance." My boss stood, straightened her tunic and long dark dress, and left.

I turned to peer at Mickey. Before speaking, he glanced around the table. "Guess we should finish the grits before it gets too cold."

#

For our closing meeting on the Digger-Lilith Murder Case, Mickey lit a fire in the fireplace and Taylor brought in coffee and tea. Roth spread her notes on her desk and began the meeting. "Based on German records and Angela's research, we know Bertha Reinhardt, starting in 1940, guarded prisoners at a Nazi concentration camp. She used an SS-trained dog to control women at the camp. She was twenty years old."

Mickey, Bruce, and I listened to her and shook our heads in agreement.

Roth summarized further. "In 1945, when the Soviets reached the Ravensbrück camp and set the captives free, female guards escaped into the general population."

Roth scanned the files Angela had given her. "Our guess has Bertha heard Soviet tanks coming, shed her uniform, and left the camp. She then got a job serving food and drink in a tavern. She met Michael Harper—stationed at a nearby army camp—and married him."

"That's how she got into the US?" Mickey asked.

Roth stopped to sip her coffee and flip over her notes. "In 1945, the War Brides Act allowed foreign-born wives of US citizens who had served in the US Armed Forces to immigrate to this country."

"But she guarded captives in an SS camp," Mickey said.

"We covered all that," Roth said. "It was just after WWII, the Soviets didn't share their archives until years later."

"Once she had a marriage certificate," I said, "she could have crossed from England to Baltimore in a week—on an ocean liner."

I reasoned bad blood existed between Bertha and Digger. I guessed Digger liked his adoptive father but frowned on Bertha. It seems Digger left Harper's home in Old Fort to get away from Bertha, moving to the house on the French Broad River.

"In going through the trunks in the Old Fort attic," I said, "Digger found the Death's Head insignia, which led him to theorize the SS had employed Bertha. As Michael is Jewish, Digger must have told her to confess, or he would tell his dad and contact Immigration."

Roth rubbed the bridge of her nose. "Digger took the Death's Head pendant to his home and happened to mention its existence to Lilith. Bertha poisoned Digger, but didn't get to take back the old SS pendant."

I thought the events, the cause, and effect, all tied together.

"The day before Bertha shot Lilith," I continued, "Lilith went to the Old Fort home and must have let slip that she had the pendant. Bertha realized Lilith would expose her. The next morning, Bertha shot Lilith and hunted for the pendant."

The search for Digger's slayer had impacted so many lives. "Digger triggered a lot of events by searching that attic."

"Hayes dug up parts of Morganton," Bruce said.

"And got arrested for a felony," I said. "And thrown in jail."

"We investigated Eigges for Digger's murder," Roth said.

I traced the scar, healing on my face. "And Palo, his gardener, cut my face with a machete and wound up in prison."

"But the tribal court delivered Eigges to prison for stealing Cherokee relics," Roth said.

Roth frowned. "One ghastly failure was the death of Lilith. Such a strong person. If only she hadn't gone to see Bertha by herself."

# # #

Roth and I relaxed in her office. We grew quiet. The only sound was the crackle of the fire. The smell of wood smoke and pinesap drifted around the room. My boss abruptly summarized the investigation. "Bertha was an abomination, cunning, full of tricks, and a destructive force."

I uncrossed my legs and leaned toward her. "From the start, you recognized the symbol Digger drew in the sugar was significant."

She pursed her lips as if about to speak but remained quiet.

"And you solved the case. Figured out the skull and crossbones meant the SS."

"I didn't figure it out in time to save Lilith."

I didn't know how to respond. Roth shouldn't take on the blame. "I'm just sorry the Confederate gold didn't work out for you."

"I take pleasure in avenging Lilith's murder. We'll find more money, but we can't bring Lilith back."

I got up and put a log on the fire. We didn't speak for several minutes. My subconscious went back over the case. "Something bothers me."

Roth cocked her head to me.

I rubbed my chin. "Bertha began by shooting at Digger and finished by shooting Lilith. Not logical to switch to poison between shootings."

She nodded her head a little.

"Had Bertha shot Digger instead of poisoning him," I said, "then he would never have fallen on the floor and drawn the symbol."

Roth didn't respond.

"So why did Bertha use poison instead of shooting Digger?"

She gave a dismissive wave of her hand. "When you have to choose between several explanations. Take the one requiring the least speculation."

"What do you mean?"

Roth stopped to rub her nose. "Did Goodman have deputies in the woods searching for the shooter?"

"Yeah."

"What if the deputies had stopped Bertha on her way to Digger's house with the P239?"

"The deputies might have found the pistol on her."

Roth gave me a smug grin. "I think she switched to aconite powder because she didn't want to carry the P239. Shrewd she was."

We went quiet again and listened to the soothing noise from the fireplace. "Do you miss Carla?" Roth asked.

"I do."

"You two worked well together."

"She's smart. Catches on fast."

"I have her parent's address in Ohio."

My stomach had a quivering sensation. "Thanks. Think I'll write to Carla."

THE END

ABOUT THE AUTHOR

 R. M. Morgan worked as an engineer in both the U.S. government and academia. In his job, he investigated mysteries like a detective, unraveling the physics of car crashes to establish how to save drivers and passengers. After years of writing articles in that world, R. M. Morgan discovered the joy of writing mystery novels. Currently, he lives in Southern California and is writing the third book in the Roth/Gannon series.

If you enjoy detective mysteries, give R. M. Morgan novels a read. The books that keep the reader guessing whodunit right up to the end.

Further information about R. M. Morgan is on his website, www.rmmorgan.com.